DANCES
IN
Moonlight

DANCES
IN
Moonlight

CHARLENE RADDON

CHAPTER ONE

1859, Upstate New York

Elizabeth Anne Webster slid her nightgown-clad bottom easily over the gleaming, candlelit hardwood floors at Runyon's Finishing School for Refined Young Ladies, made spotless by her own sweat and elbow grease, to get closer to her friend Francine Gibbs.

The two girls huddled under a makeshift tent between their beds made by spreading a blanket from one to the other. If caught, they would suffer punishment, such as mopping and waxing the dormitory floors. Four years at Runyons' had accustomed them to such chores. Both had become favorite scapegoats for the other girls, who liked to claim that the Devil had kissed Beth, causing her birthmark, and taunted Francine about being the illegitimate daughter of a rich man's mistress.

The whisper of Francine's poetic voice beside her, reading *The Last of the Mohicans,* faded as Beth stared at the roof of the improvised tent without seeing it and drifted off into fantasy. In her mind, she saw the tanned buffalo hides of an Indian lodgecover, the erratic light of a central cooking fire, and the deep indigo of night peeping through a smoke hole. Fragrant woodsmoke drifted toward the ceiling and hovered around the aromatic herbs hung to dry from the lodgepoles. In her imagination, an Indian chief stood alone on a nearby bluff, a midnight silhouette against a cream-colored moon. A breeze ruffled his scalplock and the thick hair of his buffalo robe as he gazed out into space, communing with the spirits.

Beth's small breasts pressed against the confines of her worn cotton nightgown as she issued a wistful sigh. They had smuggled the forbidden book into their room from the library to feed their hunger for adventure. "Read it again, Francie. The part about Mene-Seela."

"Shh. You'll wake the others."

Beth peeked out at their sleeping roommates. "It is all right. Read."

Francine cleared her throat. She had a beautiful voice made for recitation. All the girls there loved to listen to her. Though her face could be called plain, her figure was unrivaled for feminine beauty. Her mind was quick and clear, and she had the rare ability to see and feel what others felt and understand things she hadn't experienced herself. Beth liked to say that Francine had an empathetic soul.

"... he watches the world of nature around him as the astrologer watches the stars. So closely ...."

Finished, Francine closed the book, laid it on the floor, and pressed her cheek to its vermilion cover. Both girls stared into space, envisioning their own personal proud and handsome Mene-Seela, Francie on her stomach and Beth on her back.

"I wonder who his guardian spirit truly was?" Beth mused. "Something far more powerful and romantic than a pine tree, I would think."

"Oh, yes. A panther perhaps, or a wolf." Francine flopped over onto her back close to her friend, clutching the precious book to her chest. "Why couldn't I have been born a man so I could travel to Oregon like Francis Parkman?"

"I would rather be an Indian princess."

"Yes." Excitement filled Francine's soft voice. "We'd marry strong, proud warriors. Brothers perhaps. We wouldn't have to worry about what became of us after leaving this dreary school. And we'd always live near each other."

Beth's vision clouded like a spring meadow threatened by a summer storm. "What good is dreaming doing us, Francie? You might become a teacher in this dull old seminary, but neither of us will marry, and we both know it." Her voice deepened with the inflamed passion of a seventeen-year-old young woman. Bitterness supplied an acrid edge to her words—the tainted rancor spawned by childhood taunts and shattered dreams because of the mark on her cheek. "Everyone knows."

"You cannot be certain that is our future, Beth. We do have some control. We'll find a way to go out west. Women are said to be scarce there. They say that even those lacking dowries or good looks are soon wed."

"You know as well as I do my only chance of going west is if my mother decided to join Father at his new post in Utah Territory, and *that* will never happen." Beth's mouth curled down at the corners. She didn't understand her mother and probably never would. "She hates living on army bases and far prefers her life in Boston attending soirees and the opera. I often wonder why she married Father at all."

"How does she afford to live like that on an army officer's pay?" Francie asked.

"Her grandmother left her a small fortune in a trust, which

she seems determined to spend as fast as possible. Even if she did decide to join Father, I have no desire to live with either of them."

Beth's whisper changed to a yelp as the blanket-tent collapsed upon them.

"The candle!" Francine grabbed for it and missed. "Look out! The blanket will catch fire."

"Oh, no!" The blanket corner dipped into the flame, and the fire spread fast.

Legs and arms thrashed as they struggled to untangle themselves from the blanket and each other. The extinguished candle rolled under the bed. Smoke nearly suffocated them while blanket flames licked at their bare skin and gowns, and they began to cough.

"Beat it with the book," Beth whispered as she tried to feel her way out from under the stinking wool.

"No! It belongs to the school." Stomp, smack. "Think what they would do to us if we ruined one of their precious tomes."

Beth slapped at the flames with her hands, grimacing at the pain. "Better than burning alive. Hurry, grab the blanket from your bed, and we'll smother the flames."

Francie stretched to reach the bed, her hair falling forward over her shoulder. As she dragged the blanket toward her, she screamed, "My hair! I have a spark in my hair!"

"Use the blanket to put it out!"

Francine clamped a corner of the blanket around the long, threatened strands and extinguished the spark. "Now the blanket is smoldering."

Their thumps and thuds, intermingled with harsh whispers and yelps, filled what had been silence. Beth thought, for sure, the other girls in the room would wake up and raise the roof.

Sure enough, a cry came from one of the other beds. "What is happening?"

"Ew. Something stinks."

"I smell smoke!"

"Fire!"

A stampede ensued as the other girls fled, leaving Beth and Francine trapped between their beds, tangled in the smoldering blankets.

"Oh, my lands!" Francine rolled her eyes.

"At least the fire is out." Beth had to agree the panic was overmuch. "I think."

"Light the lamp. I need to see how badly my hair is burned."

Moving onto her knees, Beth lifted her friend's thick auburn strands and examined them in the light from the door the escaping girls left open. "It is all right. One section is slightly shorter than the rest, and the ends singed, but not badly. You got it out just in time."

"What is going on here?" A bass-drum-like voice boomed in the darkness. A familiar voice. "Is something on fire? Why is there smoke in here?"

Elizabeth and Francine fell silent, crouched between their beds, the smoking blankets tangled around them. Beth pulled one over her head to hide.

Petticoats swished into the room. Stifled giggles came from the hallway. The force of a strong jerk on Beth's blanket somersaulted her into the light of Miss Runyon's lantern. She landed at the headmistress's booted feet, her skirts tossed over her head.

"Elizabeth Webster and Miss Francine Gibbs," Miss Runyon said as the last sparks died. "I should have known it would be you two. Pull down your gown, Elizabeth, and get up from that disgraceful pose. Come with me this instant. Both of you. The rest of you get back to bed. Francine, what did you do to your hair?"

Beth and Francine clambered to their feet amid a chorus of girlish laughter as their roommates filed back inside. Barefoot and with heads bowed, the two girls followed the headmistress out and down the corridor. One step had been enough to tell Beth the big toe on her left foot had been burned. Her attempt to walk on her heel resulted in an ungraceful hobble. She wondered what punishment they were facing this time.

"What is the matter with your foot, Elizabeth?" one of the girls called.

"Oh, poor Freaky, she's a cripple now as well as ugly," another said.

Beth's head jerked up. Her mouth pinched tightly shut. She didn't have to look in a mirror to know the hated birthmark, like a lip imprint on her cheek, had flushed purple. She itched to cover the offending blemish but kept her hands down and walked as normally as possible while enduring the discomfort. Why did she always do this? The other girls cheated, snuck out at night, smuggled forbidden food and literature into their rooms, and never got caught. Beth couldn't even glance out the class window without being seen.

On reaching the headmistress's office, they were instructed to sit. A long, heated lecture followed, which the girls endured in silence.

At last, Miss Runyon ran out of words and paused. After drawing a deep breath, she said, "Tomorrow, the two of you will scrub your dormitory, every inch of it. You will make all the beds, dust the chests, and wash the windows."

Beth groaned inwardly. Nothing ever changed at Runyon's school. How she hated it here. The thought of running away niggled at her as Miss Runyon went on and on about their insubordination and lack of decorum.

"I thank Heaven you are both graduating this year." She smacked her favorite hickory stick on the desk. "Now, I have something to discuss with you, Elizabeth. Francine, you may go."

Beth frowned. What could the old shrew want to talk to her about? Had she received instructions from Beth's mother about a trip home after next month's graduation service? The thought should have excited her but didn't. She didn't know her mother and had no desire to go home.

Francine slipped quietly out the door.

Miss Runyon came to stand before Beth, hands fidgeting at her waist, a troubled look in her eyes. "I had intended to let this wait until tomorrow since I thought you were asleep, as you should have been. Now, I believe it is best to get it over with."

Beth squirmed in her chair, her stomach queasy. She sensed she would not like what she was about to hear.

"A messenger brought sad news a half-hour ago, Elizabeth. Your mother passed on a week ago, a victim of smallpox, and was buried immediately. You have my condolences."

The woman's abrupt, unexpected words failed to penetrate

Beth's rattled mind. Round and round, they circled inside her head, jumbled and senseless. Mother passed? Smallpox? Buried? She thought she might throw up. "Dead?" she mused aloud. "No. Mother cannot be dead."

"Indeed, she can be and is."

"But what will happen to me now?" Tears clogged Beth's throat, causing it to ache.

"You will leave here at the end of the term; that is certain. I assume that where you go after that will be your father's problem. Not mine."

Her father's *problem*? Yes, he would see it that way. Young as she was the last time she saw him, only eight, she'd known he did not like her. He avoided looking at her. At her birthmark especially. Must she go and live with him? She barely knew him. In her memory, she saw him as a medium-sized man with bushy sideburns, a mustache, and a trimmed beard, who never smiled. He spoke only of the army and how despicable Indians were in the West. No, she didn't want to go to him. She didn't want to go anywhere, especially *not* without Francine.

Miss Runyon returned to her desk. "You are dismissed. Go to your room. And no more shenanigans, Elizabeth. You are too audacious for your own good. I dread to think what is to become of you."

For a long moment, Beth sat there staring at the woman, unable to believe what she'd heard. The world had become surreal. She tried to envision her mother's face, but all she could remember were her beautiful ball gowns and lustrous hair falling in ringlets around her face. Her mother's beauty had dazzled her. The woman's disinterest in her only child wounded Beth like a blade in her heart.

"I said you may go, Elizabeth." Miss Runyon rose and reached for her hickory stick. Beth knew what would happen next. She stood and quit the room.

Francine waited in the corridor. "What happened, Beth? Why did she make you stay behind?"

Trance-like, she continued to walk. Francine fell in beside her, took her hand, and waited.

"My mother is dead," Beth explained as they paused outside their room. A single tear escaped despite her effort to contain it. Proper young ladies did not cry; it ruined the complexion. What did she care about her skin? It had already been destroyed by her birthmark. "I don't know what will happen to me now, Francie. If my father forces me to live with him in Utah Territory, I might never see you again. I cannot bear to think of that. To live with a man who cannot stand the sight of me. What am I to do?"

Pity and fear filled Francine's face. "Oh, Beth, this cannot be happening. I could not bear to lose you."

"I greatly fear there is no way to avoid it, Francie." Deciding she would never be a proper young lady, Beth let go and bawled.

CHAPTER TWO

Lieutenant Eggerton McCall stared at the headmistress of Runyon's Finishing School for Refined Young Ladies. The establishment occupied a large estate in the middle of a forest, which covered most of the New York countryside in this location—trees and little else. Miss Runyon reminded him of a cigar store Indian, stiff, pretentious, and fake. However, the Indian would be made of wood, and she consisted of pomp. "What do you mean Elizabeth Webster is not here? I have orders from her father authorizing me to take control of her and see her to Utah Territory to join him."

"I meant merely what I said, Lieutenant. She and Francine Gibbs vanished three days ago after graduation services. Ran away. Both girls are incorrigible hellions. I'm glad to be rid of them."

McCall cursed silently. *Why couldn't anything ever go smoothly?* "You have no idea where they are?"

"I would suggest you go to Hillsdale, the nearest town."

Beside him, Tildy Buntz tugged on his arm. "Let's do that, shall we, Lieutenant?"

He looked down at his new companion. Easy to understand her eagerness to flee this stuffy mausoleum of a place. He returned his attention to the headmistress. "Would it be possible to speak to some of her friends? One of them might know where to look."

Miss Runyon laughed. More of a titter, truly. "Elizabeth's only friend here was Francine. You find her, and you'll find Elizabeth. The two are inseparable."

Tildy tugged again.

"Very well. Thank you for your... " he stumbled for a word. Help? She certainly hadn't given much of that. "…assistance." Another erroneous word, but the best he could do.

The woman saw the lieutenant and his companion to the door. Outside, they hurried to the carriage. McCall helped Tildy up and took his seat beside her.

"Will we be staying at an inn tonight?" She placed a hand on his thigh.

He smiled down at her. "I hope so."

"Me too."

The little hussy's fiery red hair matched her spirited personality. She was a product of the best whorehouse in Albany. McCall figured he could kill two birds at once and pay for her time and skill with the Colonel's money—a chaperone for Miss Webster and a bed partner for him. What could be better? They'd have to be careful, of course. Wouldn't do to expose their relationship. The Colonel would rip his insignia off and never give it back. Tildy hadn't promised to stick around Camp Floyd after they arrived, but he was hoping she would. Besides being skilled in bed, he found her canny and amusing.

They headed for Hillsdale, through the unending forest, to find a small town with limited shops and only two hotels. McCall arranged for a room for them, ignoring the manager's raised eyebrows after noting Tildy's ringless left hand. Had the headmistress at the school seen that as well?

McCall had fitted her with a new wardrobe that put a good bite in the money Webster had given him for his daughter's care. The woman had been raised in a good family and received a proper education before her downfall. He had been confident she could easily pull off the role he required her to play. Now, he realized the life she'd lived between that education and today had made changes in her that nothing could hide.

Later, after a rest and a tumble, they ate at the hotel restaurant and took a long walk up and down the town's single main street, looking for Elizabeth. After one wasted trek, they divided up. Tildy took the north side of the street and McCall the south. This time they entered stores and asked if anyone had seen a girl with a birthmark on her cheek. At McCall's third stop, a dry goods store, the proprietor reported seeing two young ladies walking toward the school.

"Why on earth would they go back to the school?" Tildy asked when McCall found her admiring jewelry in a store window. He knew she hoped to get him to buy her something, but McCall didn't waste money on gifts for whores.

"Who knows?" He drew her from the window. "I'm certainly no expert at figuring out the female mind. We'll rent another buggy and go for a ride. Maybe we'll catch them on the road."

They had no such luck and were returning to town when McCall noticed smoke rising from the trees, probably three hundred yards from the road and an equal distance from the school. "That might be worth investigating. It's bound to be either drifters making camp for the night or our missing girls."

He steered the horse and buggy onto a patch of bare ground. "Don't forget you are now Hilary Hightower of the Boston Hightowers, a wid—"

"I know. A widow who took this babysitting job out of boredom and a desire to see the Wild West."

"Good. With your background, before you fell from grace and ended up where you were when I found you, you should be able to pull this off with no hitches."

She laughed. "Before I 'fell from grace,' huh? I did that all right. My father still tells people I'm dead."

He grinned at her. "You weren't dead last night."

"Nor will I be tonight."

He lifted her from the buggy and let her slide down his body as he lowered her to the ground.

They'd hiked about a hundred yards when Tildy wrapped herself around him. "I can't wait—"

"Quiet." McCall's attention focused on the woods. He set her aside, ignoring the woman's look of disappointment. "I see something moving through those trees."

They found two young women kneeling at a ring of stones, trying to start a fire in an open area where he assumed they had apparently been camping.

"Elizabeth Webster?" The lieutenant stepped into the clearing.

The women, no more than schoolgirls really, leaped to their feet. Miss Webster proved easy to recognize as her father had promised when he gave this duty to McCall back at Camp Floyd in Utah Territory. The unfortunate birthmark on her cheek looked like someone's kiss had seared or stained her skin. Despite the blemish, McCall thought her surprisingly pretty. Under a small bonnet, long, wavy hair the color of summer wheat hung down her back to her waist. A thin, well-worn, outgrown calico dress hugged her curvy form. Neither of her parents had spent much on her wardrobe, and she must have no cash, or she wouldn't be camping in the woods.

"Who wants to know?" Her face reflected defiance but also confusion.

"I am Lieutenant Eggerton McCall, Fifth U.S. Infantry, under your father's command. He sent me here to fetch you to Camp Floyd."

Her face fell, and she looked him up and down with disdain. "You look like an army officer, but how do I know my father sent you?"

"I have a letter for you from him." He dug into his pants pocket and pulled out a crumpled paper, folded and sealed.

Miss Webster took the missive, opened and read it. The other young woman peeked over her friend's shoulder.

According to the headmistress at the school, the second girl's name was Francine Gibbs. Her face was plainer than Miss Webster's, but her figure held appeal. The two turned their backs and exchanged whispers before facing the lieutenant again.

"Thank you, Lieutenant, for seeking me out," Miss Webster said. "However, I cannot leave immediately, if at all."

He almost laughed. "Where else would you go?"

"I have yet to decide. I have been in touch with my mother's attorney, who is on his way here with some money Mother left me. I cannot leave until I see him."

"When do you expect him to show up?" Tildy put in, much to McCall's annoyance. He'd told her to keep silent.

Miss Webster looked at her. "And you are?"

"Mrs. Hilary Hightower," McCall said. "Your chaperone for the journey."

"I see." The young woman put her nose in the air but didn't object. "Mr. Snelling is due to arrive in Hillsdale tomorrow."

"Very well." McCall walked over and picked up two rucksacks he believed must hold the women's belongings. "In that case, we'll return to town, get you settled in at the hotel, and wait until he arrives. Where would you like us to drop you, Miss Gibbs?"

"She stays with me, Lieutenant." Miss Webster took her friend's hand, her tone firm and unyielding. "Or I don't go."

He stared at her for a long time, debating whether to spank her or just do his job. Wisdom chose the latter.

"I assume my father is paying my expenses?" Miss Webster appeared determined to get her way. "I have no wish to be beholden to a stranger."

Perhaps that was for the best, McCall decided. With her friend to pay attention to, the chit would be more likely to leave him and Tildy alone. "Yes, he gave me funds for your journey. I'm sure it will cover a room for an extra night and meals for two girls. You will share the room, of course."

"Of course, Lieutenant."

"You may address me as Lieutenant when we aren't in a formal military setting."

"Very well."

"Good. Shall we go?" He gestured toward the road where the buggy awaited.

Abner Snelling, Beth's mother's attorney, sat at a table in a far corner of the hotel restaurant when Beth and Francine entered.

He rose as they approached. "Miss Webster?"

"Yes. Are you Mr. Snelling?"

"I am, indeed." He gestured to a chair. "Please, be seated. Who is your companion?"

"This is my best friend, Francine Gibbs." Beth glanced at Francine. "Is it all right if she sits in on this?"

"It's unusual, but if that's what you want, let's get started."

Beth thanked him, and the girls sat.

"First," he began, "I must explain that your mother's will contained a codicil created by her attorney before her death. It is to be included in each recipient's own will and cannot be changed. Do you understand this?"

"I believe so, sir," Beth replied.

"Good. Now, this addition stipulates that no man can touch the money in the trust your mother left you. No one, in fact, other than the person you name as your next of kin for the purposes of this will."

He signaled to a waiter who brought a pitcher of water and three glasses. After filling them and giving one to each of the girls, Snelling took a sip, cleared his throat, and continued.

"What this means is that your father will not be allowed to draw from your account, and neither will your husband once you marry, but it must always be under the control of a banker or a lawyer."

Beth felt his gaze penetrate hers as if to post his words in her brain permanently. It reminded her of one of her teachers at Runyon's. She nodded.

"Another stipulation is that you cannot withdraw more than one hundred dollars a year."

Beth gasped. "One hundred? I can't imagine ever needing so much money."

"You will be eighteen soon after you reach Utah Territory, the age of consent there, and you will no longer be required to live with your father. At that time, you may wish to purchase a house to live in or a business to provide your income."

"Oh," she said. "Yes. I can see that might be true. I don't wish to live with Father at all."

"You have no choice at present," Mr. Snelling said.

"Thank you for that information." Beth grinned at Francine. "Francine and I do wish to buy a house to share in Salt Lake City."

Mr. Snelling frowned. "At eighteen, you will still be very young. I would urge you to seek advice from your father or some other grown man regarding plans. Perhaps, you will find someone at the American First Bank in Salt Lake City, where your money will be deposited. I have written the president there, Mr. Sizewell, and explained your situation. You will need to have an audience with him as soon as you can arrange it."

He held out a large envelope. "This holds papers you might need someday, your birth record, your mother's death certificate, a copy of her will explaining your inheritance, called a death gift, and the number of your bank account in Salt Lake City. There is also a small envelope in there that contains this month's allotment of cash. I trust you will keep it well hidden while in your possession and spend it wisely."

"Thank you, Mr. Snelling." Beth took the envelope with a

tinge of trepidation. The full impact of her new situation had begun to sink in. Never had she held any responsibility before. Although she looked forward to meeting this new challenge, she feared she might fail.

"Now, we have concluded our business," Mr. Sizewell stood up, "I will take my leave of you. I wish you the best of luck on your journey and in your future life."

She thanked him again, and together she and Francine watched the lawyer limp from the room. Beth guessed him to be middle-aged.

"Francie, can you believe it," she whispered, a little afraid of saying it out loud as if someone might snatch her new freedom and wealth from her. "My mother left me enough money to allow me to have a hundred dollars every month. I'm rich!"

"I'm so happy for you." Francine squeezed Beth's hand across the table. "And to get it right when you need it, too."

Beth's excitement faded. She leaned closer, not wanting the other patrons around them to overhear. "I will always share whatever I have with you, Francie, and if something should happen to me, I want you to take charge of whatever I own."

Francine shook her head and smiled. "You are so sweet, Beth." She rose and wrapped her shawl around her shoulders. "But I could not take advantage of you like that."

Beth sighed, unsure how to interpret her mixed emotions.

The money gave her more choices regarding her future, which pleased her. The thought of going West dazzled her but having to live with her father once she arrived greatly diminished the attraction. "It would not be taking advantage since I want you to have it."

She rose and headed for the door, Francine beside her. "You know, now that I have a choice, I truly don't want to go to my father at all."

"You have always wanted to go West," Francine reminded her. "This is an opportunity to do so without paying for the trip. When you reach Salt Lake City, you can decide what you want to do."

As she walked, Beth pulled on her gloves. "I fear it might not be that easy, Francie. Until I turn eighteen, my father has control over me." The restaurant had become crowded during their time with the lawyer. Beth's long, mauve-tinted skirt caught on a chair leg, causing her to stumble. She righted herself with Francine's aid and continued toward the door. "My only hope is that he will not care enough about what I do or where I go to interfere in my decisions."

"I hope so, as well." Francine squeezed Beth's arm.

They stepped out of the hotel onto the brick sidewalk and found the Lieutenant and Mrs. Hightower waiting. They appeared to be having a calm conversation, which ended abruptly as the girls approached, and they moved apart, almost guiltily, which puzzled Beth.

She regretted having to join them. She needed more time to figure out what she wanted to do. Should she decide against going to her father, she'd prefer sending Lieutenant McCall a note rather than telling him to his face. He would argue, and Beth detested arguments.

"Everything taken care of?" McCall's eagerness to be done with her showed in his tone and attitude.

Beth did not care for him. Nor was she impressed by her so-called chaperone. Something about the woman seemed off, as if she were not what she tried to represent herself to be. Her voice and language lacked the finesse one would expect of a woman in her supposed station, and her clothing was a tad more revealing.

"Yes, the attorney gave me enough cash to buy a few necessities for the trip." She looked down at her worn, dirty, and too-tight frock. She had not had a new dress for two years and desperately wanted one. What she wore now was too short and too tight across the chest. "As you can see, we both desperately need clothing."

He rolled his eyes. "Another delay. However, I do see the necessity." His gaze lingered on her bosom. "Your father sent cash to cover your expenses, Miss Webster. Mrs. Hightower will pay for your purchases and give the receipts to me. I will allow one hour for your shopping. No more. We must catch the train by noon if we are to reach St. Louis on schedule."

"I understand, Lieutenant. We shall be quick. I promise."

With Francine and Mrs. Hightower in tow, Beth headed for the mercantile, where she selected two simple dresses, undergarments, bonnets, a portmanteau to store them in, and a few toiletries. Then she turned her attention to her friend.

"You cannot go naked on this journey, Francie," Beth told her, prepared for the argument she knew she'd get. Francine hadn't a penny but did have pride. "That silk dress you're wearing was lovely once, but you need sturdy, practical clothes suitable for travel."

"All right," Francine succumbed, surprisingly fast. "But until we reach your father and I find employment and can pay you back, I will consider myself in your service."

"Nonsense." Beth laughed. As if she would ever let her

friend wait on her like a servant. "I do not need a maid, and you know it. You are my friend, so it is my right to buy you gifts."

Francine huffed but ceased arguing.

"Neither of you will have any new clothes if we don't get going," Mrs. Hightower groused.

Beth refrained from showing the disdain she felt for the woman. Her chaperone might call herself a lady, but Beth had doubts about the truth. She also questioned Mrs. Hightower's true role on the trip after seeing how she and the lieutenant looked at each other.

Beth gave Francine no choice but to select two dresses, a petticoat, and underthings. "Now, we need suitable shoes."

The cobbler across the street proved to be a kind man who knew what he was doing and fitted the girls with comfortable but sturdy half-boots. Mrs. Hightower paid for the purchases and dragged Beth and Francine from the shop. When they found the lieutenant, the chaperone gave him the receipt, which he tucked into his pocket. Beth could have paid for the purchases but decided since her father sent money to take care of their needs, she'd let him do it.

Together, the group made their way to the stagecoach station. A coach would take them to the train depot. Their bags had been sent ahead. Glancing at each other, they grinned, joined hands, and all but skipped down the street like children as they began their adventure.

The stage portion of the trip proved dusty, exciting, and arduous. The train turned out to be less pleasant. The smells of sweaty bodies and the food brought by other passengers nearly overwhelmed Beth in the stuffy car and made her queasy. Mrs.

Hightower opened a window and shut it just as fast as soot and smoke from the locomotive streamed inside. The girls curled up on one bench to sleep while the lieutenant and Beth's chaperone made do with another.

In Independence, Beth and Francine had their first look at Indians. They were dirty, dressed in rags, and smelled like a sewer, greatly disappointing Beth. They also begged from anyone who passed by.

"They're nothing like Mene-Seela in *The Last of The Mohicans*," Beth complained.

Francine held a hankie to her nose. "They stink! And look, that woman is rubbing herself all over that man. It is despicable."

Despicable—Beth's father's favorite word for Indians. She'd learned that long ago from the letters he wrote to her mother before Beth went away to school. It saddened her to see the natives this way and to hear the disgust in Francine's voice, though she was right; they stunk.

Another passenger sitting nearby said, "It was white men who made them that way. Allow me to introduce myself. I am Caleb Stewart."

He had a charming Scottish accent Beth loved hearing. "I'm glad to meet you, Mr. Stewart. I'm Miss Beth Webster, and this is my friend, Miss Francine Gibbs. Lieutenant McCall here—" she gestured to the officer "—is escorting me to my father in Utah Territory, and Francine is accompanying me."

Almost reluctantly, she gestured to Mrs. Hightower. "Mrs. Hightower is our chaperone."

"'Tis a pleasure." Mr. Stewart bowed his head in acknowledgment. "This is my seventh trip west. If I can answer any questions you might have, feel free to ask."

"I do have a question," Beth spoke up. "Why are those Indians dressed so poorly?" She hated seeing anyone suffering, and these people appeared rather pathetic.

"They're damned savages." Sitting in front of them, McCall turned toward them, his face reflecting his disgust. "That's why."

Stewart frowned. "They are a proud people whom we have reduced to drunks and beggars. Their bodies can't handle the rotgut whiskey traders give them. We took their land and then treated them like dogs."

"That's because they're no better than dogs," McCall retorted. "Mrs. Hightower and I would like to go for a walk. Do you girls wish to join us?"

"I'd rather stay here," Beth replied. She wanted to speak to Mr. Stewart more and glean whatever knowledge she could from him about what they were facing on the journey. Besides, where was there to walk on a train?

"Me, as well." Francine, sitting next to the window, continued watching the people who were boarding.

"I'd be happy to keep an eye on them for you, Lieutenant," Mr. Stewart offered.

"Thank you, sir." McCall took Mrs. Hightower's hand. "Most kind."

Beth frowned. The man barely knew the chaperone and shouldn't be touching her in such a personal manner. One more item that made her wonder about the lieutenant.

McCall's face took on a serious expression. "I expect you girls to behave properly. Don't let them leave the train, Stewart."

"Of course." Stewart nodded. "They are lovely young women. I shall enjoy their company and protect them with my life."

Beth smiled. She liked the Scotsman immensely, finding his company far more stimulating and interesting than McCall's. His eyes reflected wisdom, experience, and kindness, a warm brown rather than the iciness of the lieutenant's.

As they continued to watch the scenery whiz past, the man entertained them with tales of life with his prominent family in Glasgow.

Beth loved hearing about Scotland. She had always had an interest in the country.

Stewart had migrated to America at a young age and earned his living as a fur trader until a few years ago when he settled in Boston for a time.

"What did you mean when you said we have reduced the Indians to drunks and beggars?" Beth spotted a new group of ragged Indians.

Stewart gave a sad shake of his head. "White traders introduced liquor to them or a vile, watered-down version that they used to get the Indians to trade pelts for a few beads. Indians can't tolerate the stuff. Makes madmen of them. Yet they are addicted to it. Sights like this—" he gestured toward the Indians staggering about the depot's boarding platform "—turn my stomach and make me ashamed to have ever been part of the trading business. Even so, I miss those old days in the mountains." He shook his head. "Miss them terribly."

"Why don't you go back, Mr. Stewart?" Francine asked.

"Caleb, lass. Call me Caleb. Now that I've come this far

west, I am seriously considering going on and returning to my shining mountains."

"You should," Beth said. "You seem to love them a great deal."

"Ah, 'twould do my heart good to see them again. Ran away from home, I did, at the age of eighteen and never regretted it. Hadn't been in New York more'n a week when I met a fur trapper. His stories entranced me, so I went with him when he left to go back west. Four years I spent trapping beaver and fighting and living with Indians. Starving and freezing, I experienced it all. Haven't felt that alive since beaver went out of favor and the floor collapsed beneath the fur market. Came back east, married, and settled down."

"Oh," Francine said, "you're married. Do you have children?"

"No. My wife died trying to give me a son. Hadn't the heart for the marital state after that." He drew out a pipe made of reddish stone and filled it with tobacco. "Would you like to hear some stories about the West and fur trapping?"

"Very much indeed, Mr... I mean, Caleb," Beth stammered.

"Well, now, have you heard the one about Hugh Glass and the grizzly?"

"No," both girls exclaimed. "Tell us."

And he did. To hear of a man fighting a grizzly and living to tell about it fascinated and amazed Beth. She wanted more. The train trip lasted for days but was far too short for her. When they switched to a different train, she discovered it had an observation car with comfortable seats and large windows. They spent daytime hours there, watching the landscape speed past. They passed through numerous towns, stopping to take on passengers or allow others to depart. Beth found it an endless source of entertainment and considered it a learning experience, for she had never traveled anywhere except when her mother sent her to Runyon's school. She had been four years younger then and frightened by all the changes.

When the story ended, they spent the time watching the passengers board and guessing at their life stories.

"See that woman over there?" Beth pointed to what looked like a housewife who had perhaps lost her way. "Her face is so sad, and I think she's frightened. I imagine she's running from a cruel husband."

"Oh, yes," Francine replied. "I think I can see a bruise on her cheek. He must have beat her, and that's why she left him. The man about a yard from her is a banker, fleeing after stealing money from the bank."

The man in question wore a typical man's suit and held a satchel. He continually glanced around as if expecting someone, fidgeting with the bag he held in front of him as if to protect it.

Beth grinned. "I believe he's abandoning his wife as well. I can see a ring on his left hand."

"His poor children will be missing him."

"Perhaps he beats them, and they're glad his gone," Mr. Stewart put in, and the girls laughed, enjoying their game.

At last, the train chugged and rumbled into action, and they pulled away from the depot. Steam clouded the windows, cutting off the view. The rattle, clank, and rumble of the train nearly deafened them. The air in the car quickly became stuffy and generously spread odors through the car, the scent of hot metal, flying dust, and unwashed bodies. Francine took her hankie from her reticle and put it to her nose. Mrs. Hightower opened a window and immediately closed it as soot and steam blew in to cover them with fine ash and dirt.

When Mr. Stewart wasn't entertaining them, they made up other games to play. Beth and Francine curled up on their bench seat to take a nap while McCall and Mrs. Hightower whispered to each other like lovers. Mr. Stewart also took a nap.

They awoke to new smells as the passengers around them brought out food and filled their stomachs. Mr. Stewart offered them buffalo jerky, which they accepted and enjoyed. Mrs. Hightower passed out apples.

By the time they reached St. Louis, the newness and fun of train travel had worn thin for everyone. McCall had grown grumpy, Mrs. Hightower snippy, and Beth and Francine weary and bored. Even Mr. Stewart had become quiet and distant.

They left Missouri and entered Kansas by crossing the Missouri River near its confluence with the Kaw River by ferry. In Kansas City, they boarded another train to Leavenworth, where they took a stagecoach to reach the fort.

It was the first fort Beth and Francine had seen, and they were fascinated by all they saw there.

CHAPTER THREE

Fort Leavenworth, Nebraska Territory

"*H*a, Colonel?" Sparrow Hawk stood at attention and greeted the officer at his desk. They had worked together at Fort Kearney and become friends. Candor had been a mentor to Hawk, and he enjoyed seeing the man again. "Have you missed me?"

Colonel Abe Candor looked up and grinned, the smile barely visible between his beard and mustache. He understood the young man's native tongue, but Hawk also spoke English. "Hawk, my boy." He stood, walked around the desk, and clasped the tall, young Indian's hand. "By gum, it's good to see you. How'd you end up at Leavenworth?"

"I came in with a wagon train that arrived an hour ago, sir." Straight black hair hung down Hawk's back with a small braid on each side of his face, decorated with beads and a hawk's feather.

"You were scouting for them, I imagine?" Candor went to his liquor cabinet and poured two glasses of whiskey. He offered one to Hawk.

Hawk smiled but waved the glass away. "Whiskey is not good for Indians, Colonel."

"That's true for some, but you're different." Candor

pointed to Hawk's broad chest. "Other Indians might go on a bender after one shot, but not you."

Smiling, Hawk took the drink and sipped, then shook his head as it burned its way down his throat. The fort commander's compliment meant much to him.

Candor carried his glass back to his seat but remained standing. "Your English has improved immeasurably. I'm glad to see you've been practicing."

"You taught me well, Colonel."

"So, I did. Tell me, what's next on your agenda?"

Hawk took another sip and set the glass down. "I have not seen my family for three years and am eager to go home, sir."

Candor banged a fist on the desk in a triumphant gesture. "Stupendous. That happens to be perfect for what popped into my mind when I saw you."

Hawk grinned at the man's enthusiasm. Whatever he wanted, Hawk would try to oblige. He held great respect for the colonel. "What is that, sir?"

"I have a supply train scheduled to head west next week. It's to be led by Lieutenant Eggerton McCall. Know him?"

"Yes, I do." The mere mention of the man's name roused displeasure in Hawk. He and McCall had been stationed at the same post once, except the officer had been only a sergeant then. Hawk had caught him trying to force himself on a young Indian girl and might have killed McCall had the girl not begged him to stop.

The colonel eyed him closely. "You don't like the man, do you?"

"No, sir."

"Could you work with him if called upon to do so?"

Hawk nodded and folded his hands behind his back. "If you ask it of me, Colonel."

Candor moved to a window. He gazed out onto the parade ground for several moments before turning back to Hawk. "I would not ask you to do this if I didn't consider it important."

"I understand, sir."

"Good. I want this kept between you and me."

A staff sergeant knocked and stepped inside. "Excuse me, Colonel. I have a message for you."

Candor motioned for him to bring it. The sergeant waited.

"Humph." Candor snorted. "My old friend, Caleb Stewart, is here. I'll need to see him about a task I have for him." He handed the sergeant the message, and they exchanged words.

Hawk welcomed the news about Stewart, for they, too, had become friends.

Candor turned to the sergeant. "Ask Mr. Stewart to come to see me. And tell Lieutenant McCall that if Stewart comes to him on the trail, I will expect and appreciate his cooperation with anything the Scotsman needs."

The sergeant nodded, pivoted, and left.

The colonel put the message down and gave his attention back to Hawk. "To get back to our conversation, I don't trust McCall, especially since a young woman will be traveling with the supply train."

"A young woman?"

"Yes. The daughter of Colonel Jonathan Webster of the Fifth Infantry at Camp Floyd in Utah Territory. The girl's mother died, so she must live with her father now. Webster made travel arrangements for her through me, but I agreed before I learned McCall would be in charge, not only of the supply train but of the girl as well." Candor resumed staring out the window. "I want you there to keep an eye on things, Hawk. She's only seventeen."

"Am I to scout for McCall?"

"That is my plan."

"As a scout, I would be away from the train much of the time and unable to protect the girl adequately."

"Hmm." The colonel returned to his desk, a frown creasing his forehead. "Tell you what I'll do. I'll inform McCall you are going with the train as a private citizen returning to your people and will make yourself available to help scout. That will give you more freedom and time in camp."

"Very well, Colonel. I accept this assignment."

"I am relieved, Hawk. I could not have lived with myself if a defenseless girl came to harm with a patrol I sent out."

"Nor could I. I will protect her as I would my blood sister." The lieutenant had best watch himself. This time, even if the girl begged him not to hurt McCall, Hawk doubted he could stop.

Mrs. Hilary Hightower bore down on Beth and Francine outside Fort Leavenworth's commissary in a wine-colored gown with Pagoda sleeves and a six-boned hoop underneath. The skirt took up the entire boardwalk, but she appeared regal with her ramrod back and high-flying chin. "Highfalutin," as Caleb Stewart would say, were he there. A giggle escaped Beth before she could stop it, and she turned to hide her grin.

"Miss Webster? Miss Gibbs? Are you ready to leave? I

saw Lieutenant McCall a moment ago. He said we would depart within a half hour. We'd best fetch our valises."

"We have ours right here, ma'am." Beth gestured to the bags beside them.

"Excellent. I'll retrieve mine from the hotel and meet you across the square, where you can see that the soldiers are assembling the carts and wagons."

Mrs. "Highfalutin" motioned to the activity on the far side of the square where soldiers scurried about, balky horses whinnied, and wagon wheels rumbled as they moved into place. Before Beth could reply, she spied two men walking toward them. "Oh, my."

"What is it?" Francine asked.

"Mr. Stewart is coming and has an Indian with him." Beth moved closer to Francine. Fear and curiosity vied for space in her thoughts. She wished to find Caleb correct in his claim that proud, noble red men did exist, and that her father's tales of ferocious, evil Indians were biased and unfounded. But Stewart was a virtual stranger. Books like *The Last of The Mohicans* were fiction, and her father had been fighting Indians for years. He might have exaggerated his tales, but they surely contained some truth. "We are safe here, are we not?" she whispered to her chaperone.

Mrs. Hightower scowled, an action at which she proved highly accomplished. "Don't be ridiculous. If that Indian were dangerous, he would not be allowed on fort property. Nor would he be in Mr. Stewart's company. Use your head, why don't you?"

"Oh, but..." Beth's gaze flashed between Francine, Mrs. Hightower, and the men they waited to greet.

"Good morning, Mr. Stewart," Mrs. Hightower sang out.

"And good morning to you," he replied, drawing closer. "You ladies look exceedingly lovely today. Are you ready to begin your overland travels?"

"Indeed, we are." Her face flushed, and she appeared embarrassed. "Or soon will be. I still must fetch my valise, but the young ladies are ready."

Beth did not respond, too engrossed in studying the men's attire. Rather than the dark gray suit he'd worn aboard the train, Mr. Stewart wore a simple white shirt with a plaid blanket thrown over his shoulder and a knee-length skirt of the same fabric that stopped short at the knees.

A man in a skirt. Shocking. And fun.

It made Beth want to laugh. Long, dark stockings covered his legs, thankfully. Never had she seen anything like his outfit, but she decided she liked seeing something new and different.

"Ah." He smiled at her. "I believe she's shocked by my attire. In Scotland, my dear, this is what men wear on special occasions. 'Tis called a kilt."

"And what is the special occasion today, sir?" Mrs. Hightower asked.

"Why, I wear it in honor of you ladies since we will be parting today and likely never to see one another again. But, please," he motioned to the man next to him, "let me introduce my friend, Sparrow Hawk of the Snake Indian Nation. His people live north of Utah Territory and are friendly with whites. I assure you; he is to be trusted."

Mrs. Hightower and Francine greeted the man.

Beth swallowed, straightened her shoulders, and summoned her courage. If neither her formidable chaperone nor Francine was frightened, she would endeavor to hide her apprehension. "I… I am pleased to meet you, Mr. Hawk."

"The honor is mine."

His well-spoken English, army trousers, and calico cotton shirt surprised her. Except for his darker skin, leather moccasins, and the long, black hair down his back, he looked much like any other man. An odd, little leather pouch hung from a thong around his neck, and a knife rested in a beautifully beaded sheath at his waist. She saw no hatchet or bow and quiver of arrows. Not even a pistol. He smelled far cleaner than the other Indians she'd seen along the way and carried himself with pride and confidence. He had an earthy sort of regal quality that brought Mene-Seela to mind.

Confusion conflicted with hope. Here before her stood an Indian who did indeed appear to prove her father wrong and Mr. Stewart right. Perhaps the truth was that some Indians were as McCall described so scathingly and others like those she'd read about in books. Enthralled, she immediately wished to get to know him better.

"Hawk here will be traveling west with you ladies," Caleb said. "He's an army scout, you see, and volunteered to help scout for Lieutenant McCall on the journey."

"Oh, my," Beth exclaimed and immediately chided herself. It would be foolish to reveal her interest in the man.

Mrs. Hightower prevented her from saying more by pinching her arm. "We shall look forward to seeing more of you then, Mr. Hawk."

He did not reply, merely giving a jerk of his chin.

"Come, ladies, we had best hurry," Mrs. Hightower urged.

Beth looked at Mr. Stewart and felt a keen sense of loss.

Impulsively, she stepped forward and kissed the Scotsman on the cheek. "Goodbye, Mr. Stewart. I shall miss your company."

"As I will miss yours, my dear." He brushed a finger over her blemished cheek. "The world is full of blind, ignorant people, Beth Webster. You are a lovely girl. As long as you know that no words can hurt you in your heart."

The sudden urge to cry surprised and embarrassed her. "Thank you." Turning, she hurried away.

With a farewell wave to the men, Francine followed.

As they strolled across the square, Beth found herself even more intrigued by the idea of getting to know Sparrow Hawk. The anticipation added to the excitement of the upcoming adventure. Even so, she wished with all her heart she did not have to go to her father at journey's end.

Sparrow Hawk watched the women scurry away and frowned. "The girl you call Miss Webster fears me, Caleb." He felt terrible to have such an effect on her. He never saw anyone with a mark on her face, such as the girl. An ache entered his heart, for he found her good to look upon, yet he knew many would scorn her and call her *dechenabuindi*, ugly, maybe even cursed.

Caleb flapped a dismissive hand. "Beth is young but also reckless. Charm her. Rouse her curiosity. She'll come around."

"How does a man charm a *hepi*, white woman?" Hawk grinned, sure that he would fail at such a task. He wished he could talk with the Webster girl but knew it to be unwise.

Together, the men strolled across the square.

Caleb took out a chaw of tobacco. "Be polite. Find ways to help her. Protect her." He bit off a piece for himself and offered the chaw to Hawk, who waved it away.

Rotten and missing teeth had always been a problem for Indians. Their food was often difficult to eat, and things like chewing tobacco didn't help, but they did what they could to protect their teeth. Hawk had noticed that many white men had severely stained teeth. He attributed it to tobacco and perhaps alcohol and wanted nothing to do with either. "I will do as you suggest, my friend."

Raucous laughter captured his attention. Two drunken men staggered out of the saloon and into the street. Hawk realized then where Caleb intended to go. "I wish very much to talk with you more, Caleb, but if you mean to enter the saloon, I will leave you here. Indians are not allowed in there."

Caleb merely smiled and led the way inside, one hand holding Hawk's arm. The bartender had a mustache bushy enough to hide a porcupine and was the only inhabitant. He looked from Sparrow Hawk to Caleb and frowned. Hawk halted just inside.

"Give us two whiskeys, barkeep, and do not give me any sass about my friend here," Caleb ordered, slapping his hand on the bar. He turned and waved for Hawk to join him. "Sparrow Hawk is a genuine U.S. Army Scout. You treat him right."

The proprietor continued scowling. Hawk held up a hand. "Nothing for me."

Looking relieved, the barkeep poured a drink and set it in front of the older man. Caleb picked it up and walked back over to Hawk. "You sure?"

"Yes. To be seen here could cause me to lose my job, and

my family needs the money I send them. The Snake people are starving, like other tribes. Forgive me, but I must go."

Caleb nodded. "I will go with you." He swallowed his drink and returned the glass to the bar, along with a coin. "It has been good to see you again, son of my old friend. I am not ready to say goodbye yet."

Hawk grinned. "Nor am I."

They left the saloon and wandered around the square, discussing the changes that had come to the fur trade in the last decade and more since Caleb worked as a trapper. A few men still managed to eke out an existence selling animal pelts, but most had switched to other trades, such as wilderness guides. Caleb expressed an interest in trying that line of work.

"At least it would allow me to live in my beloved mountains," he said.

"You would be welcome to live in our village between jobs. You know my people revere you."

"My thanks, Hawk. I might take you up on that." Caleb spat tobacco juice and took his pipe from his vest pocket. "First, I must learn what the army wants of me."

Hawk saw that the supply train was ready to leave. "I must go, my friend. Come to the village soon. Father will be eager to see you."

"And I him." Caleb gave Hawk a friendly slap on the shoulder, and they shook hands. "Take care of yourself. When you reach home, tell your father I will see him soon."

"His *bihyi*, heart, will be glad."

Hawk did not say goodbye. As was typical with him, he gave a jerk of his chin and left. Disappointment filled him at having to leave. He would have enjoyed more time with Caleb, but remembering what the man said about having business with the army, he smiled. Instinct, and an overheard conversation in the colonel's office, told Hawk he would see Caleb sooner than his friend expected.

CHAPTER FOUR

L and—as far as a woman could see from a bouncing wagon seat. Land that stretched like a waking cat, that rolled, swelled, and undulated from horizon to horizon. Empty land, except for the tall, waving grass. And gullies. Gullies the human eye couldn't detect until a person or wagon teetered on the brink. Here and there, a bent or broken tree hunched over a stream that ran only in the memories of thirsty buffalo. Above spread a blue sky, so vast and unending that a person felt tiny and insignificant in comparison.

Prairie. Surely, nowhere else in all the world but Kansas Territory could so much emptiness exist. Beth wished Francine sat beside her with the driver, Charley, enjoying the sights instead of napping in the wagon bed. Francine was missing so much.

So far, they had seen no Indians, which disappointed her. But Sparrow Hawk came past their camp each evening and stopped to talk for a moment. The more she saw of the Indian scout, the more he intrigued her. The nervousness she'd suffered at first in his presence had gone.

Unfortunately, he wasn't their only nightly visitor. Lieutenant McCall also stopped and stayed far longer than Beth would have preferred. Twice, he invited her to take a walk with him. Mrs. Hightower scolded her for not being more friendly as the officer seemed taken with Beth. Even if he were, she would have refused his invitations. The man made her distinctly uncomfortable. How he looked at her made her feel naked and as if his hands were all over her. She shuddered with revulsion.

The caravan of soldiers, horses, mules, and wagons stretched out single file, three-hundred yards ahead of the women's wagon and another three hundred behind. The procession wound over the prairie, veering past gullies or dipping down into them like one of the slithering grass snakes she had run into on her walks. The train followed a road of sorts; ruts worn in the land by previous wagons bound for Oregon or the California gold mines.

Beth's wagon took a sudden nose-dive into one of the invisible ravines, almost knocking her from her seat and tumbling the flint-eyed army mules into a confusion of legs, manes, and tails. Only the fact that she had been seated at the time and had a tight grip on the wooden bench kept her in place. Charley had no problem, and she began to wonder what secret he hid for staying put so easily.

At last, the mules found their hooves and trudged on with Charley's whip snapping above their weary backs. The wheels crunched and scraped across the rocky, sand-lined bottom of the gully, leaving indelible marks of their passing, like muddy footprints on a freshly scrubbed wood floor. Beth breathed a sigh of relief as the wagon ground its way up the other side and onto level ground.

The journey had proved more difficult and wearing than either girl expected, forcing Beth to realize how spoiled she'd been until now. Even without her parents playing an active role in her life and the lovely wardrobe many girls of her class enjoyed, she'd had what she needed and felt no reason to complain. She had hated Runyon's Finishing School until Francine came, and they discovered common interests. Life there could not be called easy, and a day never passed when Beth did not wish to leave.

But traveling across vast, open country in a wagon did have its drawbacks. Lack of privacy when a girl needed a privy, for one. Barely a day passed when her foot didn't slip as she climbed down from the wagon, and she ended up on her bottom with her skirts around her hips. Blowing dust, constant wind, and insects added to the daily discomfort they endured. At times, maintaining a positive attitude and seeing it all as an adventure became a challenge. Even so, she would not choose to be anywhere else.

With the disaster of the gully averted, Beth returned her gaze to the landscape, saw herself in her mind, and laughed out loud. She had done the undoable—trespassed into the pale, liquid world of a watercolor sketch, all blue, dun, and green washes, the details faint like smudged pencil scratchings. With this clear air, she deemed it a marvel the sky held any color.

At moments like this, when she felt on par with a sand flea yet taller than the clouds, she regretted having to share the world with others. At least Mrs. Hightower, with her unending complaints and sarcasm, had kept to her bed in the army wagon today with a supposed upset stomach. How Francine could stand staying in there with their grumpy chaperone, Beth could not imagine. Charley's favorite comment about Mrs. Hightower always made her laugh; *She'd complain if'n you hung her with a new rope,* he'd say. But Beth wished Francine would spend more time outside with her.

"There are too many bugs out there," Francine complained when Beth tried to cajole her into taking a walk. "And the wind blows my hair in my eyes. Besides, I don't want to get sunburned again as I did on our last walk."

"Then you should wear your bonnet."

A wheel struck a rock, jolting the wagon. Old Charley cursed. Beth barely had time to gather in her long skirts before he leaned across her to empty his God-fearing mouth of some not-so-God-like tobacco juice. To spit on his own side would mean spitting into the wind, something Old Charley would never do, even though his grizzled beard had already been generously lacquered with the substance. After wiping his mouth on his sleeve, he reached for his whip and cracked it over the mules' backs. Giving them a taste of the "long oats," he called it. Charley, a white-haired, chisel-faced old Lucifer, hurrying his black steeds towards the edge of life.

Beth smiled. My, she was getting fanciful. Old Lucifer, indeed.

"What happened?" Francine poked her head out from the wagon covering behind Beth and Charley.

"Hit a rock," Charley answered. "Nothin' outta the ordinary."

"Come out and join us," Beth invited as Charley maneuvered the wagon onto the backbone of a low ridge, a wise man's way of avoiding the gee-up and whoa of back-wrenching gullies.

"I don't know. Maybe."

A sharp crack interrupted the familiar creak of the wagon bed. The entire conveyance lurched, and Francine cried out in alarm as she tumbled backward out of sight. A lone wheel careened past them down the slope, and the horrifying thought that the wheel belonged on the wagon flashed through Beth's mind.

The next instant, the world tilted drastically, catapulting Beth through the air. With a startled shriek, she landed hard on the ground, her head striking something harder than dirt. Blackness descended.

"Miss Webster?" Mrs. Hightower's voice.

"Beth, wake up."

That was Francine. "Someone, get me a wet cloth to bathe her face."

Beth tried to make sense of everything, but her mind spun. A sharp scent caused her nose to smart. She opened her eyes to see Mrs. Hightower waving smelling salts in front of her. Pushing away the woman's hand, she tried to sit up. Pain shot through her head and knees.

"Are you all right, Elizabeth?" The chaperone bent over her with a concerned look.

Beth nodded as best she could without causing the pain to become unendurable. Inside, she smiled a little. Her formidable chaperone had never called her by her given name before. Perhaps they were beginning to feel more comfortable with each other. The question was whether Beth wanted her as a friend. She tested her limbs. "I hurt all over, but I don't think anything is broken."

"Good. You should be more careful. To avoid impeding the journey, I spent all day in the wagon bed, unable to see anything. Now you've gone and caused an even bigger delay. Come on and stand up. We must get out of the way so the men can mend the wheel."

Beth tried to obey with Francine's help—and only for her. Her so-called chaperone offered no help at all, only criticism. Of all the nerve to insinuate this was Beth's fault. A wave of dizziness struck, and she sank back down.

"Wonderful," Mrs. Hightower muttered. "You can't even walk."

A large set of hands clasped the annoyed chaperone's shoulders and moved her aside.

"Allow me." To Beth's shock and displeasure, Lieutenant McCall scooped her into his arms.

"Oh. This isn't necessary, Lieutenant." She did not entirely trust the officer for reasons she could not name. All the attention he paid her could not be genuine. She suspected his real interest lay with Mrs. Hightower. "I only need another moment or two for the dizziness to pass, and I'll be fine."

He carried her to a lone tree beside a narrow stream.

To Beth, it seemed to take forever before he set her down. His hand slid down her back and around so that his thumb brushed the undercurve of her breast. She jerked at the too-familiar touch and glared.

His gaze roved over her from head to toe. "You're sure nothing is broken, Miss Webster?"

As if his phony concern excused his wandering fingers.

She pushed him away. "Quite certain. Thank you for caring, Lieutenant. You may tend to your troopers now. Francie will care for me."

His gray eyes lacked kindness as he stared, his mouth a grim, straight line. "You might show a bit more gratitude, Miss Webster."

For manhandling me under the guise of helping? "I am grateful for your help, sir."

Standing, he looked at the older woman, who responded with a slight lifting of her shoulders.

Beth could see he wanted to say more, which wouldn't be complimentary. She waited tensely for the explosion. She'd always suspected he had a temper.

"We'll camp here," he said and stomped off.

That was all? Beth stared at the man's departing figure. She didn't know how to read Lieutenant McCall. She'd thought she had him figured out a little, at least. Now, she wasn't sure of anything. This journey had turned out vastly different from what she'd expected. All she could do now was wait to see what happened next.

"Francie! Francie, wake up." Beth shook her friend's shoulder where she lay in her bed inside the wagon that night, difficult to see in the dim light of Beth's lantern. Outside, the moon rode high in the sky through a bed of stars. But clouds approached from the south. For once, no wind blocked other sounds, and the camp was noisier than usual.

The girl moaned and made a half attempt to push Beth away. "Wha-is-t?"

"The soldiers are all drunk, Francie. I'm scared. Wake up."

Francine rolled over and opened her eyes. "Beth? What's wrong?"

"I told you. The soldiers are all drunk. And Mrs. Hightower is missing." Beth adjusted the lantern to give more light.

"Missing?" Francine's eyes widened. "Where'd she go?"

Beth gave a sound of exasperation. "If I knew that, she wouldn't be missing. Well, that's not entirely true.

When she left the wagon, I woke up and saw her go toward the lieutenant's tent."

Francine sat up and rubbed her eyes. "Why would she go there?"

"That's what I want to know. Get dressed. Something strange is happening, and we're going to investigate."

"Aw, Beth. I'm sleepy."

"How can you sleep with all that noise going on?"

Francine cocked her head. "Oh. Why are they yelling like that?"

"Because they're drunk. Come on."

A gunshot ripped through the air. Even though the women's wagon was fifty yards from the rest of the camp, the sound seemed uncomfortably close.

A man's voice rose in a bawdy song.

Francine twisted around to peek out from under the canvas cover. "I do not know that I want to be around those men if they are drinking, Beth."

"Neither do I, but I'm determined to find out what Mrs. Hightower is doing." Setting the lantern at the foot of the wagon, Beth lowered the tailgate. "Are you coming?"

"I suppose." Francine quickly dressed and followed Beth into the night.

At the campfire, soldiers danced with each other, sang senseless songs, and tossed empty liquor bottles into the flames, causing the fire to leap and sputter as the glass shattered. The thought of one of those men catching them off alone set Beth's pulse jumping, but she kept dragging Francine with her, keeping to the shrubbery. At last, they reached the lieutenant's tent, which also sat a little apart.

Indistinct voices carried from inside. On hands and knees, the girls crawled closer. Beth was debating how close they dared go when McCall raised his voice.

"I told you. I have good reason for courting that silly little girl. I'm going to marry her."

"Who's he going to marry?" Francine whispered.

"Shush, and maybe we'll find out," Beth whispered back.

"But why, Eggy?" Hilary Hightower asked, her voice breathy and low. "Why Elizabeth? And what will happen to me if you get married? I would miss you terribly."

"You need not fret. Marrying Elizabeth won't interfere with my relationship with you because I don't plan to keep the annoying little chit."

Beth's mouth dropped open, and she scowled. Not keep her? What did that mean?

"Beth!" Francine said, disbelief and fear in her tone.

"Shh."

"What are you saying, Eggy?" Mrs. Hightower asked.

"There are ways of getting rid of unwanted wives. Asylums, for example."

"Eggy, that would be a horrible thing to do. Elizabeth isn't crazy."

The two girls outside stared at each other, mouths open.

McCall's voice came again, sultry, inviting. "Why must you argue with me? We've more pleasant ways of entertaining each other. Let the future take care of itself."

Humph. Beth would never marry him. He'd have to look elsewhere for a wife.

Faint smacking noises came from inside the tent. "They're kissing," Francine whispered.

"Quiet!"

The thought of having McCall's mouth on her made Beth shudder. Revolted, she turned to leave. Mrs. Hightower's voice stopped her.

"Ooh, I love it when you do that." Mrs. Hightower sighed and moaned. Fabric rustled, and more moans followed. "Suckle my breast, Eggy."

Francine gasped.

"What was that?" the lieutenant asked.

"Something outside."

Francine clapped a hand over her mouth. Beth yanked on the girl's sleeve, turned, and crawled back into the shadows. No sooner had they reached the safety of the shrubbery and darkness than McCall, naked except for his long underpants, emerged from his tent, pistol in hand.

Frozen in place, the girls watched until he returned inside before they hurried back to their wagon.

Huddled together beneath a blanket beside the campfire, Francine shook her head. "I can't believe it. Mrs. Hightower and Lieutenant McCall are lovers."

"Can you believe she calls him Eggy?" Beth said with a chuckle. "I think it's hilarious."

More gunshots reverberated through the air. The soldiers

whooped and sang and laughed. One staggered close to the girls' wagon and emptied his stomach into the weeds.

Beth's mind spun with questions. Fear weighted her chest. What should they do? Fort Kearney, the nearest settlement, remained some distance away, while Leavenworth lay far behind. At any moment, she expected a drunk soldier to stumble upon them. Or, worse, come looking for them. She had only the vaguest idea of what men and women did in the marriage bed, but she'd heard whispers, none of them good. And tonight had given her new notions to contemplate.

"Why would she want him to suckle her breast?"

"What I know already is bad enough." Francine shuddered. "I don't want to know more."

"What do you mean?"

"Never mind," Francine said. "I'm just scared and rambling. And you, especially, should be frightened. My mother had a friend once who was mistress to someone high up in the government. He wasn't married, and when Mother's friend tried to get him to marry her, he had her admitted to an asylum in Connecticut."

Beth snorted. "That's impossible. He would have needed proof of insanity to do that. Only doctors can have people committed."

"I wish that were true, Beth, but it isn't. Mother said men often turn to asylums to get rid of an unwanted or troublesome wife. All they must do is pay the asylum to take the woman. Her objections are ignored."

Beth stared at her friend, praying she'd heard wrong.

"Well, I am not married to the lieutenant and never will be, so it's a moot point."

"He can say you're his wife, Beth. The asylum doctors won't interfere as long as they get their money."

An acrid taste filled Beth's mouth. She swallowed hard, fetched water from the barrel strapped to the wagon's side, and rinsed out her mouth. "Well, I will not allow such a horror to happen. Nor do I plan to remain here like a sitting duck, waiting for a hunter to come along." Her illusions of being safe because of her father had vanished. At the moment, she wasn't sure she would ever feel safe again.

"Where can we go?" Francine asked.

The full moon shone on the undulating prairie surrounding the camp. How Beth longed to be out there relishing the peace and solitude. And why shouldn't they? Who would even notice their absence? Not Hilary or Lieutenant McCall.

"I know where. Come on, Francie, and bring the blanket."

Driven by fear and the spark of wildness that so often got her into trouble, Beth wrapped a second blanket around her against the coolness of the night while Francine gathered a coffee pot, cup, and a bag of coffee grounds.

Beth collected a few biscuits left over from supper, and they stowed them in a burlap bag. Keeping to the shadows, they stole out of camp onto the open prairie. Crickets chirped and hopped out of their way. The scent of water led them to a narrow stream bordered by willows. A wet splash of water followed the throaty croak of a frog. Francine swatted at a mosquito.

Beth stopped at a grassy spot on the bank half-surrounded by a rock outcropping. "This looks good, Francie. Stow our provisions under the outcrop and help me find wood for a fire."

A search rewarded them with a few branches, a handful of

kindling, and, for Beth, a bruised great toe. Wood was sparse on the prairie after numerous wagon trains had passed through. Without the willows along the stream, there would be no wood.

As Beth took out a match from her match safe, a coyote howled some distance away.

Francine shivered and slapped at another mosquito. "I wish coyotes wouldn't do that. Such an eerie sound. How close do you think they are?"

Beth stood and pressed a stinging hand to the aching small of her back. No matter how she turned, she saw a vast, empty world lit only by a few stars unhidden by the clouds. Distances were impossible to determine. "Once we get this fire going, that would keep them away."

Not even a blade of grass moved. Nights this time of year grew cold in open country where the wind blew incessantly, and no trees existed to offer shelter. Assured they remained safe and alone, Beth kneeled and struck a match.

At last, a spark caught, and Beth cried out in triumph. Together, the girls blew on the spark, hoping to ignite their tidy bundle of twigs. The flame had barely caught when a foot came out of nowhere and kicked the fire away.

Startled, Beth gasped and nearly fell over as she craned her neck to see who had ruined the fire. Silhouetted against a three-quarter moon stood the imposing form of a man. No footfalls had announced his approach. He did not look like a soldier.

"Who are you, and why did you do that?" She used the cover of darkness and her navy-blue wool skirt to hide her action as she collected the largest rock she could reach. The stone felt cool and smooth in her aching fingers. Having a weapon gave her courage.

A low masculine voice answered, "You know me. I am Sparrow Hawk. To come out here alone was foolish."

"She isn't alone," Francine objected. "I am here."

Squinting, Beth saw long dark hair hanging down his bare chest. He wore only leather leggings, fringed along the sides and with a long flap in front. The moccasins on his feet accounted for his silent approach. She dropped the rock. "How did you find us?"

"You make enough noise to frighten off a herd of buffalo a mile away." He smiled. "I followed you."

Beth frowned. "You mean you saw us leave the wagon and followed us from there?"

"No, from the lieutenant's tent. You should not have gone there."

She stood. "Well, I guess we might as well head back now. Without a fire, it is too cold to stay here." She reached for her blanket, and something whistled over her head.

"Down!" Hawk pulled her to the ground beside him.

"What happened?" Francie dropped down too.

"A bird nearly hit me."

"No bird." Hawk tapped Beth's mouth with his finger. "Quiet. An arrow almost killed you."

He must be joking. "Who would shoot an arrow at me?" Beth asked.

"Pawnee. War party comes."

She peered into the darkness, noting the sober expression on his proud face and the worry creasing his brow. He was serious. The truth hit her then. "You saved my life."

"Indians?" Francine whispered. "They won't hurt you, Mr.

Hawk, because you're one of them, but... what will they do to Beth and me?"

He grunted. "Pawnee would enjoy killing me. They are enemies of my people. Come, you must hide."

Tall shrubs brushed against them as he led them into the tall willows along the stream. Beth shuddered at the thought of the spiders no doubt residing in her hair now.

Deep within the bushes, Hawk shoved the girls down in a small open space and ordered them to keep silent.

Beth expected him to leave, but he stayed a mere touch away.

Within minutes, they heard the whisper of hooves in the distance. Branches snapped, and a horse snorted.

Beth burrowed deeper into the undergrowth. She looked for Hawk and saw only blackness.

"Francie?" she whispered.

"Here."

She reached out and took Francine's hand, trembling like her own.

The first horseman appeared as a silhouette against the indigo sky. Feathers fluttered from his head, and a horse gave a low whiffle. A second man appeared.

Indians.

Hawk had been right. They moved noiselessly toward the camp.

Should she try to warn the soldiers? Cry out? Scream? Drunk as they were, the dragoons would be easy targets and put up little fight. What of Mrs. Hightower?

Hawk slithered in beside them, a finger to his lips.

"Now that I know you're safe, I must warn the others," he

whispered. "Stay here."

He started to move off. Beth grabbed his arm. "Wait!"

"What is it?" He kept his eyes on the ghostly shadows gliding beyond the willows.

"I... I need to know, are you and Lieutenant McCall friends?"

He looked at her. "A man like him has no friends. Only fools who want to win his favor. I am no fool."

His words eased her fears and let her see him in a new light. He was more intelligent than she'd first thought, which made lies of comments she'd heard from people like her father about Indians being stupid and more animal than man. She liked knowing that.

Six Indians rode past. Then Hawk left, as silent as the night, leaving the girls alone. But he repeatedly returned with armfuls of brush, stacking it around them until they could no longer see out.

"I leave now." His voice threaded through the branches. "No matter what you hear or see, do not move. I will use my war cry to warn the soldiers. Don't be afraid. The colonel and Caleb Stewart asked me to protect you, and I will."

"No! Wait," Beth cried, suddenly afraid for him. "Don't go."

Too late. Beth wanted to go after him, beg him not to leave them alone, and endanger himself. She strained to hear some sound of his movement, but only an owl hoot reached her ears. Another, a little distance away, answered.

"We have to do something, Francie. The soldiers outnumber the Indians, but they're all drunk. The Pawnee will slaughter them before they know what hit them."

"What can we do?"

Beth thought for a moment. "When Hawk gives his war cry, we'll join in and make as much noise as possible."

"Won't that draw the Pawnee to us?"

Beth saw her point but felt they had to do something. "You have a better idea?"

The war cry echoed eerily over the plain, terrifying enough to curdle a man's blood. Or a woman's. Beth wanted to burrow into the ground like a rabbit and pray for safety. Her pulse pounded in her temples, and she feared the fright would stop her heart. But worry for Hawk, Francine, Mrs. Hightower, and the others drove her to act.

"Come on, Francie. Yell." She stood and screamed.

They shouted for all they were worth, waving and bouncing on their heels. When their arms became entangled in the willows, they pushed the brush aside and moved into the open. It seemed like they were the only people on earth, and no one existed to hear them.

The piercing cries of "*Yi, Yi, Yi*" filled the night, causing Beth to shiver with fear. Francine threw her arms around her friend, and they both shook. Other howls and noises came, barely human.

"Wh- What is that?" Francine stuttered.

"The Pawnee, I assume."

Shouts and screams of pain added to the din. Beth felt thankful to be where she was and not in camp where the fighting ensued. Her imagination filled her head with visions of dead soldiers covered with blood. Of savages taking scalps, though she knew not how they did that.

Who all were shrieking? The Pawnee or the dragoons?

Guns blasted. Clouds of smoke scented the air and limited the women's vision.

Would the battle never end? It seemed to go on forever. Who had been hurt or killed? Visions of Mrs. Hightower, Charley, and McCall floated through her mind, the bodies contorted and covered in blood.

Not Sparrow Hawk, please. Protect him.

It shocked her to realize she'd prayed for a man her father would term a vicious killer. Yet, Sparrow Hawk had been kind to her this night and protected them. Because a colonel and Mr. Stewart had asked him to or because, despite being Indian, he was a good man? She wished she knew. It would make a great difference, though she could not say why other than that she cared about Hawk.

A horse crashed through the willows, surprising the girls, and they squealed. Beth dropped to her knees and yelled for Francine to hide. The boom of gunfire close by all but deafened her as she tried to crawl deeper into the brush.

Francine let out an unearthly howl of fear and pain. Beth's heart stopped. Had her friend been killed? She began crawling back out of the willows to find her.

The horse continued to thrash about in the shrubbery, sounding monstrously terrifying. Beth's heart lodged in her throat. She rose to look for Francine and saw a hideously painted warrior on a horse, aiming a gun at Francine where she lay in the grass.

"No!" Beth snapped off a piece of a branch and burst out of the bushes, ruthlessly striking the man and horse. "You heathen bastard! Leave us alone. Go. Get out of here."

The horse bolted, brushing against her and nearly toppling

her over.

Everything went deathly silent, sounding all the more ominous after all the commotion. The Indian had disappeared. Beth froze.

She dropped her would-be weapon when nothing else happened and crawled toward Francine. Before she reached her, a new set of thundering hooves bore down from a different direction. Instinctively, she knew she was in danger. Why had they left their hiding place? They were going to die.

A brown arm marked with slashes of red paint snaked around her waist. Her feet left the ground. She hung at the horse's side, the Indian's arm holding her in place, her legs dangling uselessly, though she kicked for all she was worth. Her heart drummed in her ears, and she felt cold all over. Detesting her helplessness, she writhed and fought to get free, striking at the man's arm and the horse's belly.

"Beth!" Francine yelled. "Beth! Help! Someone help."

In her dangling position, Beth could not see her captor. She dug her fingernails into his arm to make him let go and attempted to bite him. Grease covered his flesh, tasting of animals and dirt. She tried to spit the unpleasant taste from her mouth and shouted for Sparrow Hawk.

Instead of dropping her, the warrior began to draw her up onto his lap.

To prevent him from succeeding, Beth kicked at the horse, hard as it was to reach from her position, and pushed against the animal's hide.

The warrior grunted and tightened his grip. She found his hand at her waist and pried at his fingers. He snarled something and jerked her higher.

From out of nowhere, strong hands tore her from the Indian's grasp and threw her to the ground. Her captor followed her down, landing atop her, but didn't stay there long.

As Beth scrambled away, she became aware of two men rolling over the earth, grunting and pounding at each other. The sounds of flesh striking flesh and the smack of fists meeting jaws terrified her. She didn't know which way to go or what to do. She had to find Francine and get them both away from there.

Francine cried out her name, and Beth scooted backward on her bottom, away from the battling men, until she found her friend and huddled next to her.

"It's Mr. Hawk," Francine said. "And the Pawnee who grabbed you."

Beth recognized Hawk then. He had freed her from the Pawnee and now fought for his life. For hers and Francine's. The fear faded enough for her to think logically again. She looked around to get her bearings and figure out how to escape.

Sudden quiet fell over the small, trampled clearing in the tall willows where the girls waited, breaths held and hearts hammering.

One man lay still. The other slowly rolled off him and lay on his back, panting.

The Pawnee? Or Sparrow Hawk?

Beth smelled the metallic scent of blood. Why didn't the men move? Were they dead?

Both were brown and wore leggings with breechclouts so that she couldn't tell them apart. With her hands fisted against her lips, she waited and prayed.

At last, one sat up.

"Sparrow Hawk," she cried and crawled toward him.

He stabbed a bloody knife into the dirt, drew it out, the blade clean now, and sheathed it at his waist. "Miss Webster? Miss Gibbs? Are you all right?"

"Yes," Beth answered. "Thanks to you."

"I can't move my leg," Francine said. "I think I've been shot."

Beth whirled toward her in dread. "Francie. No. Why didn't you tell me?"

Hawk kneeled on Francine's other side. "I must move your skirts to see your wound, Miss Gibbs."

"Do what you must." Francine reached for Beth's hand. "It hurts. It hurts something awful."

"Sparrow Hawk will know what to do. We'll be all right." *Please, Heavenly Father, don't let that be a lie.*

But Hawk did know. He gently wiped the blood from the wound with a strip he tore from Francine's petticoat and examined her injury. Standing, Beth stripped off her petticoat. She ripped off a strip, wadded it up, and handed it to Hawk to press against her friend's wound. She tore off more to use as bandages.

"The bullet broke her leg," he said. "It's bad. I must get her to Fort Kearney. There is a doctor there. But first, I must set the bone."

He moved to Francine's feet. "Hold her still. This will hurt, Miss Gibbs, but must be done if you are to use this leg again."

"Go ahead." Francine's voice shook.

Without warning, he gave the leg a vicious twist. The bone jerked into place with an audible snap. Francine squealed and fainted.

Sitting with her friend's head in her lap, Beth stroked Francine's face and murmured soft reassurances while tears ran down her cheeks.

"I will be back." Hawk stood and glanced around. "Stay here."

Like a ghost, he vanished into the darkness.

Beth wanted to cry out for him to stay but knew he would do what he must. And he would return. He would not abandon them.

In the minutes that followed, sitting in darkness, Beth realized how quiet the night had become. The Pawnee had gone. The girls waited, isolated and alone. Only Hawk knew where to find them. Francine remained unconscious, and Beth chewed on her lower lip while the feeling grew in her that the entire world had forgotten them and no one else existed except them. Long, tense minutes passed. Frightened, she worried they would never be found.

What if something happened to Hawk before he could return? A soldier might shoot him, mistaking him for a Pawnee, though those savages looked far different—more naked, with feathers fluttering everywhere, even on their horses. And the paint!

But Hawk had not been harmed. Nor had he forgotten them. He found Beth and murmured words in her ear that she found comforting even though he used a foreign, garbled tongue.

And he did not come alone. He brought Lieutenant McCall, Corporal Jenks, Mrs. Hightower, and a horse.

Pulling a sachet of smelling salts from her pocket, the chaperone kneeled beside Francine and waved them under the girl's nose. Francine groaned and opened her eyes.

"How are you feeling?" Mrs. Hightower asked.

Francine blinked. "I hurt."

"I'm sure you do." Mrs. Hightower turned to Beth. "What about you, Miss Webster?"

"I'm fine. A Pawnee tried to carry me away, but Sparrow Hawk saved me."

"I'll be certain to include his brave act in my ledger." Lieutenant McCall acknowledged Hawk with a nod. "Good work, Hawk."

Busy building some sort of contraption behind the horse, the scout did not respond. Mrs. Hightower and Corporal Jenks went to help him.

"You're certain you aren't hurt, Miss Webster?" The lieutenant hovered over her.

"Yes. What is Sparrow Hawk doing?"

"He's constructing a travois to carry Miss Gibbs to Fort Kearney."

"A travois?" What a strange word. She recognized it as French and searched her memory of her lessons on that language at school but didn't think she'd heard the word before.

"You'll see when it's ready."

That time came faster than expected as Hawk led the horse over and positioned him alongside Francine. Two poles had been fastened to the saddle, one on each side. The other ends dragged on the ground. In between lay blankets supported on a web of rawhide lacings. With Mrs. Hightower supporting Francine's leg and Beth holding her friend's hand, Hawk lifted the injured young woman onto the blankets. After placing more wool blankets over her, they bundled her securely in place with extra padding beneath her leg.

Finished, Hawk turned to the lieutenant. "I will return as soon as possible."

"May I go, too, please?" Beth pleaded, terrified for her friend and not wanting to be separated from her. They had been together daily for the last four years and would be lost without each other.

"You would slow me down," Hawk said the words kindly but firmly. "I must get her there as fast as possible without causing her more harm."

She nodded, but inside, her heart ached for Francine's agony.

"I will take good care of her." He peered down at her, his gaze willing her to believe him. "Do not worry."

Beth doubted her ability to do that and said nothing. She kissed Francine's forehead and murmured a soft goodbye.

Hawk mounted the horse and slowly dragged his patient away over the bumpy, uneven ground.

The lieutenant took Beth's arm and led her back to camp. Lost in her worries about what could happen to Francine, she barely noticed him. Everything was in an uproar. Three wounded soldiers needed attention, and several horses had been stolen. Two Pawnees were killed and taken away by their comrades. Bows and arrows could not compete with rifles.

Beth looked around for fallen arrows but found none. The warriors had retrieved them.

Gradually, the camp quieted, and calm returned. Beth slipped into her bed, exhausted and anxious about Francine. Mrs. Hightower woke her when she returned, supposedly from tending to the wounded troopers, but Beth knew everything possible had been done for them before she climbed into her wagon. Her chaperone had been with McCall instead.

"Now, Miss Webster." Mrs. Hightower sat on the opposite bed. "Tell me what you girls were doing away from camp. You could have both been shot or killed."

Beth wanted to ask why the sudden concern. And why did the lieutenant wish to marry her? But she counseled herself to keep quiet. If McCall knew she'd learned of his plans, he might decide to do something more drastic, force her to wed him or send her to an asylum without ever taking her to her father.

To learn such a thing could happen infuriated Beth. She needed a plan, a way to protect herself and discourage McCall.

Meeting her supposed chaperone's gaze, she said, "I appreciate your concern, Mrs..." She barely caught herself from saying Mrs. Shrew "...Hightower. We left camp because of you. I awoke, and you were missing. We were searching for you when Hawk found us and warned us of the impending attack. Where were you?"

Mrs. Hightower glanced away and fidgeted with her skirt. "I had gone out to relieve myself. I'm sure I would have heard you had you called for me."

"I see. Perhaps it would save trouble in the future if you let us know when you're leaving the wagon so we don't fret over your absence."

The woman stiffened, and her brow furrowed. "I'll take that under advisement."

As Beth watched Mrs. Hightower prepare for bed, she questioned whether there would ever be a chance for them to become friendly, if not friends. Then she asked herself if she even wanted to have such a relationship with a woman like her.

What would the *oh-so-proud* woman do if Beth told her what they knew about her? And the captain... what would happen if she mentioned his relationship with Mrs. Hightower to her father when she finally reached Camp Floyd?

It might be amusing to find out.

CHAPTER FIVE

The first thing Beth noticed as they approached Fort Kearney was its lack of fortifications. The fort stood on a slight elevation a few miles from the Platte River that appeared to her like a broad, muddy, braided series of shallow streams and islands in a world of grasses and willows.

"Plenty o' quicksand in that river," Charley told her. "Don't wanna go wading."

"I won't, but I wouldn't mind getting a closer view."

"Looks like they're building a town over there." Mrs. Hightower pointed three or four miles west of the fort where a few new buildings stood, and hammering floated on the wind.

The moment the wagon stopped in front of the fort, Beth jumped down. She saw five unpainted houses around a large open square or parade ground while two dozen long mud buildings extended in every direction from the roads along the sides of the square. Trees lined the parade ground. The only bushes Beth saw straggled along the banks of the Platte in the distance. Intermixed with immature trees bordering the square sat sixteen blockhouse guns, two field pieces, two mountain howitzers, and one prairie piece. Her father forced her to learn useless army terms before her mother took her away years ago.

She marched down the row of houses until she finally spotted Francine sitting on a chaise on a porch. Her cheeks were flushed a pretty pink as she chatted with a soldier. Beth reveled in the sight. Francine had been so sure no man would ever want her. Now, she had to see she was wrong. The private flirted with her, and bless her, she tossed it right back.

Beth knew many things about her friend's life, but Francine had not shared everything. She did, however, talk in her sleep sometimes, a fact Beth had neglected to mention. Usually, when Francine had a bad dream, they centered around something done to her by a man when she was young, something awful. Much as Francine detested Runyon's finishing school, she dreaded returning home even more. Beth thought she understood... a little. Though unmarried, Francine's mother had a man who supported her, visited her frequently, and shared her bed. A very awkward situation for a young girl to handle. Whenever Beth asked about it, Francine became so upset Beth stopped bringing up the subject.

The private had Francine laughing. Beth loved seeing that. She waited until he left so she could approach without interrupting but made it no farther than the porch steps.

"Beth! Oh, Beth!" Francine sat up and held out her arms in invitation.

Beth raced up the steps to the porch and, bending, hugged her friend, a lump in her throat. "Francie, I have missed you more than you could know."

"If it's half as much as I have missed you, it is horrible," Francine whispered. "It's been weeks since I saw you but feels like months." Both had tears in their eyes.

Beth drew back and brushed a tear from Francine's rosy cheek. "Life didn't appear unbearable a moment ago."

Francine laughed. "No. Can you believe that private was

flirting? And he isn't the only one."

"It's wonderful, Francie. I'm happy for you."

The girl sobered. "Yes, but you will have to leave again way too soon. A few minutes is all we'll have together. I feel like crying already."

"Don't do that." Beth felt her own throat tighten. "The important thing is that you're healing well." She sat on the side of the chaise. "Captain Cooper's wife seems to be taking good care of you."

Francine nodded. "She is. I'm so grateful to her and the captain. I hope you can meet them while you're here. He says I might be able to try crutches soon. I only wish you could stay. Or I could go on with you."

Beth forced a smile. "You must concentrate on getting well so you can join one of the wagon trains coming through before they stop for the season. Otherwise, you'll be stuck here until spring."

Francine scowled. "Do not say that. I could not bear it."

"At least you will not be lonely," Beth teased.

Francine blushed again and swatted at Beth.

She laughed. "You look so pretty with your cheeks pink like that."

"Stop teasing me." Francine's eyes widened. "What I want to know is how you are faring with Hawk. He is far better looking than any of the soldiers here. Surely you are in love with him by now."

Beth felt her cheeks grow warm. "He makes a point of stopping by to chat at least once daily. But I remind myself, again and again, that dear Mr. Stewart asked him to keep an eye on me. And on you. So, what am I to make of the attention he pays me?"

"Why, you use that attention to become better acquainted and show him how wonderful you are."

Beth looked away. "If I am so wonderful, why didn't my mother ever visit me? I rarely saw her before she sent me off to school, then never again. Oh, I know part of it is my cursed birthmark." She put a hand over the offending splotch. "I hate it so. If only I could get rid of it somehow."

"It is truly not that bad, Beth. No one who cares for you will notice. I doubt Hawk does."

"How could he not?" Sick of the subject, Beth rose and went to the railing. The dragoons from the supply train were marching across the parade ground in formation. They appeared resplendent, all clean and in fresh uniforms. "You must promise me, Francie, that if you marry one of these soldiers, you will insist he bring you to visit me."

"Bosh! You are being silly now. The officers are already wed, and the privates cannot afford wives."

"Maybe."

"Miss Webster," Hawk called and waved as he crossed a corner of the field, aiming for the commissary.

"Hello, Mr. Hawk! Come and say hello to Francie."

"I have business to conduct. I will stop later."

When she turned back to Francine, she received a curious look. "What?"

"I think you *are* in love with him."

"Why would you say such a thing? We are merely friends."

Francine smiled. "A woman's face does not light up like yours did just now unless she's infatuated with a man."

"Nonsense," she said even while she felt heat rush to her cheeks. "I will confess, however, that I do admire him."

"And what about the lieutenant? Is he still trying to court you?"

Beth rolled her eyes. "Heavens. I do not wish to discuss him. The man is driving me insane. He *checks* on me constantly. Last week he brought me a bouquet of wildflowers. Before I marry any man, I intend to find out what happens in the marriage bed." Beth reached up, removed her bonnet, and placed it on the small table next to Francine's chaise.

"They... sleep together," Francine said.

"Yes, but what exactly does that entail?"

Francine looked away, her face grim. "I've heard it's painful and degrading."

Beth frowned as she gazed at her friend. Did Francine know about the marriage bed? Surely not, or she would tell Beth. "I don't know about that. I suspect it involves a lot of kissing and fondling."

"There is much more to it than that, I fear." Francine stared at her lap and fidgeted with the hem of her bodice. Her tone was that of a woman who knows, not one guessing.

"Miss Webster." A pretty woman of middle years hurried up the steps. "I'm Mary, the captain's wife. I should warn you that the supply train is preparing to leave. You had best return to your wagon."

"No." Francine reached for Beth's hands. "I cannot bear to lose you again so soon."

"Nor can I, but it cannot be helped. You know that. I must obey Lieutenant McCall's command."

Tears bathed the faces of both girls as they repeated their

goodbyes, and Beth all but ran to the caravan, not in eagerness
but to keep from falling apart in front of Francine and causing
her to feel guilty. The thought of going on without her tortured
Beth.

Sparrow Hawk sat on his horse, watching the cavalcade
prepare for departure from Fort Kearney. The banner held by
the mounted flagman snapped in the wind like a well-trained
tuukkwasun, soldier, on salute.

Lieutenant McCall led the army regiment and wagons,
including the ambulance housing Beth and her chaperone,
through the gates onto the dusty road. Corporal Jenks and a few
other soldiers in McCall's favor rode with McCall. Beth's
wagon came next. Hawk smiled at her, but she did not smile
back. Her sadness at leaving her friend behind showed on her
pretty face. He vowed to cheer her up later. The woman Beth
called her chaperone sat between her and the driver on the
wagon seat. Hawk did not trust this woman. She was not what
she pretended to be. A company of second dragoons,
replacements for Camp Floyd, followed. The supply and cook
wagons brought up the rear.

Hawk had seen more white women in the past five years
than he could count, but Beth Webster stood out from the rest.
She'd been terrified of him the first time he saw her in
Leavenworth. But after the night of the Pawnee attack, she had
changed. Her mind had not been locked against him like other
whites. She listened with her ears and heart and saw him with
clear eyes.

He reveled in her love of the prairie, for it mirrored his own feelings. The Shoshone revered all of nature's creations; rocks, trees, flowers, the four-legged and the winged creatures. They treated their *pii*, mother, the earth, with respect, not like white men who ripped up her green hair with metal tools drawn by mules. Sparrow Hawk had seen this happen too many times and heard Mother Earth's cries of pain.

Beth and others had explained the need to grow food for people and animals, and he had to accept that it must be done. Even so, it pained him to see forests uprooted to make way for grain fields.

Now, as the wagons passed the camps of whites who intended to cross Indian lands to reach those beyond Shoshone country, he saw Beth's keen, eager gaze take in everything. She devoured each image the way a starving child gobbled buffalo meat. He saw no judgment in her violet-blue eyes, only interest and sometimes concern. She had heart and the most beautiful hair he had ever seen.

A movement caught his eye. The lieutenant waved for him to head out. He always rode ahead of the caravan to scout for that night's campground. Eager to see Beth on his return, he gave the subtle gesture with his knee that put his roan gelding into a run.

To get her mind off Francine, Beth studied the emigrants huddled in scattered groups; men here, women there. She imagined the men sharing dreams of new homes and fresh chances for a new life on the frontier, better soil, and crops.

The women's expressions, however, spoke more of fear than dreams. Did these women know something she didn't? Should she be afraid instead of enthused? Perhaps such arduous journeys were easier for a woman as young as Beth.

French-Canadian hunters, lazy and complacent in dirty buckskins, with long flowing hair, occupied a separate area of the fort's outer yard, along with a dozen tipis and dark, hard-eyed Indians. Few even came close to resembling those in *The Last of the Mohicans.*

Thinking of the book she and Francine used to read together brought a stab of loneliness. She shoved it aside and concentrated on her surroundings. Old Charley stuffed his mouth too full of tobacco to reply to her questions. She watched for Sparrow Hawk but only saw him from a distance. Even so, warmth rushed to her belly at that mere glimpse.

"Charley, have you ever seen an Indian's lodge?" she asked from her perch inside the wagon.

"A few times."

"What are they like?" She crawled out and exchanged seats with Hilary. "Are they truly made of buffalo hides? How I would love to see one for myself. How do the—?"

The old man leaned across her and spat.

"Very well, Charley." She knew spitting was his way of telling her to shut up. So, she sat silently, hoping he would give in. She smoothed her skirts, re-tied the bow of her bonnet beneath her neck, unbuttoned the top button of her bodice in the hope of feeling cooler, and hummed *Oh, Susanna* twice, all the way through.

"Galdang it, girl," Charley exclaimed. "Yeah, them tipis are made of hides. The men kill the buffler. The women skin 'em, tan the hides, and build the teepees with lodgepole pines. Now, are ya happy?"

Beth grinned. "Oh, yes, Charley. Thank you. But how do the women cook their food? Do they have kettles like we do?"

Charley spat.

After three hours of travel, they stopped at a stream to let the livestock drink. Beth climbed down and walked through knee-high grass to exercise her legs and revel in a bit of solitude. Summer painted the land in shades of green. She wondered how it would look in autumn and winter. Flowers— daisies, some golden yellow and others blue, beardtongue, betony, and beebalm—bloomed everywhere. She'd learned about the flowers at school but couldn't name the blue ones. Birds flitted here and there. Bees sampled nectars. How glorious, she thought, to live in a country like this, unmarred by the smoke of hundreds of coal fires, ugly buildings, and manufactured noises. To her left, a meadowlark sang a farewell song to those traveling past. The thought saddened Beth.

By the time she rejoined Mrs. Hightower and Old Charley, the train had gone another mile or two. Beth carried a bouquet of blossoms and asked him the name of the blue daisy-like flower.

"Dagnab it!" Charley muttered when she climbed onto the wagon's bench seat. "I ain't no woman to be knowing such nonsense. They's posies; that's all they is, posies."

"All right, Charley. Maybe Mrs. Hightower will know."

She climbed over the seat into the back, fished out her most treasured belonging, a book of poetry, and pressed a few of the delicate blooms between the pages.

"You should pick a bunch of that chicory and save it in

case we run out of coffee," Mrs. Hightower suggested, pointing to the blue daisy-like blossoms.

"What does chicory have to do with coffee, and how did you recognize it?" Beth twirled the flowers.

"I wasn't born a wh... " The chaperone cleared her throat and began again. "I grew up on a plantation. Papa wouldn't supply coffee to the slaves, so they collected chicory to make their own."

"How did they do it, Mrs. Hightower?"

"They took the roots, washed them, cut them up, and roasted them. Then they ground them and used the grounds the same as coffee. And stop calling me Mrs. Hightower. Makes me feel old."

"What should I call you?"

"Hilary."

"You don't sound very Southern."

"I left there a long time ago."

Beth wondered how long it took to lose the accent a person had been born with but said nothing. "I think I'll collect some roots and try it."

"Good. I like chicory coffee. Sometimes I add some to regular coffee just for the flavor."

"I'm going to look for more." Beth moved toward the back of the wagon. "Want to come?"

"No." Hilary rolled over on her bed, facing the side of the wagon.

Beth climbed out onto the tailgate and jumped down.

"Don't go too far," Hilary called after her.

"I won't," she promised, but she knew she'd do whatever life moved her to do in her heart. Her so-called chaperone continued to sneak to the lieutenant's tent at night. But so far, Beth had not found the nerve to follow again. She feared what she might learn.

Hawk saw her fall. While the horses grazed and the bluecoats ate and napped at the noon stopping place, Beth had slipped away to walk near a cool, clear spring in a shallow ravine. Happy for the opportunity to speak to her privately, Hawk followed. She looked up at a squirrel in a tree, tripped, and fell face-down. Fear stabbed through him. She could have hit her head on a rock or broken a bone. He ran to her, but before he reached her, she reared up onto her knees with a screech. His heart plunged, and he hurried faster.

"You are hurt?" He helped her up.

"No, but look." She pointed to a small human skull and other bones scattered around. Climbing nightshade grew entwined upon a narrow, up-thrust rib cage. "It's awful. How would such a terrible thing come to be here?"

"A *nakuppeh*, grave." He glanced around. "A white child was buried here, probably from one of the wagon trains."

Tears filled her eyes. "How sad."

He knew better than to touch her but let his hands linger on her arms after she became steady on her feet. With her honeyed hair and violet-blue eyes, this slight girl made him want to do things he would never have considered doing before with a white woman. Her lips reminded him of flowers that bloomed on the mountainsides during the Moon When the Sun Was Warm. He wondered if her lips were as soft as they appeared and as warm as a summer sun.

"What the hell are you doing, you dadblasted Injun?"

Hawk and Beth whirled to see Corporal Jenks burst from the bushes, his rifle aimed at Hawk.

Hawk kept silent, dropped his hands, and waited for what he knew would follow.

"What are you doing, Corporal?" Beth stepped between the two men. "Point that rifle elsewhere. Sparrow Hawk has done no wrong. He only—"

"You can be sure he meant to, miss." Jenks moved around her; the gun leveled at Hawk. "You dirty, son-of-a-bitching redskin, how dare you put your filthy, murdering hands on a white woman? I ought to teach you a lesson." He swung the rifle around so that he held the barrel instead of the grip and made as if to strike Sparrow Hawk.

"No." Beth intervened again. "Don't hurt him. He did me no harm."

"Just touching you harms you, Miss Webster. Being alone with him could ruin your reputation. Don't you know that?"

"Don't be ridiculous. Anyone that prejudiced doesn't deserve to know me, let alone be my friend. Hawk meant no harm."

"That's crazy talk. He needs to be taught a lesson." Drawing back his arm, the corporal landed a punch to Sparrow Hawk's jaw.

Beth gasped.

Sparrow Hawk stayed on the ground where he fell.

Were the girl not there, he might fight back, but doing so would only worsen his situation. One thing he'd learned, working in the white world, was that an Indian could not win against a white. Even so, he detested having to play the coward in front of her.

Jenks danced around him, his hands fisted while taking mock swings, his long, red hair flying around his face. "Come on, you blasted Injun. Get up and fight. The girl being homely don't give you the right to lay hands on her."

Beth quickly covered her cheek with her palm.

Hawk gritted his teeth against the urge to thrash the white soldier. Instead, he waited. When Jenks came close enough, Hawk tripped the man.

Jenks stumbled, snarled, and grabbed him by the neck of his shirt, his right arm going back in preparation for dealing another blow.

"What's going on here?" Lieutenant McCall shouted as he strode toward the scene.

The corporal dropped his arm to his side and straightened. He pointed at Sparrow Hawk. "He was mauling her, sir."

"He was not," Beth spat. "He merely helped me to my feet after I tripped and fell." She positioned herself between the angry white men and Hawk. "I insist Corporal Jenks apologize to Sparrow Hawk."

"Like hell!" Jenks retorted. "I won't do it, sir. Where I come from ain't nothing lower than a man who won't defend a woman, and I learned better."

"Corporal!" McCall spoke with authority.

Jenks saluted. "Yes, sir."

"I'll deal with this. Go wait at my tent."

Jenks didn't move.

"Now," the lieutenant said in an ominously quiet voice.

Glaring, Jenks left.

That Beth had stood up for him filled Sparrow Hawk's heart with hope, though he knew his chances of winning her affections were slim. She was a white woman and, therefore, out of reach for him.

"Miss Webster," McCall said. "Are you sure that's how it went down?""

"Definitely, sir. Sparrow Hawk helped me up, nothing more. I'd barely reached my feet when the corporal rushed up and struck him. The man also called him rude names and cursed at him. I meant what I said. I want Jenks to apologize."

Instead of replying, McCall turned to his scout, who had risen to his feet. "What do you have to say, Hawk?"

Sparrow Hawk wanted to look at her, smile, and show his gratitude, but he knew it to be a bad idea. "It is as she said, sir. I saw her fall and helped her up. That is all. I do not harm women, white or red." Why could all whites not treat him as Beth did, as an equal? It took all his patience to keep calm.

McCall nodded. "All right. I believe you. But in the future, you would be wise to keep clear of the women."

Hawk acknowledged the soft-spoken order with a jerk of his chin.

"Miss Webster." McCall turned to Beth. "I regret that you had to experience this incident and that you fell. May I assume you are unhurt?"

"Yes, Lieutenant. I'm fine."

"Good." He waved for her chaperone to join them. "I will leave you to Mrs. Hightower's ministrations then and attend to Jenks."

"Sir," Beth said before he had a chance to escape. "Please, can you have one of the men bury these bones? Wolves or something must have dug up this poor child's body. I can't bear to think of leaving it this way."

The lieutenant stooped and picked up a small, crude, wooden cross bound together with rawhide thongs. It read *Mary Elizabeth Tillman, age 9*.

"Very well," he said. "Sparrow Hawk, find a shovel and help with the burial."

"*Haa'*, yes, sir." Hawk wanted to point out that he was more of a guest on this trip than an employee, but he said nothing. It would only cause more trouble.

With a sharp nod, McCall marched off toward his tent. Sparrow Hawk took a few steps and hesitated, his gaze on Beth. She ran her fingers over the letters on the cross. A violet, star-shaped flower caught on her sleeve.

"At home, we call this bittersweet," she said, plucking off the blossom. "Appropriate, don't you think? Oh, Hawk. What sort of life could little Mary have had? I cannot imagine how terrible it must have been for her mother to leave her child in such a lonely place and journey on to a new life without her."

"You want little ones of your own?" he asked.

"Oh, yes. But I do not believe I will ever be blessed in that way."

"Why not?"

She lifted a slender shoulder and let it fall. "You heard the corporal. Men find me ugly."

"They are fools. Do the thorns on the stem of a rose make the flower ugly?"

"Oh, I... " The expression of gratitude in her eyes added to the sadness he felt at what she suffered because of the mark on her face. Yearning to hold and comfort her, he lifted a hand toward her, then dropped it. "I must leave before I make more trouble," he murmured and walked away just as Mrs. Hightower reached them.

Beth wanted to object to Hawk's assertion that he might cause trouble and assure him it wasn't true, but he moved too swiftly. She placed the marker next to the skull and returned to camp.

A short time later, as she helped Hilary make biscuits, she saw Corporal Jenks stalk past, carrying a shovel.

Sparrow Hawk, a shovel over his shoulder, followed.

Beth made quick work of her meal of biscuits, coffee, and fried bacon left over from breakfast and went to watch the men bury the little girl's bones. They had shed their shirts for the dirty chore, and she knew she should avert her gaze, but having rarely seen a man without his shirt, the sight captivated her. The corporal looked thin, working beside Sparrow Hawk. Although lean, the scout's arms and shoulders rippled with muscle. Watching the play of sinew and cords as he dug the grave filled Beth's belly with a strange warmth that spread lower to her most private spot.

Sparrow Hawk turned to look at her.

Embarrassment for staring heightened the heated sensations coursing through her. She told herself to turn aside but could not.

Hawk smiled and returned to his labor.

Beth put a hand to her abdomen, marveling at the strange feelings the sight of him had aroused. What did these new sensations mean? Was she becoming ill? If only Francine were here to help her puzzle out the mystery.

That evening, Hawk stopped by the women's camp as usual.

"Is everything as it should be here?" he asked.

"Yes," Beth answered. "Thank you for asking."

Mrs. Hightower smiled as if thinking of a private joke. "I'm going for a brief walk."

Beth appreciated the woman leaving her alone with Hawk, though she knew her chaperone only went to find nature's "privy." She would be back soon. "Did Corporal Jenks cause you any more trouble?"

"No," Hawk replied. "He avoids me, which is fine with me. Did you enjoy watching us bury the bones?"

She cocked her head at him, thinking it an odd question. "Why would I enjoy seeing a poor child reburied?"

"I apologize." He straightened and bowed his head to her. "I did not think before speaking. I merely thought it might have pleased you that the task was completed."

"Oh, yes. I was glad to see it done." She did not add that she enjoyed watching *him*. "We've been lucky so far, haven't we? No cholera. No grippe? We've had it easy compared to some of the wagon trains of immigrants going to Oregon."

"We have no children with us and only two women," he said, picking a blade of grass to chew on. "That makes our journey easier, and the army is usually better organized and disciplined than a train made up of all sorts of people."

She nodded, seeing the sense of what he said. "Yes, you're right. I didn't think of that. How many times have you made this trip, Hawk?"

He glanced upward as if the answer were written in the

sky and smiled. "Four."

"Always with the army?"

He nodded. "When I was younger, before taking up work as a scout, I did much traveling with friends, mostly in what you call Nebraska Territory."

Beth began wandering, plucking at wildflowers she spotted. "Were those just pleasure trips?"

"Mostly, we were hunting." He spat out the grass and stopped to watch meadowlark sing from atop a tall mullein. "Sometimes, my friends and I would raid our enemies' camps and steal horses. I suppose you see that as a bad thing."

"I don't know." She studied him while arranging the flowers she held. "Did they raid you back?"

He laughed. *"Haa'*. Many times. We enjoyed showing each other up by stealing the most ponies. It was a competition and a way of sharpening our skills."

"What sort of skills?" she asked.

"Riding horseback, sneaking up on something or someone, staying unseen and getting away unnoticed." He hunkered down to pick up a lichened rock which he turned over in his hand, studying it. "These are important skills when hunting and in wartime as they keep you alive."

"I see." It alarmed her to think of him in a war. "Who did you war with?"

"Other tribes, the Blackfeet, Atsani, and Hidastas." He dropped the rock and stood. "Sometimes we tangled with the Dakotas and Cheyenne."

"I don't think I would like to see my man go off to fight in battles with other men," she said, not liking the thought of him possibly being hurt. "If I were an Indian woman, anyway."

"Our women consider our prowess at war and fighting as

desirable traits. Men with such skills can better protect his family and keep them warm and fed."

Beth thought about that. Such things would be necessary, of course, but she would prefer not to live where people had to fight for such basic comforts as heat and food. She reminded herself she had no idea how Indian people lived, their lifestyles, their cares, hopes, and dreams. Surely all women wanted to see their men outdo others in obtaining food, good lodging, and safety for their families. It wasn't something she'd had to worry about in her life, and she'd prefer to keep it that way. Perhaps that made her lazy or complacent. Would Hawk see it that way?

"What, then, would you think of a woman who didn't want to see her man go off to fight with others, be violent and hurt people?" she asked. "Would you lose respect for her?"

He said nothing for a long moment. "Why would anyone not want the men in charge of their lives to keep them safe, fed, and housed?"

Beth frowned. "I think I would prefer to be capable of doing those things for myself rather than having to depend on anyone else."

Hawk smiled. "You are a strong and very strange woman, Beth Webster. You have given me much to think upon. I like this."

"Good." She wanted him to like her. Wanted it a great deal. With each day she spent around Hawk, she liked and respected him more, though she wasn't sure about having him go off to steal and fight. That, she would have to think upon.

CHAPTER SIX

The ragged vee of Canadian honkers passed overhead, so close Beth heard them call to one another and saw the iridescent black of their graceful, arching necks. How would it feel to be so free? She tried to picture sailing above the earth, peering down on land where humans crawled over the mountains like ants on the march. Every spring and fall, geese traveled the same airy trail, snug in the comfort of letting instinct guide them, a skill that seemed to escape people.

Shielding her gaze from the sun flowing across the plain from the world's rim, she watched the flock diminish to a mere scratch in the blue expanse. When they vanished, she turned and followed the drunken path of the creek. The air smelled of mushrooms and rain-washed rocks. She sucked in a few greedy gulps and expelled them in soft breaths.

A herd of pronghorn antelope stood silhouetted on the skyline. Within the sheltering circle of adults, fawns chased each other on spindly legs. A doe jerked up her head, tasted the air, and blew.

At that moment, a pair of coyotes knifed past Beth. She screeched.

The pronghorn bounded away with incredible leaps, their white rumps vivid against the green and dun landscape, fawns keeping pace with adults. They soon outdistanced the coyotes.

Amazed and enthralled by the beauty of nature, she dropped to the ground, fanned out her arms and legs like a child making a snow angel, and laughed with joy. She thought about Francine back at Fort Kearney with her broken leg, and guilt brought her to her feet. Poor Francie. If only she were here.

Deep loneliness fell over her. At a snail's pace, she retraced her steps to camp, where Hilary Hightower napped in the back of the wagon. The woman slept a lot, probably because she stayed up most nights with the lieutenant in his tent, a barely believable scandal.

The next evening, as Beth sliced bacon and Hilary stirred leftover beans on the fire, a soldier brought an invitation for Beth to join Lieutenant McCall at his tent for supper. Her heart fell, and she set the knife down. So, he had decided to put his plan to woo and wed her into action. What should she do? Should she inform McCall that she knew of his scheme and would never wed him? What if he decided to get rid of her so she could not tell her father? Would he kill her? She felt sure a man such as he would not find such an act difficult. Make it look like a simple accident during a dangerous journey.

After the soldier left, Hilary rose to her feet. "Don't go, Elizabeth. Send a message that you're ill."

Beth stared, surprised by the woman's use of her given name. Could Hilary be jealous? "Why would you suggest such a thing? Are you afraid you will lose him to me?"

The woman's eyes narrowed. "Don't be ridiculous. I am only looking out for you, as I am supposed to do as your chaperone."

Beth laughed.

"What do you find so hilarious?" Hilary folded her arms

across her chest.

Weary of the charade the three of them had been performing, Beth decided the time had come for honesty. "I find the idea of you looking out for me while at the same time sneaking into the lieutenant's tent at night amusing. The man did not bring you to be my chaperone, did he? He brought you to share his bed."

Hilary jerked back as though slapped. Her hand moved to her throat and her eyes closed. Her shoulders sagged. After a moment, she straightened and looked at Beth. Her expression held sadness now, or perhaps regret, maybe even guilt. "How did you find out?" Gone was the haughty, condescending tone of voice she had used since the first moment the two women met.

"Remember the night the Pawnee attacked us? I said I was away from camp searching for you because I woke up and you were gone. I saw you go to his tent, so I followed and heard part of your conversation. Why is he bent on marrying me?"

Hilary turned away, her back rigid and her hands clenched at her sides.

Beth waited, expecting anger and denial.

Instead, Hilary huffed out a long breath.

She sat on a rock by the fire, appearing defeated. With her usual haughtiness gone, she looked younger somehow, almost vulnerable.

A trick of the evening light, Beth told herself. She felt almost guilty for causing that look of failure, dread, and perhaps fear on her chaperone's face. Almost.

"To hell with it," Hilary said, shocking Beth. "Like you, I'm sick of this charade."

"Good."

"First of all, my real name is Clotilda Buntz. I answer to Tildy. And Eggy found me in a St. Louis whorehouse."

"Eggy?"

"The lieutenant. His given name is Eggerton. I call him Eggy."

Beth grinned. "It suits him, I think. What is a whorehouse like?"

Hilary, or Tildy, rather, laughed. "You are so innocent, Elizabeth. In some ways, that annoys me, but it also has the strange effect of endearing you to me. Guilt, no doubt, for the charade, as you call it."

She stepped back and waved a hand in front of herself as if to fan her face. "My, being honest, is a huge relief. Trying to convince everyone I am a proper lady is quite wearing, not to mention boring." She let out another long breath. "It feels good to come clean."

Beth studied her. Tildy did, indeed, look more relaxed. "I don't know what to say, Mrs... Tildy. Did Lieutenant McCall pay you to perpetrate this hoax?"

"He promised me three hundred dollars if I stuck with it till Salt Lake City. He doesn't like having to go so long without... being entertained by a woman."

"I don't understand."

Tildy smiled. "Yes, I adore that about you for some odd reason. What do you know about sex, Elizabeth?"

The directness of the question surprised Beth. She decided she did not know this woman after all and wasn't sure she wanted to. "If I am to call you Tildy, you may call me Beth. And I know nothing of sex."

"Didn't you hear gossip in that school you attended? Girls love gabbing about this kind of thing. I can't believe you have no idea about sex."

That put Beth's back up. "Think what you want. None of those snobby girls had anything to do with Francie and me. They excluded us from everything except classes. Francine might know something, but I don't. I only have vague ideas in my head."

"Huh. You need an education, young lady. Better go have your supper with Eggy." Tildy waved a finger in front of Beth. "Don't you say a word about what I've revealed tonight. And don't call him Eggy to his face."

"I won't." She sighed and twisted her hands together at her waist. "But I truly do not want to spend a single moment alone with the lieutenant. I don't trust him. And I don't know how I feel about you. I should be angry."

"With good reason." Tildy took up the knife and went to work on the bacon. "No doubt Sparrow Hawk will turn up soon. That young man has feelings for you, you know. Should I tell him you're with Eggy?"

"Don't be silly. It's not like Sparrow Hawk is courting me or anything."

Tildy snorted. "Maybe not, but I'm telling you, he'd like to."

"Nonsense. He's not interested in me that way, nor I in him." She put her hands behind her to hide her crossed fingers.

Tildy laughed, a full, free bellow Beth enjoyed hearing. "Ha! I think you're quite taken with Sparrow Hawk, and I don't blame you. He's a handsome devil. Those cheekbones, oh my. And that chest." Tildy sighed. "I've enjoyed getting to know him. Always wondered what Indians were really like. Seems they aren't all the bloodthirsty savages folks make them out to be."

"I have enjoyed getting to know him as well."

Tildy gave her a long look. "And if he asks you to become his squaw? What then? Do you think you could go and live with his people, set up a tipi by yourself, and butcher a buffalo for his supper? It would be a hard, hard life. And someone is bound to make trouble over it. Your father, for instance? Eggy tells me Colonel Webster detests Indians more than anything else on earth."

Beth pretended to study her fingernails. She wasn't sure she trusted this woman yet. After all, she'd lied to her about who she was. And how much can a person believe a prostitute, anyway? She would wait before she would commit to being friends with Tildy. "You are right; my father would never accept him. But I seriously doubt I need to fret over it. Sparrow Hawk would know better than to try to court me."

"That might be, but I'd still recommend you do some hard thinking about the direction your heart is taking you, my girl."

Walking toward the lieutenant's tent, Beth wondered if Sparrow Hawk could truly love her and shook her head. No one had ever loved her except, perhaps, Francie. Her throat tightened. Soon, she would be with her father.

She did not know Colonel Jonathan Webster. He had always been off somewhere on a military campaign. Her only memories were of a complex, stiff, scary man who told terrifying tales about Indians. Tales Beth wanted desperately to believe were gross exaggerations. Her mother had left her entirely in the care of servants until Beth turned twelve and was sent to finishing school. She received letters from her mother twice a year, at Christmas and on her birthday. Cold, dry missives containing no affection or concern for Beth's welfare. Lenore Webster had been glad to have her daughter out of her life and off her hands.

"You are not happy," a gruff voice said behind her.

Whirling, she saw Sparrow Hawk leaning against a tree, watching her. She swiped an errant tear from her cheek and attempted a smile. "Thinking of my parents. My mother died of smallpox not long ago. That's why I'm going to join my father. I'm eager to see him." She didn't know why she lied.

He tipped his head and studied her. "No. I think you fear him."

Uncomfortable at his insight, she began walking again, in no hurry to reach her destination.

Hawk followed. "Beth, do you fear he will not want you once you are there?"

She sighed. "My father is all military. He eats, breathes, and drinks army life. It's all he's ever known, all he's ever wanted. Why he married my mother, I cannot say. I do know my being a girl disappointed him. And he hates my birthmark. Mother and I rarely saw him, and when he did come to the house, he was distant, rigid, and coldly formal."

Sparrow Hawk brushed a wheat-tinted strand of hair behind her shoulder, his fingers caressing her cheek. "He has not seen you for a long time?"

"Not since I was eight."

"You are grown up now. My heart believes he will be happy to have you with him."

She looked at him. Had sadness entered his voice as he spoke?

"Will you stay on at Camp Floyd after we reach there, Sparrow Hawk?"

"*Kai*, no." He sat on a log, drew out his knife, and began whittling a piece of wood he found at his feet. "When I reach Salt Lake City, I will go visit my people. I miss my family."

"Oh." Why had that news devastated her? She wasn't sure what love was or how it felt, only that she didn't want him out of her life. "I will miss you."

His gaze became intense. "Will you, Beth?"

She nodded vigorously. "Yes."

He smiled. "I will take you with me."

Excitement sizzled through Beth. Did he mean he would make her his wife?

He smiled and patted his chest over his heart. "Here."

Heat rushed to her cheeks, and disappointment filled her entire being. Thank goodness she hadn't said something and made a fool of herself. Still, it pleased her that he wanted to take her, even if it was only in his heart. "That would please me. I… I'd best go now. Lieutenant McCall is expecting me for supper."

He frowned, looking confused. "I thought you disliked the lieutenant?"

"I do. I don't trust him. But I was afraid to refuse. My well-being is in his hands."

"You are wise." He stood and put away his knife. Then he was gone. She watched him go, disappointed that she had not seen what he carved out of the wood.

Sparrow Hawk's roan skidded to a stop, scattering dust.

Beth's heart skipped a beat, thrilled to see him, then realized something was wrong. He wore a fierce expression and worry lines on his forehead.

"Pawnee coming," he shouted. "Get the women inside the wagons."

Lieutenant McCall, Charley, and Sergeant Toombs stood beside the women's wagon with Tildy and Beth.

The women fanned the air to clear away the dust. Beth's pulse leaped at the mention of the Pawnee. The memory of their first visit remained strong in her mind.

McCall straightened and turned to the scout.

The gnarled old driver shrugged. "They likely jest want some baccy."

"I believe they want more, Lieutenant," Hawk said. "It is Chief Broken Horse who comes. He and his band have followed us since the night they attacked. They know we have women. One tried to steal Miss Webster, and I suspect they are here to make another attempt."

"Best not to take chances." McCall frowned. "Never know what an Injun might take it into his head to do. Ladies, get into the wagon, please."

Tildy immediately made for the tailgate.

Beth hesitated, not wanting to miss anything.

Charley spat onto a rock. "You got a point there, Lieutenant." Turning, he said, "Best do as he says, Miss Webster. Them scroungy Pawnee get a look-see at you, they's like to take a notion o' marryin' up with ya."

"Hilary, perhaps," Beth said, careful to use the correct name since McCall was present. When the Pawnee scooped her up on his horse, she assumed he wanted to kill or rape her, not marry her. "She's lovely, but they'd not want me."

"I wouldn't count on them Injuns seeing matters the way you do, girl. Now, get in there."

The dragoons closed ranks about the wagon. They checked their rifles and muttered low amongst themselves while Hawk's horse stamped and snorted, sensing the tension throughout the camp. Hawk waited on one side of McCall, with Charley on the other.

Beth and Tildy huddled among their bundled possessions in the wagon's bed with a blanket drawn over them in case the savages looked inside. The canvas cover had been fastened as low as possible to keep out dust, enclosing the women in musty gloom. Finding a tiny burn hole in the dusty canvas cover, Beth peeked out and watched the Pawnee approach.

The Indians seemed to ride toward them forever, hazed by that unique property of prairie air that tricks the mind into thinking a mountain a hundred miles away rises just beyond the next hill. Gradually, Beth made out flashes of color and heard the jangle of horse gear. Then the riders came into view—dirty and naked, except for breechclouts and moccasins. Bows and quivers of arrows hung from their backs. Feathers and what looked like patches of long hair fluttered from the tips of their lances, and garish dabs of yellow, black, and blood-red paint marked their faces. A few carried rifles across their laps. Beth counted more warriors than she saw during the unforgettable attack when they shot Francine.

When the band came within thirty feet of the camp, Lieutenant McCall lifted a hand to halt them. Hawk spoke to them in what Beth assumed to be the Pawnee language. One, the leader, she supposed, held up his hand. The others fanned out on either side of him.

"Oh, my," Tildy whispered beside Beth, finding another peephole. "They look terrifying. Look at the big one at the front. He has a fine, strong body on him. I bet he keeps his squaws happy."

"Shh. I want to hear."

Charley and Hawk took turns speaking with the Pawnee using hand signs and that same strange tongue that sounded to Beth like an indecipherable series of grunts.

"He sez their children's bellies are swollen from hunger," Charley reported to McCall, "and their women wail because the Cheyenne burned down their village. He wants 'baccy, firewater, and food."

McCall snorted at that. "Tell him the firewater won't rebuild his village. He can have tobacco and food." He motioned to the mess sergeant, who hurried off to the supply wagon.

The chief spoke again.

"What is he saying now?" McCall asked.

"Claims he cain't guarantee his young braves won't go on the warpath," Charley said, "less'n we give 'im firewater to make their hearts good."

"To give them whiskey would be bad," Hawk advised.

"I don't intend to give them any, Hawk. Tell the chief we carry no firewater, but we'll look for the Cheyenne who raided his village and see that they're punished."

Hawk passed on the message. The Indians gathered about their leader, grunting and gesturing while casting appraising glances toward the wagons. A flour sack full of food and tobacco was handed over. Seeming satisfied with the food, the warriors prepared to gallop off, but the leader called out an order, and they stopped. Only one of the braves rode away. The leader dismounted and moved a few steps closer. He carried a tomahawk tucked in the waistband of his breechclout, and muscles rippled in his limbs as he moved.

"Uh oh," Charley said. "Chief, there's offering ten ponies for the girl with hair like honey."

Inside the wagon, Tildy swore, surprising Beth, but she was more interested in what Charley said. He must have meant her. Tildy had brown hair. "Does that mean he wants to marry me?"

Tildy rolled her eyes. "I'd say that's a good guess."

Hawk warned McCall that giving in to such a demand would be disastrous.

"Of course, I'm not giving the girl to him." McCall cursed as well. "Absolutely not."

Horse hooves shook the ground as the brave who had ridden away returned with a small herd. They must have been secreted back on the trail before the Indians approached the Army patrol.

"This is a delicate situation, Lieutenant," Hawk said. "It would be best to bring Miss Webster out and have her look the horses over, shake her head, and get back into the wagon. Only if she rejects the offer in the Indian way will the Pawnee accept the decision and leave."

McCall said nothing for several tense moments before turning to the wagon. "Miss Webster, will you come out here, please?"

Tildy put a hand on Beth's as she drew back from the

peephole. "Be careful. Do you know how to examine a horse?"

"I know nothing of horses."

"Pry their lips apart and look at their teeth, then run your hands over their sides and down their legs.

"All right." She clambered onto the tailgate and dropped to the ground, not at all certain she could do what was needed.

"Think you can do what Hawk suggested, Miss Webster?" McCall asked.

She glanced at Hawk, who gave her an encouraging smile. "I'll do my best."

Although she'd rarely been around horses, Beth had observed how Charley dealt with the mules and how the army wrangler handled the small herd of extra horses and mules they'd brought along. She walked to the first pony with a beautiful spotted coat and stroked its nose while whispering nonsense to him.

He gave a soft whinny and nudged her hand.

She took advantage of the moment to look at his teeth, trying not to grimace. After stroking his coat a few times, she moved to the next horse. Finally, she returned, shook her head at the lieutenant, and glanced at Hawk, who gave her a jerk of his chin. She climbed back into the wagon.

"How did it go?" Tildy tugged on her arm.

"Watch and see." Beth wiped sweaty hands on her skirt as she rejoined the woman at the peephole.

Outside, Hawk spoke to the Pawnee.

The same brave who'd brought the horses drove them away.

The chief frowned and shook off the Indian who tried to give him the reins to his horse.

"Please go," Beth whispered, more to herself than anyone else. The tension in the camp grew thick as cold molasses.

At last, the chief mounted his horse, signaled to his men, and they rode off.

Beth leaned her head against the wagon's side and released a pent-up breath. "Thank goodness."

Tildy chuckled. "I wonder if you'd feel so relieved if it were Sparrow Hawk who offered those horses."

She flipped her long hair behind her. "It doesn't matter because that will never happen."

"Never say never, young lady."

With that inimitable remark, Tildy left the wagon.

Her eyes wide, Beth wondered what the woman had meant. Did she know something Beth did not?

The house was small and made of white clapboard. Two windows flanked the front door, and flagstones led to the steps. A cottonwood tree grew in the yard with a rope and slat-swing hanging from a strong branch waiting for a child to put it into action. Smoke rose from the chimney, and Beth smelled the delicious scent of fresh bread. In a pasture next to the house, a cow lowed. A cat jumped down from a fence post and wound itself around her legs. As she kneaded a new batch of dough, she could see through the window the prairie spreading as far as the eye could see, the grasses tall and waving in the wind, with wildflowers scattered here and there.

And coming home through the grass, on a fine roan horse, rode—

"What are you doing out here alone, Beth?"

"Oh!" Startled out of her fanciful imaginings, she spun to find Sparrow Hawk a few yards behind her. Her pulse jumped, and heat suffused her body. She shaded her eyes from the sun to see him better. "You sneaked up on me."

He smiled. "*Kai*, no. You do not pay attention to all that is around you."

She frowned. "What do you mean?"

"*Yekwi*, sit."

She looked down at the grass and wildflowers as high as her hips. Hawk had already lowered himself to the ground, sitting cross-legged. "I won't be able to see anything."

"That is the point. Sit. Listen."

Rolling her eyes, she plopped down beside him. "Listen to what?"

He said nothing.

A bird chirped. Grass whispered in the wind. A bee buzzed from one flower to another. In the distance, a horse whinnied, and wagon wheels rumbled.

"What do you hear?" Hawk asked.

"A bird, the wind, a bee, and the wagons way off." One of which she was supposed to be riding in. Had the lieutenant noticed her absence?

"That is all?"

"What else is there?"

"If you listen hard, you will hear Mother Earth preening. She is proud, Mother Earth. And happy. The sun is warm on her, the plants—her hair—are healthy, and the natural creatures who live on her bounty are busy with life. But she is also sad and worried. Men have come. They tear her skin with their wheels, and their animals eat everything down to the ground, leaving nothing. The natural way of her world has been disturbed."

Beth stared. She loved listening to his voice when he spoke this way. It had a musical quality that relaxed her and made her want to curl against him. "Why do you call the earth your mother?"

"Because it was in her womb we were created." His dark eyes on her were warm and intense. "As your womb will one day create new life inside you."

She glanced away. The sureness in his tone when he spoke of her carrying a child sent shivers down her spine and sparked hope in her heart. "Tell me of your people and how they live."

"Why?"

"I'm curious. It fascinates me to learn how other people live and do things. I hope there is an Indian village somewhere along our route. I would so love to see one and meet a squaw."

"Squaw is a white man's word and uncomplimentary to our women."

"Oh. I'm sorry. It's only that... well, I've heard it so often from the soldiers, my father, and I've read it in books." Her neck went hot. She hated to think she might have insulted the women of his tribe. "I did not mean to debase your people."

His smile was gentle, almost tender. "I know. You have a good heart, Beth Webster. You would never knowingly harm anyone unless they threatened you."

She cocked her head, looking at him. "How do you know that?"

"You study the land, the plants, and the four-legged and winged creatures. Have you not learned much by doing so?"

"Yes." She grinned. "I suppose I have. I never thought about it that way."

He gave her that tender look again. "I study you."

Heat flamed in her neck and cheeks. "Why?"

"I care about you, Beth."

Embarrassed but also thrilled, she smiled. "I care about you as well."

"I know. Tomorrow, we will reach Fort Laramie. There will be Indians there. Sioux, as you call them. Cheyenne, and Arapaho. Some are my friends. I will take you to visit them."

She leaned forward in excitement. "Truly? Do they live in tipis? Will I meet women and children?"

He laughed and rose to his feet. "Yes, Beth." He held out his hand. It swallowed hers when she placed it against his palm. His skin was brown compared to hers, his palm rough and toughened by hard work, but she sensed a gentleness in them and knew somehow that his touch would never give her pain, only comfort, and joy. She allowed him to draw her up to stand before him.

"I would kiss you, Beth."

Her heart danced a jig in her chest. "Please do."

The first brush of his lips came soft as goose down, tentative as if seeking to learn their shape, texture, and taste. In her usual, impetuous way, she threw her arms around his neck and intensified the kiss with pressure and enthusiasm.

Hawk laughed, a sound of pure joy, and kissed her again.

She loved that his lips were soft, malleable, yet firm. They seemed to ask for more without words. As her first kiss, she could not want for more. Yet she did. She wanted a lot more but couldn't say what. She mimicked his movements, testing, exploring, savoring. His arms tightened around her.

And abruptly let go.

"What is it?" she asked, panting a little.

He stood gazing at the sky, his hands on his hips, his breathing harsh.

Finally, he looked at her and smiled. "You are everything I knew you would be and more. But we must return to the caravan. To stay longer would risk danger to us both."

"What sort of danger?"

"The kind young girls get into with men who want them too much to be cautious. Come."

He turned and headed for the wagons. Beth stood a moment, watching him and wondering what he meant.

But it didn't matter. Hawk had kissed her. Her heart soared with love, desire, and excitement. The kiss had awakened a yearning in her she'd never felt before and brought new sensations to her body. To think of the kiss caused a pleasant shivery warmth to fill her abdomen and lower. Her heart began to race. She wanted more.

After that, they found time nearly every day to spend together, out of sight of the soldiers. They walked and talked, and Hawk taught her things about nature and the ways of Indians. Beth loved it. Now and then, they kissed. But, mostly, Hawk kept her at arm's length. It frustrated her, yet she knew he did it for her own good.

"Look, Hawk," she said. "A snake."

"Keep back. It is a rattler." He looked around, found a stick, and brought it down on the snake, pinning it so fast that Beth barely saw the movement.

She cringed when he took out his knife and cut off the snake's head. He tossed away the body but not before removing the rattles, which he handed to Beth.

"A souvenir," he said.

She held them away from her as if afraid they would bite her.

Hawk laughed. "They will not harm you. Tie them to something so you can hear them rattle. It will remind you of your time on the prairie."

"And you." She pressed the rattles to her heart.

"And me," he said, pleasure dancing in his dark eyes.

CHAPTER SEVEN

Fort Laramie sat on open prairie at the convergence of the Laramie and North Platte Rivers. Beth found the terrain much as she had seen for days, mostly flat, with hidden gullies and low hills in the distance. She had begun to yearn for the towering mountains Caleb Stewart told her about, stories Hawk had added to and glorified in her mind. She could not imagine peaks as high as they claimed nor the ruggedness of such country. Until she reached those mountains, she would content herself with the sights and sounds of the first sign of civilization she'd seen in weeks.

Adobe walls reached into the sky, with a large blockhouse over the gate and smaller ones at the corners of a fence made of upended tree trunks lashed together. Inside, the fort stretched for a hundred and fifty feet, with cabins along the perimeter.

Seated on the wagon seat with Charley and Tildy, Beth spotted the tip of a canon sticking out from the blockhouse. A sprinkling of conical structures occupied the grounds outside the fort. Smoke curled upward from small fires here and there, and more significant plumes spiraled above the fort itself.

"Look, Charley." Beth waved her arm toward the ragtag Indian village. "Tipis. At last, I have seen Indian tipis. I can't wait to see inside one."

Charley grunted. "Make sure ya bathe plenty well after. Won't have ya bringing lice back to my wagon, ya hear?"

"Lice?" She made a face at the disgusting idea.

"Difficult to get rid of lice after you sleep in buffalo furs," Tildy commented dryly. "I'll stay outside, thank you."

"Well, I still want to see them." Beth refused to be discouraged from fulfilling her dream.

The dragoons made camp outside the fort, near those of travelers who'd stopped for the night. She wondered why the men bothered. In other forts they'd visited, she'd noticed the men spent all their time inside, drinking and gambling. Beth went first to the commissary to post a letter to Francine and laughed with excitement when she received one addressed to her.

"Tildy, I got a letter from Francie." She tore it open and began to read. "She says she wrote it right after we left Fort Kearney, and a trapper who was leaving for here that day brought it. I wish we could travel that fast." The moment she said it, she knew it to be a lie. Reaching her father meant an end to her adventure and the beginning of a life she did not want.

"I hope she finds a good party to travel with when she's able to continue on." Tildy studied the canned goods lined up on a shelf behind the counter and selected one of peaches. "I think I'll make a peach pie for tonight if our hosts allow me to use their oven."

"Hmm, sounds wonderful." Beth bought several colorful lengths of ribbon, which she tucked into her reticule. "And it will be a lovely gesture of thanks for Corporal Booker and his wife for putting us up for the night. I hope they're as nice as they sound. I can't wait to meet them."

A trooper squeezed in next to Beth at the counter, his shoulder brushing hers. She looked at him, and he winked.

Beth moved closer to Tildy to put space between her and the man.

"Excuse me," he said. "I don't mean nothing disrespectful, miss. It's been so long since I saw a young lady as pretty as you."

She turned then purposely so he couldn't miss seeing her birthmark. "That is nonsense, and you know it." Phony compliments annoyed her.

He straightened and looked surprised. "If you're trying to discourage me because of that little mark on your cheek, you're going to be disappointed. I suppose you think it makes you ugly."

"And you don't?" How dare he make light of her awful blemish.

He shook his head. "No. Just makes me want to put my lips there and see if I can kiss it away."

"Oh. You are entirely too fresh, trooper." Her eyes widened; she frowned, spun around, and marched out the door.

Tildy caught up with her in the yard, chuckling. "You sure gave him what for. Might as well prepare yourself for more of the same. These men are lonely, Beth. I suspect they see you as a rare beauty, birthmark or not."

Three soldiers walked by and grinned at them. One whistled.

"See what I mean?" Tildy said.

"I don't understand. Do they truly find me attractive, or are they merely being kind out of pity?"

"Did that whistle sound like pity to you?" Taking her arm, Tildy began walking. "Stop demeaning yourself, Beth. Yes, you have a birthmark on your cheek, a quite interesting one, considering that it resembles a kiss imprint." She chuckled. "Perhaps they think I've been kissing you."

"Don't say that." Beth cried. "It sounds even worse." She saw the glint in the other woman's eyes then and laughed. "Stop teasing me, Tildy. You'll have me so red in the face they'll think I'm a lobster."

"Or a squaw," Tildy said under her breath so only Beth could hear.

"Miss Webster!" Hawk came toward them through the crowd of soldiers, Indians, and other travelers bound for the West. She waved, and a large paw immediately snatched her hand with dirty fingernails.

The giant man who grabbed her twirled her around, laughing. His breath reeked of liquor and onions. "Come on, girlie. Dance with old Bearstooth. I ain't seed a gal as purdy as you since last winter when I went home to Delaware."

"Please, sir," she begged. "Let me go. People are staring."

"Let 'em. They's jest jealous." He wore a variety of clothing: moccasins, leather leggings, a new-looking linsey-woolsey shirt, and a coat made from a blanket. Feathers fluttered from an animal skull atop his long, shaggy hair. She guessed he was what Caleb called a mountain man. He looked like a buffalo.

"Sir!" Tildy poked the man on the shoulder and assumed her role as Mrs. Hightower. "This young lady is my charge, and I must insist you release her this minute."

Laughing, Bearstooth slipped an arm around Tildy and

pulled her into his impromptu dance. "Whoo-ee. I gots me two women."

"And you will let them go. Now."

The man loosened his hold.

Beth jerked away and spun to find the lieutenant behind them.

Hawk stood next to him.

"Thank you, Lieutenant." She acknowledged his aid with a nod.

"You're welcome, Miss Webster."

She saw then that he held a knife.

The mountain man froze. "Easy, friend. No need poking me with that Arkansas toothpick there." Hands upheld, he backed away.

"Well." Tildy watched him stagger off. "I'm certainly glad you came along when you did, Lieutenant. I was afraid that lummox would haul Beth off to a cabin or somewhere."

"I would not have allowed that." He sheathed the knife. "What are you two planning to do with your free day?"

Beth looked at Hawk. "I was hoping to see the Indian village and asked Hawk to take us there."

Eggerton McCall glanced at Hawk. "Are you aware, Miss Webster, of the trouble that might cause? Few men here wouldn't like to claim you for themselves, and seeing you go off with an Indian, even a good one like Sparrow Hawk, might infuriate them."

"I asked Corporal Booker to accompany us, Lieutenant, for that reason." Hawk indicated the soldier standing nearby.

"You're all right with this, Corporal?" McCall asked.

"Yes, sir. I didn't like Hawk at first, but he isn't like most

Injuns." Booker grinned. "Besides, it'd make me proud to be seen showing two fine-looking ladies like these around."

"Very well. Proceed then. Make sure you take proper care of them."

"Yes, sir." Booker saluted.

The lieutenant took his leave.

"Tildy, you will come with us, won't you?" Beth asked. "I'm sure Charley was only joking about the lice."

The woman snorted at that and brushed some dirt from her glove, no doubt from the mountain man.

"Some Indians do have lice, Miss Webster," Hawk told her. "But only those who have lost their souls to the white man's firewater and no longer bathe."

"I shall stay here," Tildy said. "I don't want to disappoint Sergeant Wilson's wife. She's eager for female company."

"We'll see you later then." Beth waved.

Hawk and Corporal Booker led her toward the fort's large gate.

Beth breathed in various odors: dirt, the river, sweat, whiskey, human and animal waste, food cooking, even the scent of lye soap as some soldiers took advantage of the fort's small bathhouse. Outside the walls, smells faded, replaced by clean air, wood smoke, and other faint odors she could not identify. The air hummed with activity. Travelers readied their wagons for the next day's travel. Children, brown and white, raced through the maze of wagons, horses, mules, tents, and campfires, playing tag. Soldiers lounged against the adobe wall smoking cigarettes or pipes. A steady stream of men and women entered and exited the main gate. Beth avoided a bear of a man stumbling and singing in an off-key voice. After that, Hawk and Booker made sure to keep her between them.

At last, they reached the corner of the massive structure, the crowd thinned out, and Beth spotted the tipis she had noticed on her arrival. Children played among them, the youngest naked and all quieter than the white children. Men sat cross-legged in a circle, passing a pipe among them. A woman hung narrow strips of meat on a series of poles set crosswise on tall sawhorses made of trees stripped of bark. Another kneeled on the ground scraping a hide. Every detail fascinated Beth.

"Is that jerky that woman is hanging on those poles?" she asked Hawk.

"Yes. Probably horse meat or cow. Buffalo are scarce around the fort."

"What sort of hide is the other woman cleaning, then?"

"Elk." Hawk led her to where the woman had the hide spread out, pegged to the ground, and spoke to her.

She smiled and kept working.

"A buffalo hip bone is used to scrape away the flesh," Hawk explained. "Thin, supple hides make the best clothing."

Corporal Booker crouched down and fingered the elk skin. "This is thin and supple, all right."

Beth followed his example and touched the skin, curious how it would feel. "It looks like a lot of hard work."

"It is." Hawk's dark eyes bored into her as she regained her feet. "Cleaning and tanning hides are part of what Indian women do, Miss Webster. The hides make lodge covers, clothing, and parfleche bags for holding food and other possessions. Every part of a buffalo is used for something. It is important work, and they do it with pride."

"At least they contribute valuable skills necessary for their homes and families. I would far rather scrape hides than embroider handkerchiefs all day."

The corner of his mouth quivered.

She smiled, knowing he was trying not to laugh.

"What are the braves doing over there?" Booker asked.

Hawk looked where he indicated. "They are playing a game with carved stones, a bit like how you throw dice."

"Is it a gambling game?" the sergeant asked.

"Yes."

Booker grinned. "Then I want to join in." With that, he walked to where the men sat playing their game.

"Come," Hawk said after the sergeant left. "I want you to meet Many Tongues. She is a healer, a medicine woman."

He guided her to a tipi and scratched on the hide door at the low entrance. A voice called out something in the Indian language, and Hawk ducked inside, drawing Beth with him.

An aging woman sat inside on a furry blanket Beth decided must be buffalo.

"Elk," Hawk said.

He must have read Beth's thoughts. Many Tongues wore a calico skirt and blouse with a trade blanket around her bent shoulders. Graying hair hung down her back, and colorful beads dangled from her ears. Beth studied everything she saw, beds made of buffalo hides, beaded bags lying about, blankets, and rawhide covering the floor. A fire occupied the center of the space. Everything was tidy and organized. Clumps of dried plants hung from the ceiling. Beth's brow furrowed as she tried to figure out their intended use.

"They are herbs dried and used for medicines, flavorings, and such," Hawk said.

"How fascinating. I would love to know what they all are and what she does with them."

Hawk grinned. "That would take an entire day. Please, sit. She offers us food."

As soon as they sat, she held out bowls of soup or stew from a blackened pot hanging from a tripod over the central fire. Hawk dipped his fingers inside and ate the chunks of meat his bowl held. Beth studied hers, wondering what sort of meat she'd been served. Her father had told her once that Indians ate dogs. The thought sickened her.

Beth drew out a chunk with her hand and put it in her mouth, finding the flavor rich and tasty. "Oh, this is very good. Tell her thank you, please."

He spoke to the woman, who smiled and nodded.

After the meal, Hawk and Many Tongues talked more. Beth was becoming annoyed at being left out when the old woman reached toward her.

"Don't jerk away," Hawk said quickly.

Beth barely managed to keep still as the woman ran her hand over her blemished cheek as if testing the texture of the birthmark.

Many Tongues spoke again.

Hawk replied.

Finally, he stood and motioned for her to follow him out.

"Wait."

He stopped and waited.

She dug into her reticule, pulled out a red ribbon, and handed it to him. "Please give this to her. A gift."

"She will be pleased."

Many Tongues grinned as she accepted the ribbon and ran it across her lips.

The door flap slapped shut behind them as they left. Hawk turned to Beth and smiled.

"You appear quite pleased," Beth said. "What did she say? Why did she touch my birthmark?"

He laughed. "She said you were marked at birth because you are special."

"Oh." Beth blinked, surprised and unsure whether to be pleased or worried. "What does that mean?"

"Many Tongues receives visions, glimpses of times to come," he said. "She predicted that you would become important one day to the *Sosone* people. My people."

"Oh, my." A shiver skimmed down her back. She still didn't understand what it meant, if it was good or bad, but she hoped for good. "Well, it sounds interesting."

Hawk laughed again. "To me, it sounds promising."

And that, too, gave her much to ponder. What had Hawk meant? Did he like the idea that she might have something to do with his people someday? How could that be? Beth would love to meet his family and learn more about the Snake Indians but couldn't imagine it happening. Not when she'd be stuck at her father's fort in the middle of nowhere.

Did Hawk have some plan in his head that concerned her?

As Beth, Corporal Booker, and Hawk started back to the fort, Beth noticed a group of men sitting cross-legged in a circle, including Lieutenant McCall and the mountain man, Bearstooth. She suspected they were playing a gambling game.

When they re-entered the fort, they were hailed from behind by a man's voice.

"Hou! Sparrow Hawk! Hold up."

They turned and saw Caleb Stewart trotting up to them on

a gray horse. He halted and rested his arms on the saddle horn. "Well, I'll be hanged. I was hoping to catch up to you but didn't figure I'd succeed this soon. How do you fare, Miss Webster?"

Hawk took hold of the bay's bridle and stroked the horse's forehead. "We are all fine except for Miss Gibbs."

"I know about that. Saw her at Fort Kearney living a life of luxury with the captain's wife waiting on her hand and foot and every soldier in the place trying to woo her." Caleb gave a hearty chuckle. "Danged if I didn't give them a run for their money, poor pups. They don't know how to treat a lady like I do."

Beth laughed. "Did you woo her, as well, Mr. Stewart?"

"Did my best." He heaved his body out of the saddle and stepped to the ground. "These old bones don't take to riding all day like they used to." He stretched his legs, back, and arms, groaning as he did so.

"You might fool some people," Hawk said. "But this warrior knows you have lived barely thirty summers. You are not old yet; you still have your teeth."

"Yeah? Well, you're a pup compared to me, you cocky whippersnapper." In return, he threw a mock punch.

Hawk dodged and smacked him on the arm.

Beth and the sergeant laughed at their antics.

"So, what brought you here, Caleb?" Beth found it difficult to believe he was as young as Hawk claimed. She'd seen him as old, at least in his forties.

"Have a message to deliver to the colonel. Then I'll head back to Fort Kearney and do a tad more wooing." He took off his hat, ran his hands through his windblown hair, and messed it up even more. He winked at Beth. "I promised a certain young lady I'd escort her west to meet up with her friends."

"Francie? You're going to bring Francie to us?" She clapped her hands.

Caleb slid his hat back on his head. "Looks that way. Don't you folks go running off anywhere while I deliver my message. Afterward, we'll get together and raise the roof in celebration."

Hawk turned to Beth. "I am not certain you are old enough to see this 'old man' raise a roof. He can become wild as a drunk buffalo."

"Huh." Corporal Booker snorted. "You'd have to go some to beat me at raising a roof."

"Well, dadgum, we'll make a contest of it," Caleb challenged. "How's that?"

"Sounds good to me," Booker said.

"To all of us," Hawk added. "We will see you later, Caleb."

No roof-raising occurred that night, but the party did meet for supper at the Corporal's house and made merry with coffee, sarsaparilla—for the more daring drinkers—buffalo steak, and peach pie for dessert. Later, Tildy and Beth retired to the room they shared.

"I'm not sure what to think about Caleb and Francine," Beth said. "I can't get it out of my head that he's so much younger than I expected. Do you think he's serious about courting her?"

"Young as you are, everyone over twenty looks old to you," Tildy retorted, brushing out her long, russet hair. "Caleb would make a fine catch for Francie." She winked at Beth. "But I'd be a better match for him. I have more experience."

Beth laughed, but her amusement changed to concern. "I do hope he doesn't take her off somewhere miles away so I don't get to see her often. Francie and I had hoped to get a house to share in Salt Lake City and find jobs there."

"How could you afford to do that?"

Wary of giving too much away, Beth averted her face. "We'll figure something out."

"Oh, wait a minute." Tildy nodded. "Eggy believes your mother left you a tidy inheritance. Was he right?"

Tildy moved behind Beth, swept her hair over her shoulder to get it out of the way, and loosened the lacings on her corset.

Beth moaned with pleasure as the garment loosened. "Thank you. It always feels so wonderful to get out of that thing." She dropped the garment onto the bed.

"There isn't a woman alive who wouldn't agree." Tildy gave Beth her back. "Here, undo mine now."

"Thank goodness, my travel clothes are looser and more comfortable." As she unlaced Tildy's corset, Beth wondered how the woman felt about McCall courting someone other than her.

Tildy slipped out of the garment and turned to face Beth. "You didn't answer me about Eggy. Are you sure you won't marry him?"

Beth laughed, her imagination working double-time as she remembered the woman begging him to suckle her. "The man makes my skin crawl. He reminds me of snail slime."

Tildy roared with laughter. The sound brought a smile to Beth's face. During the last few weeks, she and Tildy had become friends. Beth's mother, and probably her father, would disapprove, but Beth didn't care. She liked Tildy. The woman was fresh, open, and natural. Beth found it a pleasant change from the snide, back-stabbing girls at school. Or the manipulative snobs her mother kept around her.

"Remember Bearstooth?" Tildy asked. "The trapper who danced with us?"

Beth nodded.

"He got mad and hit a man so hard, they had to take him to the infirmary. He might have died. We need to make sure to stay away from him."

Beth frowned. "I doubt the man would accost us after the lieutenant threatened him on our behalf. I saw them playing a game together with other soldiers as we returned to the fort."

"That's a surprise, but Eggy's determined to marry you." Tildy shrugged. "Your father mentioned to him that your mother had inherited a fortune that would now be yours."

Beth's mouth fell open. "A fortune?" She didn't know how to answer. Why hadn't she asked Mr. Snelling how much money she had? "He only gave me five hundred dollars. To me, that's a fortune."

Tildy gave Beth a canny look out the side of her eye. "But is that all there is? Did you ask the attorney for the total amount of your inheritance?"

"No. I didn't think of it." So foolish. She would send a message to the attorney in the morning requesting more information, but it would take a while for his reply to reach her as it would have to wait for a party traveling east to come through and agree to take it.

Tildy fell asleep, but Beth continued writing a letter for Caleb to return to Francine. In it, she described the events of the journey since leaving Fort Kearney and shared her growing feelings for Hawk.

He's a good man, Francie. I do not care that he is Indian. That means nothing. Hawk saved my life and yours; that says a great deal about him. He is always a gentleman, kind, gentle, and caring. Loving him is not wise, but I cannot help my feelings. And if I turn my back on him, how can I know I will ever find another man as wonderful?

CHAPTER EIGHT

The cavalcade had been back on the road for two days when Hawk walked into the women's small camp and glanced around, eager to see Beth.

Mrs. Hightower sat on the wagon tailgate talking with Sergeant Toombs, Beth on a grassy spot a little distance apart, mending a tear in a skirt. She looked beautiful as always.

"Come," he said, motioning for her to get up.

"Why? What is it?"

"I'm going to teach you to shoot a bow."

She grinned. "Wonderful. Oh, Hawk, I'm excited. Let's hurry." She stuck her needle into the fabric, jumped up, and headed for an open spot beyond camp.

He chuckled. "Not so fast, little one." He called to Mrs. Hightower and the sergeant: "I'm going to teach Beth to shoot a bow. Will you come and chaperone, please?"

"Why not?" Mrs. Hightower jumped down, and she and Toombs followed Beth and Hawk from camp.

He wedged a piece of bark into the vee of a large broken rock. "That is your target." He walked back to Beth.

Shading her eyes with her hand, she studied the object. "It looks tiny from here."

"Only twenty feet away." He handed her the bow and slipped a quiver of arrows over her shoulder.

She positioned the bow as she'd seen him do once.

He moved behind her. "Hold the bow steady." Hawk braced her hand with his. "Now, pull an arrow from your quiver and nock it."

She glanced over her shoulder to see the quiver.

"Keep your eyes on your target, Miss Webster, or it will get away."

With a low growl of frustration, she aimed her gaze forward again and reached blindly for an arrow. "I've got one."

"You have two. Drop one back in." Hawk swallowed the chuckle that rose to his throat. She amused him, so different from the women of his people. Innocent, naive, and always dreaming unlikely dreams, like a child with a woman's body. But with a woman's needs. To resist fulfilling those needs became more difficult by the day.

She rolled her eyes at him. After fumbling around a bit, she managed to let go of one of the arrows.

"Good. You did well," Hawk said. "Now, let me see you nock the arrow on the string."

"It is odd-looking string."

He smiled. She found a great many things strange. "I made it from buffalo sinew."

"Eww." She nearly dropped the bow and arrow.

Hawk couldn't help laughing. She scowled.

"Continue." His bare chest brushed against her back and made his blood sing as he steadied her. He wore leggings, moccasins, and a breechclout today and enjoyed the way she stole glimpses of his near nakedness when she thought no one noticed. Her chaperon watched from the sidelines, along with Sergeant Toombs, who wore a frown.

No doubt, he disliked seeing Hawk so close to a white woman. And touching her. Hawk would have to be cautious.

He reached around her to help her nock the arrow and caught a whiff of her scent. Grass, coffee, and a pleasant smell he decided belonged to her alone. He drew in a deep breath, savoring the sweet aroma.

"Like this?" she asked.

"Yes. Now bracket the arrow with your fingers and draw back the string."

The arrow wobbled, but she managed not to drop it. He had expected her to give up by now. It pleased him that she had not.

"Draw it back until your hand meets your chin."

Pulling a tree down with her hands might be easier for her. He watched her grit her teeth with the effort. Small as she was, she hadn't the strength to pull a man's bow. She needed one made for a boy. When he had time, he would make her one.

"Pull harder," he coached.

"I do not think I can. This is hard."

He knew how difficult it was. Leaning close again, he reached around and put one finger beside hers. "I will help this time."

He showed her where to hold her hand near her chin and straightened the bow a little. "All right. Let go."

The arrow flew three feet and dropped to the ground. Behind them, Mrs. Hightower chuckled.

Beth turned to glare at her over her shoulder.

"Ignore them." Hawk wished their audience would disappear, though he knew they needed them. "Try again."

This time the arrow flew properly but missed the target by a wide margin.

Her shoulders slumped.

"That is enough for today." Hawk reached to take the bow.

She snatched it away. "No. I will get this right if I have to stay up all night to do it."

"Beth, shooting a bow takes many moons of practice. You will not get it right today, whether you spend all night at it or not."

"But—"

"Trust me. You are going to have a sore shoulder and arm as it is. If you keep it up, you will not be able to use your arm tomorrow."

"Oh, all right." She handed over the bow.

He slipped the quiver off her shoulder and carried it and the bow to where he'd stored his saddle and other belongings.

She trailed after him.

Hawk opened his mouth to scold her but noticed Mrs. Hightower and Toombs were too busy flirting to see Beth's action.

"Walk with me, Hawk," she pleaded. "I want to get away from the camp for a while and enjoy the peace and quiet of the plains."

"We will walk but keep to ridges so anyone watching cannot accuse us of misbehavior." He feared his own possible actions more than hers. The urge to kiss and hold her left him aching with need, a need that became harder to ignore.

She plucked a blade of grass and chewed on the end. "Who cares if they think we're misbehaving? I don't."

The temptation to take the grass from her with his own

mouth made him smile. He stepped away. "You should, Beth. If the soldiers spread it around that you kept company with an Indian, your reputation would be ruined. No man would want you then."

She pinned him with her gaze. "You mean no white man. What about a red man?"

Halting, he gazed at her for a long time. Did she know what she asked? "You court trouble, Beth. Beware what you ask for."

She spat the grass from her mouth, spun on her heels, and ran.

Hawk blew out a breath and went after her. He caught up and halted her escape with a hand on her arm. "You behave like a child, Beth. Why do you—"

He saw her face then. Tears shone in her eyes. He brushed them from her cheeks, loving the feel of her silky skin. "I am sorry. I did not mean to wound you."

"I'm not a child, Hawk. I'm a woman, and I—"

He could not let her finish. He put a finger to her lips. "Remember what I said, be careful what you ask for. You have much to learn before you can face the world you think you want to occupy."

"What must I learn?" Annoyance tinged her tone.

He glanced out over the rolling plain, aching with the need to throw her on his horse and ride away with her the way his ancestors would have done. Those days were gone. Too dangerous, especially with a white woman. Hawk had no desire to be put in the white man's prison or hung from a tree. Somehow, he had to make her see what she courted. "The ways of the people you would live among. The language. The beliefs."

"Teach me."

"Beth, you know not what you ask."

She peered up at him.

He saw a clearness in her eyes that told him she was serious.

"I do know, Hawk. You are more of a man than any other I have ever met. You are honest and open. No tricks and no agendas to hide. You are what you are, and you intrigue me more every day. I want to know your people, your tongue, and your beliefs. I want to know you. Teach me."

Hawk did not answer. He turned to look back toward camp. Through the soles of his moccasins, he felt the earth quiver. Someone approached on horseback.

"Hawk?" Beth prodded.

He held up a hand to silence her so she would hear the hoofbeats in the distance. "Company comes. Now we will be in trouble."

At that moment, Corporal Jenks crested the hill on his dun mare and headed toward Beth and Hawk. When he came within hearing range, she surprised Hawk by nearly shouting.

"I appreciate your concern, Mr. Hawk. I truly do, but I came out here for some solitude. Perhaps it seems strange for a woman to seek to be alone, but I happen to enjoy it."

Jenks drew up beside them. "Hawk bothering you, ma'am?"

She turned toward him. "Not really, Corporal. He saw me here and came to scold me for being so far from camp."

"Well, Mrs. Hightower and Sergeant Toombs are looking for you, and Lieutenant McCall sent me to bring you back. Best come with me now." He removed his boot from the stirrup and held out a hand. "Here, get up behind me."

Beth looked at Hawk. He tipped his chin to encourage her to go. The corporal did not seem disturbed at finding them together, but McCall might be. Hawk suspected the man was trying to court Beth, which infuriated him. The idea that Beth might fall for McCall's lies bore down on Hawk like a prairie tornado. He could no longer deny she had crawled inside his heart, and he knew not how to get her out. Giving into his desire for her would likely get him killed.

She did not look happy but did as the corporal told her and mounted behind him. Seconds later, they were lost to view beyond the hill, leaving Hawk alone.

The next morning, Hawk rose hours before the rest of the camp. He slipped away unnoticed, walked out onto the drifting plain, and climbed a gentle hill. There, he stood with arms out, embracing the world before him: Mother Earth, Father Moon, the four directions, the winged creatures, and the four-legged. His voice rose to the heavens as he greeted the day. He thanked the All-Father for another day of life and prayed for his family and Beth to remain safe.

Finished, he waited for the peace that always filled his heart at such a moment.

It did not come.

Once more, he lifted his arms and his gaze to the sky. "Hear me, Ancient Ones. Your wisdom and guidance are needed. If it is meant for Beth to belong with me, give me a sign. If it is not to be, give me the strength to resist her, for she lives in my heart. To give her up will end my being."

Still, the peace he sought failed to come.

For a long minute, he considered going home. Not even

returning to camp for his pony.

He looked to the west, where home lay.

He looked to the east, where Beth waited.

And he began walking.

"Is the lieutenant angry with me?" Beth scrubbed her hands and rinsed her face in the wash pan.

Tildy handed her a piece of toweling. "I don't reckon he's pleased."

"Because Hawk was with me? Or because I left camp?" Beth took the towel and dried off.

"Both, likely. Hurry up. He's waiting."

Peering into the small mirror propped up inside the wagon, Beth checked her hair, tucked a few errant tendrils back in place, and smoothed her shirtwaist. "I truly do not want to do this."

"It's only supper. You'll survive."

They climbed out the back of the wagon, and Beth wrapped her shawl around her shoulders. "If he touches me, I'll scream."

Tildy laughed. "I'll come and rescue you. Or would you rather I sent Hawk?"

Beth smiled. She had come to enjoy the camaraderie developing between her and Clotilda Buntz. "I don't want to get Hawk in trouble."

"But it's all right if I get in trouble, is that it?"

"No." Ready at last but wishing for some reason to delay, she drew in a deep breath, squeezed Tildy's hand, and headed for the lieutenant's tent. As she walked through the army camp, it fell suspiciously silent. She glanced at the troopers. All grinned. A few tipped their caps. At the journey's beginning, she'd overheard uncomplimentary comments about her birthmark, but the troopers seemed to have changed toward her. They were much friendlier. Sometimes, too much so, though never truly out of line. Just more familiar than she was accustomed to, which left her flustered and tongue-tied.

A folding table stood near a fire outside McCall's tent. No tablecloth or fine china, but she hadn't expected such amenities. Tin plates and cups were the best the Army could do. Beth wouldn't mind if she were anywhere but this particular spot. A lantern hung from a pole, illuminating the area and exaggerating the shadows outside its perimeter.

The lieutenant stood waiting.

"Evening, Miss Webster."

She nodded. "Good evening, sir."

A private stood by with a coffee pot in his hands.

McCall chuckled. "I won't expect you to use my given name, Miss Webster, but please, no 'sir.' Lieutenant will do. Sir makes me feel like my father, and he was an ornery old cuss."

He held out a folding chair for her, the height of luxury on the trail.

She sat. "Thank you."

"Coffee? Or would you rather wait until after the meal?" he asked. "I fear I have no wine."

"Coffee is fine, Lieutenant."

The private poured and vanished.

"I'm very pleased you were willing to join me tonight." McCall offered her a sugar container.

She shook her head.

"I've been attempting to get to know you better, Miss Webster. Your father is a fine man and a top-notch officer. I have great respect for him."

"I appreciate you saying that, Lieutenant." She sipped her coffee and nearly choked. It was thick enough to make into mud pies.

He looked at her for a moment, pursed his lips, and tried again. "I'm not trying to curry the Colonel's favor through you, Miss Webster. He and I get along just fine as it is. No, I'm interested in you. Being in the army, I don't meet many young ladies, but I find you more fascinating than any I've met before. I admire your spirit and courage."

"That is kind of you, Lieutenant." She knew he was trying to be nice and complimentary, but she could not forget the conversation she'd overheard the night she followed Tildy to his tent. Nothing he did or said could change how she felt about him.

"Do you know your father well?"

"I fear not." She put down her cup and folded her hands in her lap. "I have been in school the last four years and seen neither my mother nor my father during that time. I believe I might have been eight the last time Father visited us. All I remember is that he talked excessively about how terrible Indians were."

McCall put an elbow on the table, evidently thought better of it, and rested his arm on his leg, bent slightly forward. "Yes. He has a powerful hatred for the cursed heathens. Most army men do. It's because we've had to fight them, you understand. We must deal with them on their level, savage to savage. One cannot see what they do to their victims without being affected by their viciousness. Their sheer blood-lust and cruelty."

"Are you saying all Indians are that way, Lieutenant?"

"Pretty much, ma'am. The Snakes aren't as bad as most. They try to be friendly to whites."

"Snakes. That is the tribe Mr. Hawk belongs to, is it not?"

He chuckled. "Mr. Hawk, huh? He must enjoy hearing that." A furrow formed on his brow. "Miss Webster, I've noted your interest in Sparrow Hawk and must, for your own sake, discourage that line of thinking. Injuns aren't like us. They don't think the same, believe the same, or act the same. Another species altogether, if you get my meaning."

"I see. What color is their blood, if I may ask?"

His eyes narrowed. "Red, like ours, but that doesn't mean anything. You persist in letting your curiosity and impulsiveness rule your decisions, you're going to end up in big trouble, I can promise you that. Now, no more about Injuns. Let's eat."

He waved a hand.

A private emerged from the shadows with two plates loaded with fried steak, beans, and biscuits. Beth looked for a napkin and found none.

"Here." McCall handed her his handkerchief.

It appeared clean, to her relief.

"Thank you."

He picked up his knife and fork. "Well, dig in. Private Simpkins is as good a cook as I've found in the military."

She cut off a small bite of meat and put it in her mouth. The delicious flavor burst inside, and she nearly groaned with pleasure. Not even in Boston had she tasted steak this good.

"Excellent, Lieutenant. Your private is indeed a good cook."

A low "Thank you, ma'am" came from the darkness.

McCall motioned for him to leave.

"So, are you enjoying the journey?" He chewed a bite of steak.

She watched his jaw move vigorously and the food slosh about in his mouth and decided she wasn't very hungry. "Yes. The prairie is beautiful. So immense, it takes my breath away."

He chuckled again. "You've not seen it during a storm. I've witnessed ferocious tornadoes on the prairie, sometimes one after another at certain times of the year. So far, we've been lucky not to have encountered bad weather or grass fires. Such fires can blaze for weeks on end, leaving miles and miles of land blackened in their wake."

"It sounds terrifying. I am most happy to have escaped that experience."

"I would have kept you safe." He leaned toward her. "No harm will come to you as long as you are in my care."

Beth swallowed a mouthful of beans and laid her utensils on her plate. "If only that care had extended to Francine Gibbs while she was with us, she might not have been shot."

Anger darkened his eyes. "Had you not left camp's safety that night, she would not have been hurt."

Her gaze narrowed. "Had you and your men not been drunk that night, we would have stayed in camp."

His hands on the tabletop clenched and unclenched, and a tic began in his jaw.

Beth realized she should be more careful not to offend him. After all, her well-being did lie in his hands for the moment. Yet, she could not regret baiting him.

"The men work hard, Miss Webster. They face danger daily, keeping us all safe from Injuns and other perils. They deserve to let off steam now and then."

"Perhaps, Lieutenant. I mean Eggerton. Do you not recall, however, that had it not been for Sparrow Hawk and Francie and I screaming our heads off to warn you, a lot more of us might have been injured that night?"

Red-faced, he rose from the table. "I believe supper is over, Miss Webster. Walk carefully as you return to your wagon."

She stood, leaving the soiled handkerchief on the table. His anger had surprised her, but she was grateful the supper had ended. "I will, I assure you. Thank you for the lovely meal, Lieutenant."

He grabbed her arm and swung her back around as she turned away.

"Damn you, woman. I am trying my best here to court you proper."

"I am aware of that, Lieutenant." She pulled her arm from his grasp, took a deep breath to calm herself, and decided wisdom might be better than total honesty. "Forgive me. I'm afraid I'm quite tired and a bit out of sorts. Perhaps we should try this another night when circumstances are more favorable." She added a smile and saw his shoulders relax. His hands unclenched.

"No. This is my fault. I fear I am too eager and get ahead of myself. Instead of sending you an invitation you could hardly refuse, I should have come to speak to you myself and make sure you were up to spending an evening with me." He bowed to her. "Forgive my clumsiness."

"Certainly, Eggerton." She widened her smile for effect and offered her hand.

In a seeming effort to act the gentleman, he kissed her knuckles, then called for the corporal to escort her to her wagon.

Tildy was waiting. "How did it go?"

"The food was good." She went to the fire and helped herself to a cup of coffee.

"That's all you have to say about it?"

"Only after tonight, I doubt McCall will be as interested in wooing me. As I walked away, I heard him call me a spoiled brat under his breath."

Tildy laughed. "Well, heck. Things might be a bit different around here from now on."

"What do you mean?"

"I mean, Eggy isn't the kind of man to take rejection with a smile. I'd watch my back, were I you, little girl, and stay as much out of his sight as you can."

"Gladly. It will be fine if I never see him again."

"Long as it doesn't mean being left here in this wilderness, all by yourself," Tildy muttered.

Alarm settled inside Beth. "You think he would do that? My father would have him court-martialed."

"Maybe. Or you might meet with an unfortunate accident along the way."

"Surely not." But Beth felt little confidence in her words. After all, hadn't she had the same thought once, herself?

CHAPTER NINE

B eth awoke later from a sound sleep to a scratching on the canvas wall near her head. She glanced over at Tildy's bed. It had not been slept in.

"Beth?"

"What is it, Tildy?"

"I'm going to Eggy's tent to soothe some ruffled feathers, but you won't be alone. Hawk will be within calling distance."

"Thank you."

"I'll see you later." She chuckled. "Much later."

For several minutes, Beth lay there thinking about Hawk being outside and listening for any sign he was indeed there. Crickets chirped, an owl hooted, and a man laughed over in the army camp. Nothing more.

"Hawk?"

"I am here, Beth. Go to sleep."

She peeked through the gap at the bottom of the canvas covering and saw a shadow move beneath an old tree a dozen feet from the wagon. "I can't sleep. Come and talk to me."

"It would not look good for me to be seen standing beside your wagon."

"Come inside, then."

He said nothing for long moments. "That is not a good idea, Beth." She heard laughter in his voice.

"Then I will come out." She did not bother to dress, simply pulled a shawl around her shoulders over her nightgown and slipped into her shoes.

She found him leaning against the tree, dressed as usual in his long, fringed leather shirt and army trousers. A gun belt circled his hips, and a rifle leaned beside him. With his dark hair and bronzed skin, the lack of light made his expression difficult to read. "Hawk, don't you want to talk to me?"

"It is not wise, Beth. You should not be out here."

She sat on a rock and drew the shawl tighter against the cold breeze ruffling the leaves. "I miss Francie."

"Caleb will probably catch up with us at Fort Bridger. You will see her then."

"I hope so." She peered up at the moon, playing hide and seek with a flotilla of clouds. "But what if they miss us?"

"They will keep going and find you at Camp Floyd."

Standing, she walked a few feet to where a creek swirled around a bend, widened by the swift water's current. A frog hopped out of her path and into the water. "I don't want to go there. I don't want to live with my father."

"Why do you feel this way?"

She turned to face him and found that he had moved closer, away from the tree. "I don't know him, Hawk, and he dislikes me."

"You said that before, but I find it difficult to imagine."

Out from under the branches, his face became more visible. Moonlight emphasized his high, prominent cheekbones. He looked so handsome, she yearned to touch him. "I heard him once telling my mother how ugly my birthmark made me. He was embarrassed to be seen with me."

Hawk frowned. "I am sorry for this, Beth. Perhaps he will feel differently when he sees you grown up. You are a beautiful young woman now."

She reached out to feel a feather hanging from his braid. "You think so?"

"Yes." He put his hand on hers. "You know how I feel about you."

She would have thrown herself at him had he not swooped down and captured a baby frog, which he deposited in her palm.

She laughed. "That tickles. He's wet."

"Frogs like water."

The tiny amphibian escaped.

Beth wiped her hands on her shawl. "Hawk, do you have a wife or a girl waiting at home?"

He smiled. "Why do you ask?"

"I want to know."

"No, curious one, I do not. Does that please you?"

"Maybe. Do you want a wife someday?"

"Yes. Do you want a husband someday?"

"Yes." She laughed. "I know what a wife does around the house. What do Indian wives do besides scrape hides and make clothes?"

"Much the same as white women do, I imagine. They keep the tipi and clothing clean, make new garments, care for the children, cook, and prepare food for winter."

"But they always cook over an open fire, like we do here. Have they no stoves?"

He shook his head. "Compared to your people, we lack many luxuries, but my people are happy. They enjoy living close to Mother Earth."

Beth found a daisy growing along the stream, picked it, and brushed the soft petals over her lips. "I would like to learn what it is like to live in a tipi."

"It is much like you whites live, except our homes are conical, and yours are wooden or made of stones."

"Do you have beds?" She reached over and fluttered the flower against his jaw. She already knew the answer to her question. She merely wanted to keep him with her.

Hawk grabbed her hand and put it away from him.

Beth frowned but didn't object. "You didn't answer my question."

"Yes, we sleep on buffalo robes on the ground. They are comfortable. Did you not notice the beds when we visited Many Tongues?"

"Yes." She cocked her head, puzzled. "Don't you get bugs and spiders in them, being on the ground?"

He shook his head, more from wonder at her persistence than as an answer. "Our women scatter certain herbs that discourage the insects from invading our homes."

Her eyes widened. "Oh. How clever. What herbs?"

"Beth, you are *kitsaan*, bad. What is Caleb's word... incor... incorrable. Yes. This means hopelessly naughty, does it not? You ask too many questions."

She laughed. "Incorrigible? I guess you could call me that. I remember my mother calling me unmanageable. That's the same thing."

"Unmanageable. I like this word better. Easier to say."

Beth sobered. "You wish to manage me? Why?"

He sighed, then chuckled. "No, I don't. What is it you want

from me, Beth? I think sometimes you try to tease me into doing things I mustn't, like kissing you. This is a risky game you play. What do you hope to gain?"

"I am not teasing. I'm serious." Scowling, she marched away but turned back. "What is so wrong with me wanting to feel your mouth on mine? To have your arms around me? I like you, Hawk. Very much."

He took her hands, keeping her in place. "I feel the same for you, my Beth. This makes what we do here even more unwise. Do you not understand what can happen between a man and a woman when they kiss and touch each other? What if I can't stop? I want you. More than anything. What if someone saw us?"

"I…I don't want to get you into trouble. What do you mean about what can happen between a man and a woman when they kiss?"

He stared. "Beth, do you know how babies come to be?"

"Not entirely. I know it happens to married couples and has something to do with the marriage bed, but I don't know what. Kissing and touching, of course. But it doesn't make sense that babies can be created so easily."

He shook his head. "You are a wonder."

"Well, tell me. What happens?"

"Ask your chaperone. A woman can explain such a matter better than a man. Now, go to bed before someone catches us together."

She argued, but he was adamant. Frustrated, curious, and angry, she stomped back to the wagon and hauled herself inside. But the night proved long, and her mind and imagination were hopelessly busy.

In the morning, she awoke to find Tildy abed across the narrow aisle in the middle of the wagon. Beth rose and dressed, preparing to leave the wagon.

Tildy woke. "Is it time to get up already?"

"Almost. You'd better hurry." Beth sat on her mattress. "First though, were you able to soothe Eggy's feathers? Is he still upset with me?"

Tildy sat up and ran her fingers through her long ruddy hair. "I think that man will stay upset until you agree to marry him. It amazes me how serious he is about this idea."

"Well, he'd best give up." Beth fetched the brush and set to work on the other woman's hair. "I cannot believe he feels any sincere affection for me. The silly, foolish man. Money is no reason to marry."

She gave Tildy's hair a last stroke and put the brush away.

"Maybe not, but that's how it's been done for centuries among the finer families."

"Well, at least now I know how to get him to leave me alone. I'll tell him the money is in a trust my future husband cannot spend."

Tildy frowned. "To tell him such a thing is not a good idea, Beth."

"Why not?"

"Because he'll know then that I told you of his plans." Tildy shuddered. "I dread to think what he'd do to me."

"He doesn't have to know. I will work it into the conversation when it seems right."

"The man is no idiot. What type of conversation would be appropriate for you to disclose such personal information? You must be very careful."

"I will. You'll see."

"Drat it, Tildy. I'm in huge trouble because of that little brat."
In a violent gesture, Lieutenant Eggerton McCall swiped
everything off the table onto the tent floor a few days later. The
glass he'd brought, so he didn't have to drink water from a tin
cup, struck a tent post and shattered. Ledgers, pencils, pen, and
inkpot went flying.

"Oh, Eggy," Tildy chided as she watched the tipped
inkwell turn his pillow black. "Now, what good did that do?"
If he weren't careful, he'd wake up the whole camp, including
Beth.

Grabbing her, he glared with bloodshot eyes. "It made me
feel better. Is that a good enough reason for you?"

Froth peppered his lower lip and Tildy's face. She shoved
him away and wiped her face with her sleeve. "You don't have
to take it out on me."

He poked a finger at her. "If you'd done your job and
convinced the girl to marry me, we wouldn't be in this
predicament now."

"What's with the *we*? This is your problem, not mine. If
Beth doesn't want you, I can do nothing about it. You need to
be nicer. Romance her."

"Romance the chit!" He threw up his arms. "I don't even
like her. How do I romance a spoiled child I can't stand? With
that birthmark, I'd have to put a sack over her head to bed her."

"What a cruel thing to say. Besides, it's not that bad."
Tildy stood back and watched as he stomped about inside the
tent and ranted. And he called Beth a spoiled child. Tildy had
never seen him like this before and didn't like it. No wonder

Beth didn't want to marry the man. He was a donkey's ass. "Eggy, calm down and tell me what this is all about. What trouble are you in?"

He sank onto a chair, looking deflated now. "Aw, hell, Tildy. I gambled away the money Colonel Webster gave me for Beth's travel expenses. What I hadn't already spent, anyway."

"Gambled it? To whom? One of the dragoons?"

"I wish it were a dragoon. I might have a chance to get it back." He folded his arms on the tabletop and rested his forehead on them. "It was Bearstooth. You remember that giant of a mountain man back at Fort Laramie? The one who nearly killed a man with one punch without breaking a sweat?"

"That overgrown grizzly?" Tildy picked up the other chair in the room where it had been knocked over during McCall's temper tantrum and sat. "Well, you won't be getting it back from him."

"Get it back! Hell, it's worse than that." He lifted his head.

"Wait a minute," she interrupted. "If you're broke, how will you pay me?"

He straightened and heaved a sigh. "Darned if I know. I don't have two nickels to rub together. But what has me scared half to death is that I gave Arkansas Jack an IOU for ninety-five dollars he intends to collect, even if he has to take it out of my hide."

Tildy wanted to tell him he deserved it but kept quiet.

"He said he'd catch up with me in Salt Lake City, and I'd better have the money for him or... as he put it, 'Dead men don't need cash.'"

"What are you going to do?" She asked more out of

curiosity than concern. Tildy was fast losing what respect she might have had for the man initially.

With a shrug, he rose, stuffed his hands deep in his pockets, and paced the floor. Glass crunched under his boots. "I planned to marry Beth the first chance I got and use her money to pay him back. Confound it. I've got to find a way to make her marry me."

Tildy blew a silent whistle. McCall was a bigger fool than she thought. "I suppose you think that lawyer in Hillsdale gave the girl her inheritance then and there?"

"No. The man's no fool. He wouldn't give a fortune to a seventeen-year-old girl. He might have given her a couple hundred dollars, but no more. She'd have to go to a bank, get the money and hand it over." He rubbed his chin. "Maybe all I'd have to do is show the banker a marriage certificate."

"You mean a fake certificate?"

His eyes brightened. "Do you think I could get one that would fool a banker?" Pacing the tent again, he seemed to forget Tildy's presence.

"Yes," he mumbled under his breath. "That would work. In a town the size of Salt Lake City, I should be able to find a forger. Consarn it. Why didn't I think of this before?"

Because you're a stupid jackass. She stood, thinking to slip away.

He turned. "I have to get this supply train to Salt Lake City as fast as possible, Tildy. Before Bearstooth gets there. If the girl refuses to marry me, I'll seek a forger who can give me a marriage certificate."

She laughed.

He scowled. "What are you laughing at?"

She shook her head. And lied. "The thought of you as a married man."

"If I have my way, I won't be married for long."

Silently, Tildy watched him.

"I'll figure out something." He paced the floor. "I'll see about transferring out of the Tenth Infantry to some other location where Webster won't have any idea what I'm doing. Then I'll find a way to get rid of the brat."

Until now, she had considered the man all talk and no action. Now, she wondered. He didn't need to marry Beth. He could easily force her to give him the money he wanted unless that wasn't all he intended to have. "Why marry her at all if you can get your hands on a fake certificate?"

He grabbed her by the shoulders, his fingers digging into her flesh. "That girl caused me a lot of trouble, having to go fetch her in New York and all. She's made this trip miserable with all the special arrangements that had to be made because of her. By damn, I deserve to get a piece of that young body after all she's put me through."

He shoved Tildy away so hard she nearly fell. But she'd learned what she wanted to know.

He turned and started back across the tent. "Besides, marrying her would be simpler and more certain to give me what I want."

Tildy wasn't so sure. She eyed him as he flopped down on his cot, ignoring the ink-stained pillow, and continued to plot in his head. Tomorrow, they would reach Fort Bridger, where he'd be more likely to find a chaplain. Could he force Beth to marry him there? It would be easier to arrange an accident for her on the trail than it would once they reached Camp Floyd.

Did Salt Lake City have a sanitarium he could lock her up in and tell her father she died in an accident on the way?

She might have underestimated McCall's desperation. Somehow, she had to find a way to protect Beth. Could Tildy get her hands on a six-gun? Maybe steal one a soldier left unattended? She needed to get Hawk aside and warn him to take Beth away from the wagon train as soon as possible. Beth was too sweet to die so young.

It wasn't the first time Tildy had witnessed a man's cruelty to a woman. In her line of work, it was almost a daily event. One she was good and sick of. She'd seen it as something unavoidable, just part of life. But, by heck, it didn't have to be.

If she had to kill McCall herself, she'd do it. And it might very well come to that.

CHAPTER TEN

B eth and Tildy rode side by side on the wagon's tailgate as it rumbled along deep ruts in a muddy road through tall prairie grass. Ahead, in the distance, misty mountains rose from the plain, and Beth wished she could explore them.

Charley said they'd arrive at Fort Bridger before dark, and Beth could hardly wait. She and Hawk would be able to see each other more there. She swatted futilely at the flies that buzzed around them. If only a breeze would arise and chase the insects away. They were one of the things she didn't like about traveling in a wagon. They couldn't escape the bugs even when they closed themselves inside. The dust and dirt didn't help. Beth thought surely, she would never be clean again. When she talked, she felt the dirt grind against her teeth, so she tried to keep her mouth shut.

She felt the older woman's eyes on her and knew her friend awaited a response to what she'd told Beth this morning, but Beth had yet to decide what she'd heard.

"You asked me." Tildy touched her sleeve. "Don't you believe me? Is that why you're upset and won't talk to me?"

Beth felt guilty for her silence. Couldn't Tildy see she was thinking? But her silence came from more than that. All around them, life went on as usual. Deer grazed in meadows while hawks floated on breezes high in the sky. So much to see and learn, and she loved it all.

Peeking out between the wagon cover and the bed, she saw a ground squirrel run across the road and vanish in the grass. A second, smaller one started across, stopped, and watched the wagon with curious, beady little eyes. The little animal raced back the way it had come at a sharp bark from the verdant growth, no doubt from the rodent's mother. To the north, in the distance, lay a series of low hills, blue and gray against the green prairie and blue sky. But it was the view south that captured and held Beth's attention. Magnificent, white-tipped mountains rose into the heavens like the thrones of gods. How she yearned to explore them.

Would Hawk take her there if she asked? They had grown closer the past several days, spending as much time together as they could. Mostly, they talked. At times, they became caught up in kissing and holding each other until he set her away from him, got up, and walked off, saying he needed to cool down. Was what Tildy had described as lovemaking what he wanted to do with Beth? "Do you think I'll like making love with a man?"

"It can be wonderful, with the right man. One you love." Tildy smacked at a mosquito on her wool plaid skirt.

Beth glanced over, her brow furrowed. "*Can* be? Meaning it isn't always?"

"No, not always. If you're with the wrong man." Tildy pointed at the road behind them. "Look. Deer."

A doe and fawn bounded across the double row of ruts that made up the road and were soon out of sight in the high grass.

"For working girls like me," Tildy continued, "it is rarely pleasant. It's a job. But if you love the man and he cares about you, that's another story altogether."

Beth thought about that but found it hard to imagine herself doing such a thing. Would she feel differently with Hawk? Probably. She loved it when he held and kissed her. "Did you ever love a man?"

"Yes." Tildy blew out a breath. "Seems like a long time ago, but it wasn't really. I was seventeen, like you are now. He was twenty-three and very experienced. We planned to be married as soon as he returned from a trip to New Orleans."

"What happened?"

"I don't know. I never heard from him again. A year later, I heard he had been killed but had no way of knowing for sure."

Beth straightened and stared at her. "Why didn't you go look for him? That's what I would do."

Tildy laughed. "Yes, but you're more adventurous than me. Besides, he left me with child. My father kicked me out."

"I'm so sorry. What an awful thing for a father to do. What happened to the baby?"

"It was stillborn. A boy." Tildy scraped flecks of mud from her skirt hem with her fingernail. "I needed to find work, but no one would hire me. I survived by stealing, but hunger weakened me. A man tried to rape me, and I fought him. He beat me in the belly again and again until I passed out. When I woke up, I lay in a pool of blood, and the babe was coming. I couldn't get him to breathe. In some ways, my life ended that day."

Beth's throat closed up, aching with unshed tears. Not knowing what to say, she merely squeezed her friend's hand.

For a long time, neither spoke until a cry came from farther up the caravan.

"Fort Bridger ahead!"

Carefully, Beth climbed onto the seat next to Charley and straightened to full height, trying to see the fort. Smoke spiraled into the sky in the distance—the only sign of civilization.

"What do you see?" Tildy asked.

"Smoke. Just smoke."

With Tildy steadying her, Beth regained her place. She wanted to get out and walk, but yesterday's heavy rain had left everything wet and muddy. At the sound of an approaching horse, she leaned to the side to see past the wagon ahead of them. Hawk was coming from the direction of the fort.

"We will be at Bridger soon." He grinned. Beth thought she had never seen him look so happy.

"Have you already been there?"

"Yes, I rode ahead and just came back. Some of my people are there. I am going now to visit with them. I will see you when you arrive."

She barely had time to say goodbye before he was gone. The minutes passed like hours until, at last, the wagon pulled off the road and came to a stop. Beth jumped down at once. The sides of the fort, a hundred yards away, had been built of upright poles at least ten feet high. Another wagon train sat alongside, and people came and went through the entrance. She looked for the tipis of Hawk's people but saw none. "Come on, Tildy, let's go see."

She all but dragged Tildy through the wide-open gates. Low log huts ran along the inner walls. Indians stood here and there among the troopers, travelers, and several men who looked like mountain men.

"Oh, I wish Francie were here. Look." Beth entwined her arm with Tildy's. "Indians. And they look exactly how I envisioned Mene-Seela."

"Who in thunder is Mene-Seela?"

"A character in a book," Beth answered, laughing.

"There's Hawk." Tildy pointed toward a few Indian men standing inside the gate. "He doesn't look happy anymore."

"No, he doesn't." He appeared troubled. Beth's enthusiasm faded.

He spotted them and hurried over. "Beth. Tildy. My people brought bad news. My mother is dying. I must leave at once for the *kattainten*, village."

"I'm so sorry, Hawk." Her heart ached for him, yet she couldn't help worrying about what would happen to her without him. It was selfish, she knew, but he had become her world. "Will you be gone long?"

"I cannot say." He glanced at the older woman.

"Don't mind me, young man. I know you two are crazy for each other. Go ahead and give her a proper goodbye." With that, she strolled away.

Hawk turned back to Beth. "I want to kiss you but must not. Forgive me for leaving. I will come back and find you as soon as I can."

"I understand." She fought to keep from crying and begging him not to go. "Don't forget me. Please?"

"Never, my Beth. I could never forget you. You are my heart."

"And you are mine."

He gazed at her for a long moment, then wheeled about and ran for his horse. Within seconds, he was gone.

And Beth was alone, terrified she would never see him again.

Beth paid little attention when the call came two days later.

"Wagons coming."

She had yet to leave the room she shared with Tildy at the home of Fort Bridger's sutler, William A. Carter. Hawk's departure had left her with an overwhelming sense of melancholy she had no will to fight.

"You've got to cheer up, Beth," Tildy told her. "This moping around is doing you no good. Hawk said he'd be back. Don't you believe him?"

"It isn't that." Beth answered from the bed where she sat still in her nightgown, even though noon would be upon them soon. "I'm afraid he won't get back before I reach my father, and then it might be too late. Besides, I do not want to spend more time with the lieutenant than I have to, and he'll be there."

Tildy frowned. "What does *it might be too late* mean? What nonsense have you got planned, girl?"

Rising, Beth moved to the window, sweeping the curtain aside with her hand as she gazed out on the parade ground. "No nonsense. If only Francie were here. She and I hoped to get a house in Salt Lake City." She turned to Tildy. "I don't want to live with my father. And I will not marry Eggy." Beth had grown sick of seeing the man everywhere she went.

"You're only seventeen. The Colonel still has legal control over you."

"I know. I'll be eighteen soon, though. October fourteenth."

"Congratulations. Unfortunately, you won't be free until then."

Beth wandered to the dressing table and picked up Tildy's bottle of lavender water. She uncorked the container and sniffed the sweet fragrance. "How old did you say you were when you left home?" She recapped the bottle and put it down.

Tildy laughed. "Seventeen, but... now, don't you go getting any crazy ideas, young lady. If I hadn't lost the babe and been able to earn a living on my back, I would have starved and the child with me. Take my word for it, Beth; you do not want to be an unwed mother living on your own."

Beth sat on the bed again. "I know."

Wagon wheels rumbled outside, and a horse whinnied. The newcomers had arrived. From which direction? Beth wondered but didn't care enough to ask.

"Listen." Tildy sat beside her and took her hand. "I understand how you feel, but believe me, Beth, there are worse things in life than living with your father."

"I am sure you're right."

Tildy cursed under her breath. "I can tell you've shut your ears. I'm going down for the noon meal. It wouldn't do to be late after Mrs. Carter invited us to stay with them. Are you coming?"

"I am not hungry."

"Huh! Hawk'll come back and not recognize you for the toothpick you will have become. Now, get up from there and—"

Someone knocked on the door. Before either woman could answer, the panel swung open, and Francine Gibbs stepped inside, a grin on her pretty face.

"Francie!" Beth jumped up and ran to her friend.

Hugging each other, they rocked back and forth while Beth sobbed and Francine muttered soft, soothing sounds. "Here, here, Beth. I'm glad you're happy to see me, but I hate that I've made you cry."

Beth drew back a little, bracketed Francie's face with her hands, and hiccupped.

They laughed.

"I'm sorry," she said. "It's just... "

"She's been moping around here for two days," Tildy offered. "Hawk left and went home to his people."

Francine looked at the older woman and back at Beth. "Did you... are you in love with him, Beth?"

Instead of answering, Beth hid her face in Francie's neck, her arms wrapped around her friend, and nodded.

"Oh, my." But Francine's voice held little surprise.

"Should I come back later?" a man asked with a Scottish brogue.

Beth peeked over Francie's shoulder. A tall man in his early thirties stood in the open doorway. He looked familiar, but she couldn't place him. His face was clean-shaven except for a mustache. The lack of tan on his cheeks and jaw indicated a recent shave. She saw nothing remarkable about his clothes except the tasseled cap on his head. An image formed in her mind. "Mr. Stewart?"

He grinned. " 'Tis me, lass."

The two girls broke apart.

Conscious, suddenly, of her skimpy apparel, Beth grabbed for her robe and drew it on over her nightgown. "It's wonderful to see you, Mr. Stewart. And even more wonderful that you brought Francie to me."

"Now, lass. I distinctly recall telling you to call me Caleb."

With a smile, she offered him her hand. "Welcome, Caleb."

"'Twas my pleasure to accompany her here, I assure you."

A look passed between him and Francine that Beth didn't know how to interpret.

"All right," Tildy said, "let's have it. Something is going on between you two."

"Is that true?" Beth noted the pretty color on Francine's cheeks and her new dress.

Then she saw that Caleb was holding Francine's hand, and his expression as he gazed at the young woman displayed clear adoration.

"Francie?"

"Beth, Mrs. Hightower…" Francine's cheeks pinkened, and she grinned. "I'd like you to meet my husband, Mr. Caleb Stewart."

"Francie, I can't believe this," Beth exclaimed when the door shut behind Tildy and Caleb, leaving the two girls to their reunion. Tildy had told Caleb she had something she wanted to discuss with him, which Beth thought odd. "You and Mr. Stewart? How did it happen? Do you truly love him?"

"Yes, Beth." Joy suffused her voice, and moisture glistened in her eyes. "I love him so much. He is the kindest, gentlest, and most generous man I have ever met. We plan to reside in a place called Jackson Hole in Washington Territory.

Caleb says it is the most beautiful spot in the country, and we'd love for you to live with us. Will you, Beth? Please?"

Beth paced the room as she considered Francie's request. "Oh, I don't know, Francie. You and Mr. Stewart—"

"Caleb."

"Caleb. You're on your honeymoon. I wouldn't want to be in the way."

"You won't be, I promise. Caleb says he'll build you a separate cabin next to ours. He says Snake Indians frequent the valley sometimes. That's the tribe Hawk belongs to, isn't it?" Francie sat on the bed.

Beth rubbed her neck, uncertain what to do. If she went with Francie and Caleb, she would at least be away from her father. But she wasn't eighteen yet. Would he come after her? "Tildy says I can't make such a decision without permission from Father because I'm still underage."

"Oh." Disappointment filled Francine's voice. "I suppose I should have had my mother's permission to marry, but you and I both know she doesn't care what I do. Perhaps we could go with you to see your father, and Caleb could talk to him."

Beth rushed to the bed and sat beside her friend, feeling a surge of hope and excitement. "That might work. Do you think Caleb would mind?"

"I don't think so. Why don't we ask? Mrs. Carter invited us to join them for the noon meal. Let's go down."

"All right. Help me get dressed."

Beth wore her rose-colored, sprigged cotton dress with the pink satin sash tied in the back. "I wish I had nice slippers instead of these clunky traveling shoes."

"They don't show anyway. Just take small steps." Francie

pushed Beth onto the stool at the dressing table and brushed her long hair. After tying it back with a pink ribbon, the girls left the bedroom and descended the stairs to join the others in the dining room.

Caleb pulled out chairs for them, and they sat. The food occupied the center of the table so everyone could help themselves. Beth found herself seated between Tildy and Corporal Gray, who smiled at her as she took her place beside him. Mr. Carter occupied the head of the table, Ann—Mrs. Carter—the foot. Opposite Beth were Francine, Caleb, and Lieutenant McCall. The Carter's two small daughters could be heard chattering in the kitchen where they had their own meal.

"Miss Webster," Ann Carter said, "I understand you might be traveling with Mr. and Mrs. Stewart to settle in Jackson Hole. William went through the valley once and told me it's sublimely beautiful."

"What's this?" The lieutenant glared at Beth; his eyes dark with anger. "You have not discussed this with me, young lady."

Beth glanced at Francine and Caleb before turning back to him. "I did not realize, sir, that I needed to discuss possible future plans with you."

"Well, you damn well better."

Ann gasped. "Please, Lieutenant. No swearing in my house." She looked toward the kitchen where her daughters waited.

"I apologize, ma'am. Colonel Webster placed his daughter in my care. Until I deliver her safely to him at Camp Floyd, I cannot allow her to go off alone or with anyone else." He scowled at Caleb and Francine.

"I understand, Lieutenant." Beth clenched her hands

together at her sides, hiding them in the folds of her skirt. It took a moment before she could look him in the eye again without exposing her fury. "Perhaps it would be best to discuss this later privately?"

"Of course."

She hazarded another glance at her friends. Anger turned Caleb's ruddy face bright red, and she noticed that Francine held his arm as if to keep him from rising. His willingness to defend Beth surprised her. But their feelings about McCall paled compared to Beth's. McCall did not care about her welfare or delivering her safely to her father. His concern was getting his hands on her money. That she would not allow, no matter what she had to do.

At the end of the meal, the men retired to Carter's study for cigars. The women prepared to move to the sitting room, but Beth had barely stepped outside the dining room when the lieutenant stopped her.

"Shall we speak now?" he said.

"Very well. Where?"

He looked around and motioned toward the empty parlor. Standing nearby with Francine, Caleb glowered and stepped toward them, but Francine stopped him. Beth followed McCall inside and sat on the sofa, fanning her skirts to discourage him from sitting next to her. Instead, he paced the room in sizzling silence. At last, he drew a chair in front of her and sat down.

"Miss Webster, I feel a need to apologize. I do not mean to overburden you with my presence, but you must understand I have come to care for you a great deal. Everything you do matters to me." He hesitated, cleared his throat, and began again. "I want very much for you to become my wife, Beth.

May I call you that?"

She nodded, keeping silent for fear she'd spew her anger all over him or empty her stomach.

"Good, I shall consider that progress." He reached across the space between them and took her hand. "I know you told me once you had no wish to marry, but I beg you to reconsider. I'll provide well, build you a fine home, and give you everything you want."

She opened her mouth to reply. He forestalled her with an upheld hand.

"Don't answer now. Think about it. I'm truly not the villain you seem to think I am, and I'm sincere in my affection." He rose to his feet and offered her a hand up. "Should you change your mind, come to me at once. Otherwise, I will wait until we reach Salt Lake City to re-approach the matter. Now, shall we join the others?"

She let him help her up and followed him into the foyer. Music came from the sitting room, and masculine laughter from the study.

McCall went to join the men.

Beth slipped inside the sitting room where Ann Carter played a piano. Beth took a seat beside Francine.

"What happened?" Francine whispered. "Did he hurt you?"

"No. It's fine. I'll tell you about it later."

To wait until Salt Lake City to tell McCall how she felt about him seemed a waste of time. Beth would never change her mind, but remembering Tildy's warning, she decided to allow the lieutenant to think he had a chance.

CHAPTER ELEVEN

"There it is." Beth, Tildy, and Francine stood side by side, gazing down at the small city in the valley below. "Salt Lake City."

The Mormons had chosen a site at the northern end of a valley that seemed to stretch forever southward. Beyond the town to the north lay the enormous lake Beth remembered Hawk saying contained so much salt a person could float in the water without fear of sinking. She wanted to see it, taste the water, and try floating in it. She wanted to spend days exploring the city, meeting the people who had founded it, and seeing for herself if they indeed had horns on their heads. Their leader, Brigham Young, reportedly had fifty-five wives, an unbelievable number for Beth to imagine.

Francine took Beth's hand and squeezed. "It seems we traveled forever to get here."

Tildy snorted. "We *did* travel forever."

"Three months," Beth replied. "It amazes me to think this valley was empty a little over ten years ago. Not one sign of civilization. Then the Mormons came."

"Now it holds a tidy little city." Francine shaded her eyes with her hand.

Beth laughed. "A little city? I thought that was what they called a town."

"You knew what I meant," Francine chided with a grin. "But imagine... before people came here, the valley was natural, the way God made it. The town almost appears a blight upon the land."

Gazing out on the grassy valley with its river running through the middle, Beth had to agree that she preferred looking at the unpopulated section over the city. Deer grazed in a meadow, and a hawk soared overhead, free and unfettered, the way Beth wished to be.

Lieutenant McCall walked up wearing a clean, tidy uniform and holding new gloves. "The land wasn't as empty as you might think. As I understand it, a band of Injuns lived along the river running through the valley."

"I bet they didn't stay long," Tildy muttered.

"Didn't they fight to keep their land?" Francine asked.

"I don't rightly know, Miss Gibbs... excuse me... I mean, Mrs. Stewart. They might have been outmanned or not have wanted to stay once the whites moved in. To Injuns the land doesn't belong to anyone. They call it their mother. I do know there have been battles between the Injuns and the Mormons. Black Hawk, the Ute chief, hates the whites being here. His people used to camp down there. I expect he'll cause serious trouble sometime in the future."

"That's good to know." Tildy's voice held sarcasm.

"I hope he doesn't go on the warpath before we all reach our new homes." Francine shuddered.

McCall slapped his gloves together and motioned to the cavalcade waiting on the trail. "Can't think of a better reason for reaching there as soon as possible. Shall we return and get going?"

Beth hurried to keep up with his long legs. "I'm looking forward to seeing the city, Lieutenant. Would it be possible to stay a day or two?"

"Your father is expecting you, Miss Webster. Besides, we aren't going into town. As you can see, it sits at the north end of the valley. Camp Floyd is to the south, beyond those mountains that nearly enclose this valley. We'll travel in that direction and camp on the far side of the river. That way, we can arrive at the fort late tomorrow morning."

Disheartened, she fell back to walk with Francine and Tildy. "Did you hear what he said?"

"Yes. It's a huge disappointment." Francine lifted her skirts and stuck out a foot. "My shoes are worn out, and so are yours. You could insist on staying to buy new shoes."

"Do you think that would work?" Beth wanted to curse their poor luck out loud. She had been counting on having an opportunity to check out lodgings in the city and do some shopping. "Maybe I could use my charms to convince him a layover would help me make up my mind about his proposal."

Francine laughed and fanned away the flies that hovered around them. "What a sneaky idea. I like it."

Tildy said nothing, appearing particularly glum. Beth wondered why.

The lieutenant aimed for the head of the caravan while the women kept going until they reached their wagon, where Caleb waited for them with two saddled horses.

Beth's heart instantly fell. At times, she forgot her best friend was married now. Since Caleb and Francine rejoined the supply train, Francine had shared the wagon with Tildy and Beth. During the day, Caleb rode his horse, occasionally with the lieutenant, often with Hawk. At night, he slept under the women's wagon and complained about not having his own wagon.

"Time for us to leave, my dear." He held out a hand to Francine.

"What a shame," Tildy said. "Caleb, might I have a word with you while these two say their farewells?"

"Certainly, Mrs. Hightower." They walked away several feet.

Beth threw herself into Francine's arms. She wanted to beg Francine not to go but resisted. To lose her friend again tore her heart into little pieces she feared could never be put together again. "I'm going to miss you so much." She fought the tears that threatened.

"I'll miss you, too."

"Yes, but you'll have Caleb and soon, maybe, a babe to care for." A hawk gave a mournful cry overhead. It matched Beth's mood. No, it didn't. She believed her sorrow to be much deeper than anything a hawk could feel. She wanted to beg the newlyweds to take her with them, yet didn't have the courage. She tried to appear cheerful, but Francine knew her too well and gave her a look of deep sympathy and concern.

"You'll find new friends at Camp Floyd, Beth," she said. "I'm sure of it. How could anyone not love you as I do?"

"If you met my father, you'd know."

Caleb and Tildy returned.

"Beth, will you be all right if we leave?" Caleb asked. "It bothers me to go without knowing McCall won't give you too much trouble. But we have matters we must take care of before winter comes."

"I'm sure I'll be fine, Caleb," Beth lied. Her world had shattered around her and left her stranded on a lonely island she feared she'd never escape. The prospect of living with her father, with no friends nearby, made her want to scream, beat the earth with her fists and die. "After all, I'll be with my father."

"Very well. Come along, Francie." He held out his hand to his wife. "Prolonging these goodbyes only makes the parting worse."

The women hugged again, and Francine took her husband's hand, the other held by Beth until their fingers slipped apart. To Beth, it felt as if her heart had been torn from her body. She wanted to snatch Francine back. Instead, she watched the couple walk to their horses, mount, and ride out of her life.

Beside her, Tildy muttered, "Tarnation."

Beth could find no word suitable to express her feelings.

Lieutenant McCall led the supply train along the base of the foothills of a mountain range that bordered the eastern side of the valley in the opposite direction from where Beth wanted to go. They passed a few distant farms, each moment taking them farther from Salt Lake City. Eventually, they crossed over to the west side, using a Mormon ferry to ford the Jordan River. Beth observed everything with her usual fascination. Yet, her heart grew heavier with every mile that took her farther from her friend.

"Whoever said these Mormons have horns never visited

here," she whispered to Tildy as they watched the ferryman load their wagon onto the ferry. The women stood on the landing, awaiting the ferry's return to get them and goods from the wagon. They'd had to lighten the load.

"Mighty hard to believe." Tildy rolled her eyes.

"Yes. I never believed such a thing possible." Beth turned to watch the water. "How will I convince the lieutenant to take us into town when we're so far away?"

"I don't know."

Tildy seemed different since leaving Fort Bridger. She rarely let Beth out of her sight, and her mood was somber. Beth suspected she dreaded their separation as much as Beth did but wondered if something didn't have Tildy worried. Perhaps she still felt she should get a job and stay in Salt Lake City. Beth had told her that would be silly, that she was sure her father would welcome her.

"You gals have some sorta scheme goin', doncha?" Charley said, ambling up to them. "What're you up to now?"

"Nothing, Charley. We're merely disappointed not to get into Salt Lake City."

"Now, you oughtn't to be wantin' to go there, pretty gals like you. Them Mormons'ud snatch you up and make you their third, seventh, or sixteenth wives." He cackled at his own humor.

The women ignored him.

"Well, I'm going to complain to my father when I see him," Beth said.

Charley laughed again, a sound that put her in mind of a donkey they'd seen at Fort Bridger. "You do that, little girl. You do that."

She glared at him, incensed at being called a little girl, and said nothing more. She knew chiding him for what she considered an insult would be a waste of time. Little girl was exactly how he saw her. Remembering back to the beginning of their journey, she could understand it; she had been a child then. No more.

They traveled through the pass between the two mountain ranges that enclosed the valley's south end and made camp not far from a freshwater lake. As soon as everything was in order and she had a moment to spare, Beth went to hunt down the lieutenant. She and Tildy had hatched a plan she was eager to put into action. She found him sitting outside his tent, writing in his ledger. Tildy had followed and hovered just out of sight, but Beth knew she was there.

"Good afternoon, Lieutenant. May I speak with you?"

He stood and gestured to the chair he had been using. "Of course, Miss Webster. Have a seat. I'll fetch the other chair from inside."

A moment later, they were both seated, and Beth searched for the best way to word her request so he couldn't refuse. She started with a smile she hoped looked inviting. "I've been thinking about your proposal, Lieutenant, and wondering where we would live."

He looked pleased. "There is an empty house in the officer's quarters at Camp Floyd that I'm quite certain we could claim. Nothing fancy but adequate, I believe."

"I see. And where would the wedding take place?"

"Wherever you want."

She widened her eyes and her smile. "In Salt Lake City?"

He frowned. "That would require a long ride from Camp

Floyd. Your father would not appreciate being taken away from his duties."

"None of that would be a problem if we had the ceremony tomorrow."

He stared and then grinned. "Are you agreeing to become my wife, Miss Webster?"

"I'm seriously considering it. I would truly prefer not living with my father, whom I barely know. I know you."

He jumped up and danced a short jig. Good, the conversation seemed to be going as she wished, though she worried tremendously about how he would react when she changed her mind later. He could be a violent man. "But I have nothing to wear that would do for a wedding. All my dresses were made for a schoolgirl, you see. None would be suitable...unless I could go to Salt Lake City to do some shopping. Having a special dress for the occasion would mean a great deal to me."

She lowered her head and did her best to blush. "And garments for the honeymoon." Then she peeked at him from under her lashes.

His face lit up, adding to his good looks. What a shame he was so slimy at heart. "I'm very pleased. I believe your idea has merit, Beth." He reached over and took her hand.

A shiver ran down Beth's back, but she didn't pull away. "Of course. So, we can plan to layover here a day or two?"

"I think that can be arranged."

"Excellent." She stood. "I'm so excited. I can't wait to share the news with Hilary."

He stood as well, his smile gone now. "But we have plans to make."

"There is plenty of time for that, Lieutenant." She rushed off, thankful to get away from the man.

Tildy appeared from behind a tree a dozen steps away.

"Were you listening? He went for it." Beth tried to look jubilant, though she still felt too low over Francine for it to be gen. "We're going into the city tomorrow."

"I hope it doesn't backfire." Tildy did not look as confident as Beth felt. Typical of late. "You might find yourself truly wed to that buffoon."

Beth's heart jerked inside her chest. "No, I cannot allow that. We must be very, very careful."

"And lucky," Tildy added, her chin firm and with a hard look in her eyes.

The streets of Salt Lake City were wide and lined with young trees. People strolled the sidewalks and came and went from the shops like every other town Beth had seen. The women's fashions also appeared the same. A little behind the times compared to New York, but Beth had heard this was to be expected in the west.

As the lieutenant drove the Army ambulance down Main Street, she wondered if he knew someone here he wanted to find. He kept looking right and left at every person they passed. He seemed nervous. He secured the team when he found space to park, then helped Beth and Tildy from the wagon.

"The shops look very inviting," Tildy said. "This will be fun."

"Yes." Beth cajoled.

McCall slipped a hand around her waist. He continued to study the people. Somehow, she sensed he worried about seeing someone he didn't want to meet up with. Then she remembered about Bearstooth. That must be who Eggy was watching for. "Enjoy yourself," he said with little enthusiasm. "I'll meet you back here in, shall we say, two hours?"

Pouting a little, Beth peered up at him. "Three?"

He squeezed her waist, and she thought she felt his hands shaking. "All right. Three. Mrs. Hightower, may I have a word with you, please?"

"Certainly."

He moved Tildy a little way apart from Beth and whispered something to her. Beth couldn't help wondering what it was all about. The whole time he watched the street. When he finished, Tildy joined Beth, and the women headed for the first interesting-looking shop. The lieutenant vanished into the closest saloon. Beth couldn't wait to start shopping, hoping it would banish the darkness clouding her soul.

"We did it. We got our way," Beth said as they strolled the walkway. She wanted to cover her birthmark; she'd already noticed a few people staring. "Now what?"

"If we were smart, we'd jump on a stagecoach and get out of here." Tildy scanned the shops. "I wonder where the stage office is. Maybe they have a stage going to Jackson Hole."

Beth stared at her. "We can't do that. The lieutenant would think we'd been kidnapped. My father would likely start a war to find me."

Tildy turned imploring eyes on her. "I can't convince you it's in your best interest to leave?"

"Of course not. Once I see my father, then I will consider

it, but not now."

"In that case—" Tildy linked her arm with Beth's "—we shop."

"Yes, I'm so eager. But what about later? How will I tell the lieutenant I've changed my mind? What if he flies into a rage?"

"It wouldn't be a problem if we were on a stage for—"

"No, Tildy." Beth couldn't believe it; Tildy began acting as nervous as McCall had been, her head constantly turning as she scanned the people on the street.

Tildy heaved a heavy sigh. "We'll have to hope that being in a public place will make him think twice about behaving badly. It would be more likely to happen after we leave town, and even then, he'll be cautious about how he acts in front of me."

"I pray you're right." Beth didn't feel convinced. She began to wonder if Tildy was telling her everything she knew. Ever since before Fort Bridger, the woman had done everything she could to talk Beth into escaping somewhere.

"Maybe we'll run into Hawk. You'd like that, I know."

Beth nodded. It would cheer her immensely to see him. "Oh, how I wish we could. It's been so long since he left us, I'm afraid to count on seeing him again." She stopped to peer into a jewelry store. "I pray his mother is all right."

"If he loves you, he'll come for you."

Beth gaped, shocked Tildy would doubt Hawk that way. But perhaps she might be right. No matter how much the thought hurt, she had to be realistic and accept that something could prevent Hawk from coming. His mother might die. She would not expect him to come right away then. "I suppose you might be right. He could decide it would be wiser to stay away."

Tildy patted her back. "If that's the case, there's nothing you can do about it. Look at that bracelet. Let's go inside and inquire as to the price."

They exited the store moments later, laughing at themselves for thinking they could afford such a piece. The price amounted to three times what Beth had expected.

"My, oh my." Tildy scrubbed at the tears her hilarity caused. "I never dreamed it would cost that much."

"I hope we find some reasonable buys here." Beth pointed to a tea house across the street. "I'm hungry. Let's have a bite, shall we? We can discuss strategy, and afterward, I'll go to the bank."

A Scottish woman ran the tea shop. Listening to her speak reminded Beth of Caleb, which exacerbated her loneliness for Francine.

"Everything looks delicious." Beth studied the menu. "I'll have a scone. I've never had one, and it sounds just the appropriate amount of food for a midmorning snack."

"Ah, ye will love it, ye will," the woman said.

She brought the tea in a pot covered with a colorful cozy. The biscuit-like scones arrived with bowls of elderberry jam and clotted cream, neither of which Beth nor Tildy had tasted before. Beth fell in love with the pastries on the first bite. "These are wonderful. I love this clotted cream. It's perfect with the sweet jam."

Tildy finally began to relax and seem more herself. When they finished, they moved to the counter, where a showcase displayed scones and other treats. Beth chose several to save for later and paid for them.

"Please tell me how you make that delicious clotted cream."

"Och. I canna be giving away me secrets now, can I?" The shop owner smiled as she bundled up Beth's purchases. "Ye'd make them at home and not come back."

"You needn't worry about that," Beth assured her. "I'll be living on an army post miles from here and doubt I'll get back often at all anyway."

"What a pity," she said. "Verra well, I'll write it down for ye, but ye must promise not to share it."

"I do. Thank you so much. You are so kind." Beth left a tip when they departed, the recipe in her pocket.

They stopped at a dressmaker's shop on their way to the bank. A lovely dress hung in the window. Inside, Beth found more on a rack. She chose two and ordered two more in similar styles. It would give her an excuse to come into the city. Camp Floyd might be nicer than the other forts she'd see, but she doubted it and knew she'd be eager to get away now and then. She also bought a hat, new gloves, a bottle of French perfume, and a silver dresser set with a brush, comb, and mirror.

Out on the boardwalk, she tried to give the dresser set to Tildy.

"No," the woman said, backing away. "I'm not taking that. It's too expensive. I told you I have some pride."

"Pride be damned," Beth said emphatically. "I already have one, and I'm not wasting my money. Either take this, or I'll throw a noisy fit here on the sidewalk." To prove her point, she opened her mouth as if to scream.

"All right." Tildy held up her hands to calm her. "All right.

I'll take it. Thank you."

Beth laughed and hugged her.

Next, they located the American First Bank. Beth went inside.

Tildy opted to explore a dry goods store next door.

The bank president, Mr. Jeremiah Sizewell, took care of Beth himself, leading her through a low gate to his desk at the back of the room, where she took a seat. "Now, what can I do for you... Miss Webster, did you say?"

"Yes, sir." She studied him, noticing a large mole beside his eye. She hoped it didn't grow larger; it might affect his sight. "I wish to set up an account. An attorney, Mr. Abner Snelling, instructed me to come to this bank when I arrived."

"Ah, Mr. Snelling." The portly man began digging through a stack of paperwork on his desk. "I remember. He sent a telegram with instructions regarding your account."

Finding what he sought, Sizewell put on a pair of spectacles and scanned the papers. "I see we've already set it up, Miss Webster, with funds Mr. Snelling sent."

Taken aback, Beth blinked in surprise. "He sent me more money?"

"Yes, indeed. A lot of money, in fact." Sizewell removed his spectacles. "But, you understand, he gave strict instructions as to how much you could withdraw at a time."

"I don't understand. How much money did he send?"

He donned his spectacles again and looked at the papers. "Two hundred and twenty-two thousand, one hundred and sixty-seven dollars, to be exact."

The room spun, and she clasped the edge of the desk to steady herself. She'd had no idea her mother had that much money. It explained how she could afford to send Beth to Runyon's School for Refined Young Ladies but not why she never seemed to think to send money for her daughter's clothing and other needs. Fanning a hand in front of her face, she said, "Oh, my. That came as an enormous surprise."

"I can see that." Sizewell beamed, then sobered. "Now, you must remember you are only allowed to withdraw two hundred dollars each month. Should you require more for some special reason, you must come to discuss the matter. I will wire Mr. Snelling for permission if I feel your need is warranted."

She fanned her face again. "I could never spend that much money in a month. I came to deposit most of the money Mr. Snelling gave me in New York before I traveled here. I spent very little of it."

"We can certainly take care of that." He gestured for a clerk to come over. A man with a long, thin face appeared at his side. "But I'd advise you to keep enough to see you through an emergency. You never know when you might need it."

"That sounds like good advice." Beth took the money from her reticle, separated out one hundred dollars, and handed the rest to the clerk.

The man took it away.

"Mr. Sizewell, may I ask if Mr. Snelling told you anything else about my inheritance?"

He folded his hands on the paperwork. "Of course. What is it you wish to know?"

"I was wondering what would happen if I were to marry." She hoped she didn't sound selfish. If Hawk received it, that would be all right. McCall, never. "Will my husband then control my money, or do I retain that right?"

"As I understand it, Miss Webster, your husband would have no say in handling your inheritance. Your great-grandmother created a trust to be passed down from first daughter to first daughter. No man can touch it."

Hearing that brought great relief. She didn't know who she might marry, but it didn't matter; they couldn't have her money. "What if I die without a daughter?"

"I'm glad you brought that up." He fished through more papers and came up with a legal-looking form. "I need you to name a beneficiary who would receive the money should something happen to you. But remember, it must be a female, preferably a relative. The money cannot be left to a man."

Beth had no relatives she knew of but answered quickly. "I know exactly who I want to have it. Francine Gibbs Stewart, wife of Caleb Stewart, Jackson Hole, Wyoming."

Sizewell wrote down the information.

Beth signed the document, shook hands with the bank president, and departed in a daze. When she told Tildy what happened, the woman broke into laughter.

"What is so funny?" Beth asked.

"I had a vision of Eggy's face when you tell him that." She doubled over, still laughing. "The man is in such a sweat to marry you to get your money and can't touch it, even if he gets you to the altar. It's hilarious."

Beth smiled. "I had no idea I had inherited so much until Mr. Sizewell told me." The smile turned into confusion. "Why is Eggy so desperate for money he'd marry a woman he dislikes?"

Tildy sobered and shook her head. Her lip curled. "The idiot lost the money the Colonel gave him for your expenses to a man who swore he'd beat it out of his hide if he didn't pay up. You remember Bearstooth at Fort Laramie?"

"That huge man who grabbed us and wanted to dance?" Beth's eyes widened. "I remember seeing the lieutenant playing a gambling game with him and other men."

"Yes. They were supposed to meet here in Salt Lake City. Eggy was counting on marrying you and getting the money before the brute found him. You know he could give Eggy a thorough thrashing without effort, even if Eggy had a knife."

"Oh, Tildy. That poor man." Beth glanced up and down the street for a glimpse of him. "We need to find him before Bearstooth does and inquire where to find a doctor in case he gets hurt. Perhaps I should marry him or, better yet, give him the money he needs; I have enough."

"Why would you do that? If he finds out I told you about the money, it will be me you'll need to find a doctor for."

"We won't tell him that, but we must make sure he's all right. I couldn't live with myself if he came to harm because of me."

Tildy fisted her hands on her hips and glared at her. "It wouldn't be because of you. It would be because the lackbrain is too stupid to know better than to gamble his money away, especially to a man like that."

Beth gave her a stern look. "All right, but we must find him. And watch out for Bearstooth. How much did Eggy lose?"

"Over two hundred, the fool."

"All right. As soon as we find him and know he's unharmed, I'll go to the bank and try to get the money he needs."

"No, you won't." Tildy grabbed her and whirled her

around. "You will not give him a penny. Have you forgotten what he intended to do with you after you married him? I wouldn't put it past him to smother you in your sleep, bury your body, and report you missing."

"Truly?" Alarm heightened Beth's pulse.

"Yes. I wouldn't lift a finger to help that man if it weren't for you. He can't pay me what he owes me, either. I'm going to have to go back to work."

"Not if I can help it. If you insist on living here, I'll pay your rent."

Tildy laughed, but the sound held no humor. "You will not. I have some pride, you know."

"You can't argue against me paying you what Eggy owed you. You can write out a receipt, and my father will reimburse me. Right now, we need to find the lieutenant."

"Very well." Tildy nodded. "I'll agree to that. I do need the money."

They walked up and down the streets, peering into shops and saloons, and found him, finally, waiting by the wagon as if nothing were amiss. He smelled of whiskey and appeared tense but unharmed. Motioning to a large parcel Beth held, he asked, "A dress?"

"Yes, it is." She didn't bother to tell him it was an afternoon tea dress.

He grinned, looking pleased and hopeful. Taking her arm, he drew her away from Tildy and passersby. "Shall we go find a minister?"

Now that he stood before her, perfectly healthy, Beth's concern for him faded. He was not a small man; he should be able to defend himself. His over-eagerness to wed her renewed her anger over what he'd intended to do after she became his wife. "Oh, Lieutenant. I'm so sorry. I've been thinking and remembered Father saying once that under no circumstances was I to wed without him being present. I'm afraid the ceremony will have to wait until we reach Camp Floyd after all. Probably for the best. I still have a few concerns about marriage."

His mouth tightened, and his face darkened. Beth expected him to start cursing and braced herself for it. Instead, he looked up and down the street, forehead creasing. He made a visible effort to bring himself under control. "I'm disappointed, but I understand. Let's get back to camp. I want to make an early start tomorrow. I'll speak to your father as soon as possible."

"Thank you, Lieutenant."

Clouds darkened his gray eyes. "I thought we'd advanced to a first-name basis."

She smiled. "Of course, Eggerton. I'm just not used to it yet."

"Well, get used to it." His brusque tone sounded more like an order. "We'll soon be getting a good deal more intimate than that."

Beth's temper flared. *Not if I can help it.*

When McCall helped her onto the wagon seat and turned to help Tildy, Beth noticed that her chaperone stood on the walk, her bags at her feet. She must have taken them from the back while Beth had her confrontation with Eggy. "Til— Er, Hilary, what are you doing?"

"I'm staying here, Beth. There's no place for me at Camp Floyd. We all know that."

"Mrs. Hightower," McCall said. "We discussed this. I told

you I would find lodging for you."

Beth hid a smile at his ridiculously formal tone.

Tildy straightened and lifted her chin, staring Eggy in the eyes. "Yes, but I've decided I'll be better off here. While Beth was in the bank, I slipped into the Woodbury Hotel and secured a room. You may bring my pay to me there, Lieutenant. Thank you for everything. I believe I am going to enjoy Salt Lake City very much."

"But Hilary." Beth climbed down from the wagon. "I'll miss you so much. I'm sure Father would allow you to share my room."

"Uh, Miss Webster." McCall looked doubtful. "I'm not sure that's a good idea."

"No," Tildy put in. "It's not. I'll miss you as well, Beth. More than I ever would have expected when this journey began. I've come to admire you a great deal. You have courage and spunk, not like most of the mousy little misses you see running around these days with nothing on their minds but tea cozies and dress patterns."

Beth laughed. "You mean I'm impertinent, impetuous, and impulsive."

"That too." She joined in Beth's laughter, then sobered. "But don't ever change."

The two hugged.

Beth came away with damp eyes, surprised and pleased at the moist sheen she'd seen in Tildy's. They had become friends in the months they'd spent traveling together.

"Promise me, you'll come to see me now and then," Tildy said. "I'll need to find work, you know, and you won't be able to visit me there, but we'll find a way."

Beth knew what she meant. Tildy would seek a job at a whorehouse and live there. "Yes. Write me, care of Colonel Webster at Camp Floyd, and let me know how and where to find you."

"I will. Goodbye, Elizabeth Anne Webster. Have a wonderful life."

"Goodbye, Mrs. Hightower. Thank you for taking such good care of me."

Tildy glared at the lieutenant. "I just hope *you* take good care of her. I don't want to see anything untoward happen to her."

He scowled back and looked ready to snarl a reply but said nothing.

Chuckling, Tildy picked up her bags and briskly crossed the street to the hotel. Unlike the first time McCall had helped her into the wagon, Beth needed his guidance this time. Tears blinded her, and it was all she could do not to sob openly.

CHAPTER TWELVE

Colonel Jonathan Webster stood behind his desk—at ease, hands clasped behind his back, feet spread, shoulders squared, head high. The image of the perfect military man.

Except for the slight tic in his right eye.

Beth knew that tic and what it meant. He was not happy to see her. But she felt the same about him. He looked smaller than she recalled but every bit as cold and formal as he had been during his short visits during her childhood. She felt no fear of him, which seemed odd since she'd dreaded this meeting so much for so long. He was only a man like most others, whether as kind or not, remained to be seen.

His gaze scanned over her. "Your birthmark isn't as big as I remembered it."

She allowed herself a small smile. She wasn't as he expected, either. Perhaps he might accept her after all. "Plainly, it didn't grow at the same rate I did."

"Yes, well." He harrumphed and looked at his boots for a moment. "You must understand, Elizabeth. The only reason you're here is that I had nowhere else to send you. Your mother's people are in England, and mine are dead. An army post is no place for a young lady your age. I expect you to occupy yourself and contribute to the household."

"I'll do my best not to be in the way, Father."

"I also expect you to behave properly. No fraternizing with troopers, you understand?"

That came as good news. She could avoid Lieutenant McCall. "Yes, Father."

"There are few wives here and only one with children. I will inform Captain Pickens you are available to watch his two daughters when needed. At least you can help in that way."

"Certainly. I adore children."

He cleared his throat, reminding Beth he expected only silence from her.

"You may walk the parade grounds when they are not in use by the troops or over by the creek. Watch out for snakes, however."

"Yes, Father. Thank you for the warning."

He cleared his voice. "I will expect you to accept all invitations from the officers' wives. Otherwise, you will keep to my quarters."

She kept silent until he cleared his throat again, though she wanted desperately to ask if there was anything she could do there. It seemed everything was forbidden. "Yes, sir."

"You are dismissed. Corporal Sims will show you to my quarters. Be polite but distant, understand? With both me and Mrs. Sparks, my housekeeper. She's the widow of one of my officers and resides in the rear bedroom next to the kitchen."

She shifted on her feet, becoming antsy. She hoped the woman would welcome her and be friendly. "I will ensure Mrs. Sparks knows I am willing to help her all I can. May we speak of another matter, Father?"

A furrow formed in his brow, and his voice held annoyance. "What is it?"

"I thought you'd want to know Lieutenant McCall has expressed a desire to marry me and will mention it to you soon. At first, I thought taking him as my husband might be a good idea. It would get me out from under your feet and give me something to do. But the more I think about it, the more I realize I am too young to wed. Don't you agree?"

He frowned. "Young women do wed at sixteen, Elizabeth."

"Perhaps they are more prepared for the responsibility than I am. At Runyon's Finishing School for Refined Young Ladies, we learned embroidery, sewing, painting, dancing, serving tea, Latin, French, literature appreciation, and letter writing." She tried to keep her disgust out of her voice. "We were not taught how to be wives."

His eyes widened with surprise. "They did not teach you cooking or how to deal with servants?"

"No, Father. They expected us to marry wealthy men and have cooks and housekeepers." She smiled. "I did learn how to cook beans on the journey here, and I can bake biscuits in a pan over a fire. Oh, and coffee. I make good coffee."

He rolled his eyes. "Those skills will not be needed here. Whether or not you marry the lieutenant or any other man will be your decision, Elizabeth. I will not interfere in such matters so long as you are sensible in your choice of a husband."

"Thank you, Father." She turned to the door to hide her great relief and waited for him to open it.

Colonel Webster preceded her into the anteroom and instructed the corporal to wait. Lieutenant McCall rose from a chair and sent her a confident smile. Beth returned the smile without confidence and left with the corporal.

"This way, miss." Corporal Sims led the way outside and along the row of buildings made of reddish mud bricks to the residential area. Each structure held two identical, adjoined houses. Beth thought them quite ugly. Living in them would be like living in dirt. How did the women keep them clean?

"Corporal, what are those scrubby bushes at the sides of the buildings?"

"Sagebrush." He waved a dismissive hand at the plants. "Ain't much else grows around here, except rabbitbrush, like that clump over there, and prickly pear cactus. There are grasses and weeds, of course. Lots of prickly stuff here. Over at the creek on the south side of the camp, you'll see some cottonwoods and willows."

She shaded her eyes from the lowering sun and surveyed the surrounding hills. "What about the trees on those hills? I don't think I've ever seen any like them before."

"Locals call 'em cedars, but I can tell you that ain't what they are. We had real cedars back home, and they were nothing like these."

He turned onto a path to a set of houses. She would have to be careful to ensure she entered the right one; they looked so much alike.

"As we were arriving. I saw a town just east of here. Will you tell me about it?"

He nodded. "That's Fairfield. There's a smaller one next to it we call Frogtown. There's two distinct parts to it, miss— the Mormon section and the part occupied by camp followers. Young women like you don't belong in either one."

"Why not?"

"Mormons don't like us *Gentiles,* as they call us. Nothing

in the other part but saloons, gambling halls, and houses that aren't exactly homes as you know them. You don't want to visit there."

"You mean whorehouses?"

He blinked and coughed. Beth suspected he was trying not to laugh.

A platoon of troops marched toward them in formation on the parade ground. Others lounged outside the enlisted men's barracks. Three men brushed down horses at the stable while a blacksmith fitted a new shoe to a spotted pony.

When they reached the house, Corporal Sims climbed the steps to the small porch, opened the door, and waited. Giving him a smile and a nod, Beth went inside.

The door shut behind her, and footsteps sounded outside as he returned to camp headquarters.

A woman came from the back, dressed in a simple shirtwaist, skirt, and apron. She was younger than Beth anticipated but still older than her.

"Miss Webster, I am Mrs. Sparks, the Colonel's housekeeper. Welcome. I will show you to your room."

Beth followed the housekeeper upstairs to a plain but adequately furnished room with a pale blue counterpane on a brass bed, an oak bureau, a washstand, and a wardrobe. A single window looked out over the sagebrush plain behind the camp. She found it far more likable than the room at her school she shared with Francine and six other girls, although she missed the forest surrounding Runyon's.

"Will this be satisfactory?" Mrs. Sparks asked.

Beth turned to face the woman. "Oh, yes, thank you. And please know I will help with the cleaning and whatever else is needed."

Looking as if she'd been eating lemons, the woman nodded. "I imagine you'll want a bath?"

The question sounded more like an accusation than a question. Beth started to say no and changed her mind. She refused to be cowed by a servant. Besides, she hadn't had a bath for months, which sounded pleasant.

"Yes, please. But first, I'd like to rest from my travels. I'm exhausted."

"Very well. Supper will be in an hour." With a nod, Mrs. Sparks departed.

Beth removed her hat and gloves and laid them on the bureau. She stripped down to her chemise and drawers, crawled between the sheets, and closed her eyes. Sleep refused to come; too many new images, questions, and unsettling emotions rattled around in her head and heart. Her father did not want her here. The message came through loud and clear via his posture, tone, and words. She found it impossible not to let his rejection hurt. Mrs. Sparks didn't want her here, either. Would Beth find anyone here willing to befriend her? What would she do with her time? Crochet doilies?

Hugging herself beneath the covers, she thought of Tildy, Francine, and Sparrow Hawk. Her throat tightened. How she missed them. Had Hawk's mother recovered? Would he come for her as he'd promised? She pictured his dark, handsome face, the high, chiseled cheekbones and jaw, the ebony eyes that saw more than they should, and the long, sleek hair she yearned to run her fingers through. She would beg him to take her away if he appeared at this moment. But he didn't come. Only tears.

A bell awakened Beth. Rolling onto her back, she stared

at the ceiling. The shadows had deepened, so the bell must mean supper. Instead of rising, she continued to lay there, a heaviness in her heart like an anvil on her chest. She glanced at the window where twilight settled over the land.

The bell rang again. With a tired sigh, Beth forced herself from the bed, washed, and dressed. Downstairs, she found the Colonel sitting at the head of the table, his napkin in his lap, his long fingers tapping out a rhythm on the tabletop. He rose when she entered.

"From now on, Elizabeth, I expect you to come to the table promptly before Mrs. Sparks must ring for you. Understand?"

"Yes, Father. I apologize." She seated herself to his left, where a plate and flatware marked her place. "I was fatigued from traveling."

Mrs. Sparks entered with a tureen of soup, and the meal began.

A silent meal that ended the way it started.

Colonel Webster retired to his study with nothing but a nod to acknowledge his daughter's presence. He had not seen her for eight years and, no doubt would be happy to go on the rest of his life without seeing her again.

When Beth began clearing the table, Mrs. Sparks cast her a heated look and took the plates from her. Feeling as though she weighed two hundred pounds, Beth continued to clear the table and offered to help with the washing up.

Shooed out of the kitchen, she wandered into the parlor. The furnishings were sparse but serviceable. A settee, two upholstered chairs, and a pair of small tables sat in front of the fireplace. An empty bookshelf occupied the space next to the hearth. Deep shadows filled the room. Seeing an oil lamp on a side table, Beth thought about lighting it. The need for freedom and fresh air drove her outside. Curled up in a wicker chair on the veranda, she watched the camp close for the night. The smell of cabbage and fresh bread wafted in the air. The troopers were at supper, she supposed. A gray cat jumped up beside her and mewed.

"Hello, kitty." She petted its furry head, watched its eyes close in pleasure, and listened to it purr. "Are you lonely, too?"

When full darkness descended, Beth returned to her room on the second floor. A lamp had been lit, and a small fire crackled on the grate in the fireplace. With slow, measured movements, she undressed and crawled into bed.

A bugle woke her the following day. She yawned, pushed herself up, and sat on the edge of the mattress. With nothing to look forward to all day, the temptation to go back to sleep loomed large in her mind. She forced herself to wash, dress, and join her father for a quiet breakfast of eggs and toast.

She spent the rest of the morning exploring the camp— what few areas weren't forbidden to her. The commissary proved a pleasant distraction. She studied a Godey's Ladies magazine, something she and Francine enjoyed doing at Runyon's. It perplexed them why Miss Runyon subscribed to such a publication. Her clothes were all dark, plain, and the same.

Beth perused the limited selection of fabrics and trimmings the commissary offered and decided that an army post left a good deal to be desired regarding women's interests. Her father had an account there, but she saw nothing she wanted. Leaving, she wandered down the street, surprised by the number of homes she saw up ahead. She walked over, wondering if this was Fairfield—or Frogtown. A pharmacy stood at the near end of the street. A young woman her age emerged from the building. Hoping perhaps to find a friend, she greeted her. "Hello."

"Excuse me," was the girl's only response as she started to walk away.

"Please," Beth pleaded. "Can you talk to me for a moment? I was hoping you could tell me if this—" she gestured to the stores and houses. "—is part of the army camp or if it's a town?"

Turning halfway back to Beth, the girl said, "It's Fairfield and certainly not part of the military camp. Good, honest people live here."

Beth tried a smile. "I'm glad to hear that. Have you lived here long?"

"Long enough." With that, the girl hurried away. "Try Floyd Street. I imagine the people there would welcome you."

Staring after her, Beth wondered why the girl had acted with such hostility. Would she find a single person in Cedar Valley who would befriend her?

The sound of women's voices, some low, some high-pitched, filled the parlor of the captain's home. Beth surveyed her companions from beneath her lashes as she sipped tea from a Royal Doulton china cup. The cherrywood table had been set with only the finest in tableware, the silver gleaming with fresh polish and the crystal spotless. Having just made the trip across the country from the East, she marveled that such fine furnishings had reached Camp Floyd safely.

"Elizabeth, how long do you plan to stay with your father?"

Beth looked up and scrambled for a name to put to the face of the slender woman who'd spoken. Hunt. Yes, Lieutenant Hunt's wife, Ida. Or was it Ivy?

"I truly don't know. Until I marry, perhaps. I have nowhere else to go."

"Goodness," Mary Heart, a sergeant's wife, said. "Finding a husband here shouldn't take long."

"That is what my father said." The thought made her nauseous.

"I heard about your mother, Elizabeth," a gray-haired matron put in. "I'm so sorry, dear. I hope you were able to spend some time with her before you lost her."

The sweet tea curdled in Beth's stomach. The woman wanted the gritty details. Very well, she'd give them what they asked. "I'm afraid not. You see, my mother died all alone. She had smallpox, and no one would go near her. She had lain for days in a soiled bed, unwashed—"

"Please, Miss Webster, such gruesome details." Mrs. Dawes, who hosted the afternoon tea, rose and moved around the table, refilling cups with lukewarm tea. "It was wrong of us to pry into such a painful event. Forgive us." She cast a baleful glance at the gray-haired matron who opened the subject.

"Yes," agreed Lola Smith, a corporal's wife. "Let's change the subject. Have you heard there's to be a harvest ball in Fairfield in a few weeks?"

"No. Who is hosting the event?" Ana Hunt's eyes shone with excitement. "Have we been invited?"

Mrs. Dawes laughed. "By the Mormons? You're joking, are you not? Gentiles are never favored with invites from them."

Adelia Sparks, the Colonel's housekeeper, set her cup and saucer on the table and dabbed at her lips with a napkin. "That's not quite true, Katherine. Colonel Webster was invited."

"That makes sense," Ana said. "They might not like us, but they do know protocol, and it would be an insult not to invite the highest fort officer."

"Well, then, Adelia, you must find out from him what it was like and tell us all about it the next time we meet."

Beth rose. She'd had all she could take of this boring gossip. The thought of having to endure many more of these occasions bore down on her like an avalanche. "Excuse me, please. I must make a trip to the back lawn."

"Go through the kitchen, Elizabeth. Much shorter that way."

"Thank you." In the kitchen, she nabbed a sweet roll from a tray the cook had just taken from the oven. She bit into it as she crossed the boot room and opened the rear door. A kitten slipped inside and wrapped itself around Beth's feet, mewing.

"Oh, aren't you adorable?" She kneeled and petted the cat's soft fur. When it climbed onto her knee and showed interest in the bread she held, she broke off a piece and dropped it to the floor. The kitten leaped down and snatched up the treat.

"I feel so badly for that poor child," someone in the parlor said. The softly spoken words reached Beth in a whisper she didn't want to hear, and hadn't been meant to hear.

"I know. Bad enough she has to live with that stuffed-up curmudgeon of a father, but she's bound to be terribly lonely, as well, with none of us being close to her age."

"Yes. How sad."

"I find it difficult to imagine Colonel Webster being married, let alone having a daughter. I vow he probably sets a schedule for when Elizabeth can visit the necessary."

Titters of laughter followed.

Not wanting to hear more, Beth picked up the kitten and was about to leave when she heard, "By the by, have any of you heard what happened to Lieutenant McCall?"

"No, what?"

"Well, I don't know. That's why I asked. It seems he's disappeared."

"We should ask Elizabeth when she returns. Her father might have mentioned it."

The Colonel hadn't mentioned it. Beth had heard nothing about the lieutenant being missing and had no interest in discussing it with those old biddies. What had happened to him? Had Bearstooth found him? She hoped whatever happened had nothing to do with her. She felt guilty for leading him on and not being more honest. Yet, he hadn't been honest with her. He had proposed marriage while planning to put her away in an asylum or somewhere afterward while he spent her fortune. No, she neither wished him harm nor regretted turning him down.

Going out, she eased the door shut behind her without a sound. A lump formed in her throat as she walked to the small, white-painted structure in a corner of the back garden. That the women pitied her hurt more than a dagger thrust to her heart.

Instead of going back inside after using the necessary, she went home, closed herself in her room, and told her best friend all her troubles in a letter. With every word she wrote, she wished Francine were here and not heaven-only-knew-how-many miles away in her new home with Caleb.

At supper that night, she asked her father if Lieutenant McCall had spoken to him about wanting to wed her.

"Yes, Elizabeth, he did." The Colonel picked up his wine glass and drank from it. After putting it back down, he said, "I told him you were too young. He was not happy but did not argue. He's gone missing, incidentally. Do you know anything about that?"

"No, Father. I heard someone mention it today at the luncheon, but no one knew what happened." She had hoped he would tell her she'd heard wrong. If something had happened to McCall, she'd have to consider that it might partly be her fault. Although he'd been wrong to gamble, getting himself in trouble for it did not lie on her shoulders. However, that didn't ease her sense of guilt.

Her father gave her a pointed look. "I believe his vanishing has something to do with you. Not with anything you did except to refuse him, but it's too much of a coincidence to have happened so soon after asking for your hand and being turned down. He appeared quite upset about it. I hope I don't have to hunt him down and court-martial him."

"I hope not, too, Father. I would feel terrible if he deserted or something happened to him because of me." She laid down her utensils and clasped her hands under the table, worried that what she was about to tell him would make him angry. "I should have told you this sooner, but I learned from Hilary Hightower, my chaperone on the trip, that Lieutenant McCall wished to marry me because of the money Mother left me. It seems he lost not only the funds you gave him for my trip here but more to a man who threatened to kill him if he didn't pay up."

Colonel Webster looked astounded. "The devil, you say! Is this true?"

"Yes, Father."

"How did this chaperone come to know such a thing?"

"Oh, well, it seems the lieutenant hired her from a—" heat rose to her cheeks. To say such a word in front of him filled her with trepidation, unsure how he would react. "—a house of ill repute, Father, to entertain him on the trip."

Webster soared to his feet. "I will have that man court-martialed. Of all the audacity!" He stalked from the room, yelling for Corporal Sims.

The housekeeper collected his plate and utensils and carried them into the kitchen. Alone, Beth stared at her uneaten squash, ham, and potatoes, worrying whether Lieutenant McCall had met an untimely end because of her.

CHAPTER THIRTEEN

The woods along the stream drew Beth, though they amounted to little more than willow bushes and a half dozen cottonwood trees. She walked as close to the gurgling water as the weeds and shrubbery allowed. The sagebrush grew as high as Beth's waist. Lizards and ground squirrels darted here and there over the sandy soil, leaving tiny tracks behind. Sticker weeds grew everywhere, snagging at her skirts, even though she tried to hold them out of the way. She saw a few flowers, all tiny and colorless.

Her walk became a stroll, not because she found it too pleasant to waste on speed, but because she learned caution. One accidental step too close to a prickly-pear cactus cost her several painful minutes picking cactus spines from her kid-leather slippers. Next time she came this way, she would wear her worn but sturdy travel shoes made of good leather and thick soles.

Thoughts darted through her mind, leaping from one to another with the speed and agility of the numerous grasshoppers in the area.

Would Hawk ever come for her? With every day that passed, she felt more confident of her love for him but less assured of his for her. She would leave and search if she had any idea how to find him. She feared his absence had to do with his mother and meant she was not doing well or had died. It made her sad, knowing how much Hawk loved his mother. Caleb might know how to find Hawk. Plans formed in her head for paying a visit to Caleb and Francine. Surely once she was there, Caleb would help her. And seeing Francine again would be so wonderful. Beth only had to devise an excuse for making the trip her father would accept.

Where was Tildy, and what was she doing? Did she know anything about Eggy? Beth hadn't heard from her since that afternoon when they said goodbye. It hurt that Tildy hadn't cared enough to write her.

A rabbit darted out from under a rabbit brush and vanished into the willows. Beth chuckled, thinking how appropriate for it to hide in that particular bush. An errant breeze burst the seed heads and sent them flying. Feathery seeds scattered everywhere, some catching on Beth's woolen skirts. She missed the lush green of the forest, the streams, and ponds, finding this arid land in the low valleys depressing at times. She tried to concentrate on the animals she saw—deer mostly, rabbits, squirrels, and mice. A badger threatened to attack her once until she backed away and took a different route. She loved spotting foxes and coyotes, although they frightened her a little. The coyotes' forlorn howls at night sometimes seemed to match the loneliness that plagued her daily.

If only she had someone to talk with, to share her thoughts and worries, a friend like Francine or Tildy. No one here at the camp seemed willing to have anything to do with her, and it hurt like a knife thrust into her heart. Only the men paid her attention. The troopers she'd met on her journey had made her feel better about her birthmark and appearance. Even so, she couldn't take their declarations of admiration seriously.

Silence ruled her days for the most part. In the distance, as she walked, she heard isolated shouts from dragoons, a hammer banging, and the neighing of a horse. Soft sounds, far away. Closer, she listened to a new sound she thought came from the trees up ahead. This, too, was faint and challenging to make out.

Hesitant to trespass on the woman's grief, she stayed where she stood among the weeds and bushes. The trunks of the trees a few feet away blocked her view. They were huge, old trees with diameters more than her outstretched arms could span. Overhead, the leaves rustled. Some, already brown, broke free and fluttered to the ground. Others clung to the yellow shades of autumn. On the high mountains across the valley, she could see swathes of orange and red as fall settled in for the season. She wished she could walk up there, where it was bound to be prettier, but it was too far away.

The sobbing increased. When Beth could stand listening no longer, she coughed to warn of her presence and stepped around the trees.

"Oh." A young woman, maybe two years older than Beth, with dark brown hair and blue eyes, rose from a stump, tears raining down her cheeks. "I-I thought I was alone."

Beth's heart wrenched at the sight of her, for half of the girl's face bore horrible bruises. Someone had beaten her.

"Forgive me for intruding," Beth said. "I was out for a walk and did not realize you were there until too late. You've been crying. Is there anything I can do to help you?"

The woman glanced around as if making sure they were alone. Looking back at Beth, she mopped her face with an embroidered handkerchief. "I guess there's no denying my bruises, but please don't mention them to anyone. My husband would be furious and think I had been complaining."

"No, I won't speak of it," Beth assured her. "Is he who did this to you?"

"Yes. Sorry, I'm Annaliese. I live in that house yonder." She pointed to a simple one-room structure made of adobe bricks Beth estimated to be a few hundred yards away.

"Are you Mormon?"

"Yes," Annaliese said, peering at her strangely. "Aren't you?"

"No. My father is commander of the Fifth Infantry at Camp Floyd."

"Oh." Annaliese stood. "I should not be speaking to you."

Disappointment filled Beth. "Why not?"

The woman thought a moment and sat again. "To tell the truth, I'm not sure. I shouldn't talk about it, but I don't understand much about my religion. That's why Abram beat me. He says I ask too many questions. I should accept what the elders tell me. He says I must be simple-minded for not understanding."

"You don't strike me as stupid at all." Moving to a log, Beth sat. "Is Abram your husband?

"Yes, Abram Christianson. Thank you for telling me I'm not stupid. I was good in school." Annaliese scrubbed at her face as if to remove all signs of her tears.

"Well, that proves you're not simple-minded."

"Maybe." Annaliese motioned to Beth's skirt of lavender-sprigged broadcloth. "I love your dress. Did you make it?"

"No. I purchased it back east before I came here." She had

foregone the hoop she usually wore underneath because of the bushes. Even so, the skirt was voluminous and dragged on the ground.

"Oh." Annaliese sounded disappointed. "My mother taught us girls to sew, but I do so poorly."

"So do I, I'm afraid." Beth plucked at a piece of grass and smoothed the thin green blade between her fingers. "I find sewing boring. I'd rather be outside in the fresh air working in the gardens or almost anything else."

Annaliese smiled for the first time. "Me too. I like growing flowers. Abram says they're a waste of time and water. He insists I grow vegetables instead. Of course, having vegetables is important, and I don't mind growing them. I wish I could grow some flowers as well. Sometimes, I long for something pretty to look at instead of so much brown."

"But Abram won't let you?"

"No, and I don't dare go against him. Mormon women are taught to obey their husbands implicitly. Weren't you raised that way?"

Beth made a soft snorting sound. "Even if they tried to teach me such a thing, I would ignore them. What is so special about men that we should obey them like dogs?"

With widened eyes, Annaliese stared. "Would your father not strike you for speaking such a rebellious thought?"

"I don't know. I have spent most of my life in a school in the east while my father was in the army fighting Indians."

"You and your mother do not live with him?"

"Not since I was a toddler. Mother did not like army life and had her own money, so she took me and moved back to Boston. For the past eight years, I have been in a finishing school in New York. Mother died recently, and I had to come here and live with my father."

Annaliese's eyes widened. "You traveled clear across the country?"

"Yes, with an army supply train. I had a friend with me and a chaperone." The thought of Tildy as a proper chaperone made Beth smile.

"I envy you. What an exciting life you've led. I've never been anywhere except Fairfield."

"I went there, but no one would talk to me unless I bought something."

"No. We're discouraged from being friendly to Gentiles." Annaliese glanced around again. "But I'll be your friend. Your secret friend if you'll be mine."

"I would like that very much." Beth smiled. "I find it lonely here. There are no women near my age, only the older army wives, and I have nothing in common with them. They pity me because of my birthmark and my father not wanting me here."

"I'm sorry. Why doesn't he want you here?"

Beth shrugged. "He finds me a bother, I guess, and dislikes looking at me because of my face."

"I don't think your birthmark is ugly. It barely shows, really," Annaliese said. "I'm sure it wouldn't bother the soldiers. They seem very lonely, too."

"They try to talk with me, but I'm not interested." She wished she could speak of Hawk but feared Annaliese would be shocked at her loving an Indian. No one seemed to understand.

"I'd better go before Abram comes looking." Annaliese

stood. "But I can meet you here almost any day. I come here a lot to get away from the house."

"I will look for you." Beth rose and took the girl's hand. "Thank you for being companionable to me. I've so longed for a friend."

Annaliese smiled. "So have I. There are plenty of women in Fairfield my age, but I cannot be honest with them about my feelings the way I can with you. Thank you for listening to me."

"I can easily sympathize. We are both in situations not of our choosing. I'm thrilled to have met you."

In the distance, a man screamed Annaliese's name. Her face went white, and she took off at a run.

The next day, Beth found her new friend waiting by the trees. "Hello."

"Oh, Beth, I'm so glad to see you," Annaliese jumped up and hugged her.

Surprised but pleased, Beth hugged her back. They separated and sat, Beth on a stump and Annaliese on a log.

"Have you other friends in Fairfield?" Beth asked.

"No." Annaliese poked at a small hole in her dress. "I'd receive a huge lecture for associating with you, but I don't care."

At last, a friend. Beth grinned. "Me either."

Annaliese leaned closer. "May I share a secret you can never reveal to anyone?"

"Of course." Beth bent toward her.

"I don't love my husband." The girl jerked back and glanced around. "Abram would kill me if he knew."

"I won't tell. But why then did you marry him?"

Annaliese sighed. "Because my father ordered me to. That's part of what being a dutiful daughter means."

"A lieutenant I cannot stand asked me to marry him on my way here," Beth said. "I pretended like I might, then told my father I wasn't ready to marry yet. He promised not to interfere in that part of my life as long as I was sensible about who I chose for a husband."

"You are so lucky. If I had my choice, I know who I would marry," Annaliese said, a dreamy look coming over her.

"Who? Is he Mormon?"

A mischievous grin spread across the woman's pretty face. "No. He's a soldier at Camp Floyd."

"He is? What is his name? Maybe I've met him."

"If I tell you, will you take him a message from me?"

"If you like."

"Thomas Coltrane. He's a private in the Tenth Infantry and works at the blacksmith shop." Annaliese squirmed on her log. "Oh, Beth, he's so kind, and I'm so in love with him."

Beth frowned. The girl might not be stupid, but neither was she wise. Instinct told Beth it would be equally foolish for her to become involved in such a delicate situation. She considered saying as much to Annaliese, but that would mean losing the only friend Beth had here. "Does Thomas love you as well?"

"He says he does, and I believe him."

"What about Abram?"

"Thomas wants me to run away with him to California and get married. No one there would know about Abram, so it would be safe. We could start a new life together. And I want that new life, Beth. I want it desperately."

Pity filled Beth's heart. She could not blame the girl for wanting to leave a man who beat her, especially when a nice man like Thomas Coltrane wanted her. Beth would make a point of checking on him when she returned to the fort. "Thomas would be a deserter then, Annaliese. He could be shot if they catch him."

The girl's face blanched. "I know. We have to be very careful." A look of terror filled Annaliese's eyes. "You won't turn him in, will you?"

"No." Beth reached over and patted the girl's hand. "In fact, I will do all I can to help you, though I would hate to see you leave. You're the first and only friend I've made here."

"I'm glad for that, and I'll hate losing you, but if I don't go, I'm afraid Abram will kill me one day. He's such a bitter man, Beth. He's older than me. Forty-three. His last wife ran away too. I'm his third wife. The first one died in childbirth. He's afraid I'm barren because we've been married for over a year now, and I haven't gotten with child. That's partly why he's angry all the time. He's talking about getting another wife." Guilt filled the young woman's eyes. "It is my fault. I learned of an herb that keeps a woman from becoming pregnant, and I've been using it."

Shocked, Beth froze, then glanced around to ensure they were alone. "Where on earth did you learn such a thing?"

"From a Ute woman who came to my door begging."

Beth thought of Tildy. To discuss that private act, married people or lovers shared that she knew nothing about embarrassed her. "I met a woman on my journey here who worked at a whorehouse once, and she told me that prostitutes soak cotton wads with vinegar and stuff them inside themselves before lying with a man, and it keeps them safe from pregnancy."

"I'll remember that," Annaliese said. "Except, I won't need such methods if Thomas and I succeed in escaping here."

"You and Thomas need a plan."

"I know. That's why I need you to take him a message to meet me here tonight at eight o'clock. Abram will be at the church ward house with the elders then. You'll know Thomas when you see him. He's the most handsome soldier there. At least, that I've seen." Annaliese blushed. "He has brown, wavy hair and light brown eyes that remind me of honey. And he whistles all the time."

"All right. I'll tell him. If somehow I can't, if he's out on patrol or something, I'll come and meet you instead."

Again, Annaliese looked around. "I had better get home now. I left bread rising, and it will fall if I don't return in time."

Beth stood. "Go then, and I will seek out Thomas."

The young woman took Beth's hands in hers. "Thank you so much. You have no idea how grateful I am to have found you."

"I'm glad, as well. Go now."

Annaliese scurried off through the shrubs and willows. When Beth could no longer see her, she turned back home. She would have to be careful going to see Thomas. Disaster could result if anyone figured out her interest in the private. Best to find him on her own.

The stables stood on the south side of the grounds, away from the living quarters and close to the horses. Beth approached slowly, her hands clasped behind her back to give the impression she was merely wandering in no special direction. Two men worked a horse on a long tether in a corral. The sound of hammering came from a small structure at the other end of the stables, and someone was whistling. *Thomas!*

Horses whinnied from the stalls she passed, despite her efforts to shush them. At last, she reached the blacksmith shop. Peering around the corner of the wide doorway, she saw a man about twenty years old pounding a horseshoe on an anvil. Brown, wavy hair hung over his brow as he worked. She saw no one else.

She stepped inside. "Excuse me."

The hammering stopped, and the young man looked up. His eyes were, indeed, the color of honey, like a darker shade of Beth's hair. "Can I help you?" he asked.

"Are you Thomas Coltrane?"

"Yes. Who are you?" He put down the hammer and stepped toward her.

"My name is Beth Webster. I'm Colonel Webster's daughter."

He smiled. "I heard we had a pretty young woman at camp now, but no one said how pretty."

"Nonsense. You've no need to flatter me. I've come with a message from Annaliese."

Fear replaced his smile. "Has something happened?" He began to tear off his apron.

She held up a hand to halt him. "No, she's fine, as much as she can be under the circumstances."

"What is the message then, and how did you become involved?" He gazed at her with eyes dark with suspicion.

"Don't worry. I may be the Colonel's daughter, but I have my own way of thinking, and I will never reveal to anyone what I know about you and Annaliese."

Thomas relaxed. "You're sure she's all right? That bas— excuse me—man she's married to needs to be taught some manners."

"I agree. Abram is a bastard. He's beaten her, and her face is all bruised. But that's not the message." For caution's sake, she stepped to the doorway and peered out to be sure they remained alone. "She wants you to meet her at the trees by the stream at eight o'clock tonight. Abram will be with the elders at the ward house."

"I'll be there. Is that all?"

"Yes." Beth moved closer. "Thomas, you do understand that they'll shoot you on sight if you desert."

"I know. I enjoy being in the army. But I love Annaliese, and if I don't get her away from that heavy-fisted husband, I'm afraid he'll kill her."

"You will be laying down your life for her, you know."

"And gladly, if it means spending the rest of my years with her."

Beth smiled. "Good. I wish you all the luck in the world then and will help in any way I can."

"Thanks." He laughed. "You're not only prettier than I expected, but you're also nice. Never would have expected the Colonel to have a daughter like you."

Beth did not walk home. She floated, feeling a rare satisfaction in doing something to help others. She liked Annaliese and Thomas; they genuinely seemed to love each other. *Please, Lord, don't let their plans go wrong.*

Fetching her shawl the following morning, Beth let herself out the front door and went down the steps. She wandered toward the stream, breathing in the crisp air. The trees swayed in the wind, the trunks creaking. An officer barking orders on the parade ground drifted to her, along with the gurgle of the creek. Fall leaves littered the ground in shades of rust, orange and yellow. So many that she expected the trees to be bare, yet they appeared to have as many leaves as ever. Appearances did indeed deceive, she mused. Perhaps her looks did, also. Her birthmark did not seem to put the troopers off. Several had tried to approach and speak with her, and two had asked her to marry them. Certain they were not serious, she politely turned them down.

She found Annaliese sitting on the same stump as before. "Beth, hello."

"Good morning. I'm glad to see you."

"I was hoping you'd come."

Beth studied the girl. "Your bruises look better."

"Yes. I'm trying extra hard to please Abram, so he won't suspect I plan to leave him. Thank you for giving Thomas my message."

"You're welcome. Have you decided when you will leave?"

Annaliese's eyes lit up, and she bounced a little on the stump. "Tonight. Can you believe it? I'm so excited." She grabbed Beth's hands and leaned closer. "Can I tell you something private?"

"Something else?" Beth laughed, tickled that she had someone to share secrets with. "Why not?"

The girl glowed as she whispered, "I'm with child. Thomas's child. Isn't that wonderful?"

Beth frowned. "But what about the herb you use to avoid

pregnancy? How do you know it's Thomas's?"

"Because Abram hasn't touched me that way in months. He's usually too drunk and unable to... well, you know, and I didn't use the herb with Thomas."

"How far along are you?"

"Three months and two weeks, I figure."

Beth squeezed the young woman's hands. "How fortunate you're leaving soon. If you waited much longer, it would become obvious. I'm happy for you."

"Thank you."

"Annaliese!" The call came from Abram. They could see him through the trees, standing outside the house, looking for her.

Fright distorted Annaliese's bruised face. "I must go." She jumped up and started toward home but turned back and smiled. "Goodbye, Beth. I'll miss you."

"I'll miss you, as well." Sadness filled her. She'd finally made a friend, only to lose her. "Good luck. I hope you'll be very happy."

That night, Beth slept little. Having a new friend in Annaliese helped ease her loneliness and gave her something to do, but that had come to an end. And she still agonized over Sparrow Hawk's continued absence. Where was he? What about his mother? And why hadn't she heard from Tildy? Or Francine? Indeed, enough time had passed for a letter to reach her from Jackson Hole. Had something happened to Francine? To Hawk? Had she been abandoned by everyone she cared about?

She dozed fitfully, awakening in the wee hours. Unable to return to sleep, she rose and lit a candle, deciding to go downstairs to look for a book she'd left in the parlor. She opened her door and heard a noise from her father's room down the hall. He must be getting up, perhaps needing the necessary. Not wanting to speak with him, she blew out the candle and waited with the door cracked so she would know when he was gone.

Instead of her father emerging, Mrs. Sparks crept from his room, easing the door shut behind her. The lamp she held made her identity plain. Dressed as she was in rumpled nightclothes and her hair a mess, Beth had no doubt what she had been doing. Mrs. Sparks was not only the Colonel's housekeeper but also his mistress. Did anyone else at Camp Floyd know? Did everyone know?

Wider awake now than ever but not wanting to go downstairs and let Mrs. Sparks know she'd been caught out, Beth curled up in the chair by the window. There, she watched the clouds drift across a half-moon and mulled over her unsettling discovery. She found it less disturbing than she would have before her journey west. Looking back, she could hardly believe she was the same naive girl who foolishly ran away from Runyon's Finishing School for Refined Young Ladies all those months ago. Her journey across the country had taught her much about life. She had matured.

"Oh, Hawk," she whispered into the night. "Why haven't you come for me? I miss you so."

Staying in her father's home now that she knew his secret would be more unpleasant than ever. She could not imagine being around him and Mrs. Sparks. What would she say? She doubted she could look either in the eye.

Eventually, she dozed off, waking late so that she had to rush to be in time for breakfast. With every step, she took down the stairs toward the dining room, her trepidation over facing her father grew. To her surprise, breakfast took place as it always did. Her father already sat at his place. Mrs. Sparks placed the food on the table and took her seat. The Colonel read the paper, and everyone ate in silence. Afterward, Beth helped clear the table and offered to wash the dishes. The housekeeper refused her offer as usual.

As Beth expected, Annaliese was not at the stream. Beth sat and waited a while, just in case, then headed home, feeling anxious and lonely. Annaliese's absence must mean she had run away with Thomas, but what if they were caught? It would be horrible if he were killed, especially if it happened in front of Annaliese, and what would happen to Annaliese then? Would her husband divorce her? Would she be kicked out of Mormon society? Beth knew nothing of the Mormon church except that they disliked non-members and practiced polygamy.

The questions circled round and round in her head. Hawk, his mother, Tildy, Francine, Annaliese, McCall; where were they, and were they all right?

When she returned home, her mind heavy with worry, she found Corporal Sims sitting on the headquarters steps. He stood as soon as he saw her and walked out to the pathway. "Good afternoon, Miss Webster. I was waiting for you."

She couldn't imagine why he would do such a thing. "Can I help you in some way, Corporal?"

He hemmed and hawed a bit, shuffling his feet, before finally getting his words out: "I'm hoping you'll allow me to court you, Miss Webster. I've already spoken with your father, and he's given his permission. By the way, my given name is Gage. May I call you Elizabeth?"

"No, call me Beth, Gage."

He smiled and nodded.

Beth looked at the young man, probably for the first time. He had brown hair and the usual mustache popular among the men. Gage's was at least well-trimmed and tidy. Green eyes gazed back, showing hope, trepidation, and determination. Was he earnest about courting her? Privates earned only about forty dollars a month which would hardly support a family.

On the other hand, the corporal could supply her with a decent, if not fancy, home. He was an attractive enough man in his twenties, tall and slender. She liked his smile and the softness in his green eyes that hinted he would be kind and gentle.

"Gage, you have me at a disadvantage. I never expected this."

"I cannot imagine why not." He gave her that pleasant smile. "A pretty girl like you has probably already received a few proposals."

She laughed. "Not really. At least, none I took seriously."

"So, may I call on you this evening? We could walk or sit on the porch and talk."

"Let's try for a walk." Agreeing to see the Corporal made her feel disloyal to Sparrow Hawk. But she needed to think of her future and face the fact that Hawk might never come for her. "More private that way."

"I agree. Sounds nice." He gave her a little bow. "I look forward to seeing you then."

He sprang up the steps and went into the office. Beth continued home. At least, her father might be happy with her for allowing the corporal to visit her.

For supper that night, she chose her favorite dress, one she had bought in Salt Lake City. The black, waist-length jacket had pink buttons and pink lace at the throat and along the edges of the three-quarter sleeves that came fashionably short of covering the long, puffy sleeves of her pink dress. She drew up her hair and fastened it at the back of her head with curls dangling down her shoulders.

"You look lovely tonight, Elizabeth," her father greeted as she joined him at the dinner table.

"Thank you, Father. Corporal Sims will be visiting later." He passed her a bowl of mashed potatoes. She helped herself and offered the bowl to Mrs. Sparks.

"Good." He handed her a platter of roast beef. "He's a fine young man."

Beth didn't respond. Her father buried his face in a newspaper, leaving her frustrated. She'd tried to please him, yet he showed no approval or satisfaction. Was there nothing she could do to please him? After dinner, he went to his study. Standing, she reached for some dishes to remove.

"Don't bother," Mrs. Sparks said. "Go wait for your young man."

The housekeeper's rare smile froze Beth in place, uncertain what to make of it. She went out onto the veranda and sat on the porch swing. Corporal Gage Sims arrived ten minutes later. Both stumbled for topics to discuss as they walked. They talked more about the weather than anything. After half an hour, Beth excused herself, saying she was tired. Gage was a nice young man, but she had become bored. She slept that night, thinking that at least one man wanted her. Or did he also know she was an heiress, like Lieutenant McCall?

Poor McCall. Where was he? Had Bearstooth found him? If only she could talk with Tildy and learn what she might know.

The next day went much the same way, including a surprise afternoon visit from Gage Sims. She enjoyed his quiet sense of humor and thought they could become friends, though friendship would not satisfy him, and Beth doubted her ability to love him.

When she went inside for supper, her father was absent. Mrs. Sparks rushed in, placed a plate loaded with ham, fried potatoes and onions, and snap beans in front of her, and hurried back out. No place setting waited at her father's spot. Too curious to eat, Beth went into the kitchen.

"Mrs. Sparks, where is Father? Has something happened?"

The woman glanced over her shoulder while she removed biscuits from the oven. "The camp is in an uproar. One of the troopers and a girl from the Mormon town are missing. They found her husband hanging in his barn. Dead."

Beth spun to face the window, hiding her alarm. So, she'd been right. Thomas and Annaliese were gone. What had happened to Annaliese's husband? Had he been murdered? She could not imagine Thomas or Annaliese doing such a thing. Perhaps Abram hung himself because Annaliese left him.

Had her father gone out with his troops to search for the missing couple? Dread turned her stomach sour and caused her whole body to tremble. Dread and guilt. Needing to confirm her fear, she asked, "Do you know who the missing trooper is?"

"No, Elizabeth. Nor do I have time to chatter away the evening with you."

Beth returned to the dining room and sat, but her appetite had fled. Mrs. Sparks brought a small plate with a biscuit cut open, steam rising above it, and dabs of melting butter on each half. Guilt forced Beth to eat half, all she could choke down. She had too much on her mind to eat.

Had Thomas killed Annaliese's husband? What would happen to them now?

Dark fell, and Beth climbed the stairs to her room. She heard a door slam downstairs and wondered if her father had come home but didn't look. She feared facing him. Would he be able to see through her and recognize her guilt?

Dawn found Beth pacing, glancing continually out the window, and trying to gauge the activity in the camp. She felt confused as to what to call this place where she lived. Camp Floyd differed from every other fort she'd seen. It was not a camp such as she'd stayed in on her trip here. A wall enclosed the grounds, but only six feet tall, and a single guardhouse stood at ground level at the main gate.

It took until the wee hours for her to fall asleep, so she slept late. Her father had already left the house, and getting information from Adelia Sparks was like pulling prickly pear spines out of leather shoes.

A door closed, and heavy footsteps sounded in the foyer below. Her father had come home.

Beth flew down the stairs and found the Colonel in the dining room sipping a cup of coffee from the pot on the sideboard.

"Father?"

He glanced up but said nothing.

"Mrs. Sparks told me a trooper was missing. Did you find him?"

He put down his cup. "No. Blasted fool deserted and took a girl from town with him, the bastard." Pulling his chair out from under the table, he sat heavily. "But we'll find him, and when we do, there will be a trial."

"Oh, no! How awful." She slapped her hands over her mouth to keep from saying more.

His eyes narrowed, and he sat forward. "Why does it matter to you? Do you know the soldier or the missing girl?"

"No. Of course not, Father. I merely feel sorry for her. She must have been in love to run away with him like this. The soldier was foolish to take her, though."

"Damned right. Stupid girl will probably end up—"

He cut off his words.

But she could imagine what he'd been about to say. Annaliese would be banished from the church and town with nowhere to go.

"I'm sorry you have to deal with such a problem, Father. I won't disturb you further."

With that, she hurried back upstairs.

What had happened? Kneeling beside her bed, she prayed for the safety of Annaliese and Thomas and asked forgiveness for her part in the event. All her life, her mother and her teachers had warned her that being reckless and impulsive would get her in trouble someday. Instead, it appeared that she might have aided in putting Annaliese and Thomas in danger. Had she stayed out of it, would the couple still be here, safe, though unhappy?

Acknowledging her guilt, she determined to act more wisely in the future, reason out her decisions before acting, and be less hasty and impulsive.

CHAPTER FOURTEEN

The next day, Beth went for a walk to get away from the fort. She had so much on her mind and could think better out on open land. Before leaving the house, she'd written a letter to Tildy and another to Francine, begging them to write her. She felt lost without anyone to talk with and discuss her problems.

She told Tildy about the lieutenant being missing and how worried she was about his fate. Why hadn't she given him the money he needed? His ill intentions toward her didn't justify her being mean-spirited to him.

Of course, she'd asked Francine for any news she could give her regarding Hawk. She feared his mother had died, and he was too deep in mourning to think of her. Every night, she prayed for his mother's health and safety. It seemed Beth's life was falling apart. Everyone she loved had gone away and left her behind.

Stop it, you selfish girl.

She had to learn to accept her situation, stop yearning for Hawk, and thinking up ways to escape and search for him. Her happiness didn't depend on Hawk, Francine, or Tildy. It rested on her shoulders. She alone held the responsibility for her actions, thoughts, and deeds. She must grow up and find a way to become helpful to someone.

A hawk soared overhead; so beautiful. She drew in a deep breath of the clear air and started a list of things to be grateful for: adequate housing, good food, family, and her health. Many suffered worse fates than hers.

Was Lieutenant McCall one of them?

A ground squirrel popped up from his hole and watched her, standing on his hind feet, front paws held before him. She smiled as he sniffed the air, peered in every direction, barked out, and raced off into the sagebrush. The land here housed a veritable hoard of creatures and mice. She'd learned to keep her ears open for the many rattlers in the area. And keep her eyes out for dangerous holes in the ground, abandoned mines the owners hadn't bothered to board up.

Up ahead, she spied a fence and questioned its purpose. She'd heard of no farms or ranches out here, and the only building she spotted looked more like an outhouse than anything more significant.

She reached the fence and followed it until she came to an unlocked gate. Then she noticed the crosses stuck in the earth.

A graveyard. On the far side of the gate, she found a small sign that read Camp Floyd Cemetery.

So, the crosses marked the graves of soldiers.

Curious, she opened the gate and went inside, reading the names carved into the wood. Some gave birth and death dates. Many of the men interred here had been young. She wondered how they died. If they found and killed Thomas, she supposed this was where he'd end up.

She gazed out over the empty plain, devoid of trees or buildings except for overgrown sagebrush, a few dead cottonwoods, and the outhouse. Such a lonely place. The idea of being buried there horrified her. Deciding she'd seen enough, she turned to go.

A shout stopped her. Where had it come from? It sounded like an angry man.

Scanning her surroundings, she realized she wasn't alone after all. Someone stood by the privy. No, two men.

One cried out in pain as the other struck him.

Beth gasped. Her pulse leaped.

That poor man. She hurried toward the spot. "What are you doing there? Stop that."

The giant attacking the other fellow halted and looked at her. Then he turned and ran in the other direction. He was soon lost to view.

Beth kept going. At last, she reached the building, which was larger than she'd thought; a storeroom, she decided.

A man lay on the ground. She ran to him. "Are you badly hurt?

He moaned. So much blood covered his face it took her a moment to recognize him.

Lieutenant McCall!

"Eggerton. What happened here?" She knelt beside him and inspected his injuries. "Who was that man that ran away? Are you hurt badly?"

He looked up at her through blurry, bruised eyes. His lower lip had been split, and she saw holes where teeth should be in his gaping mouth. He'd been severely beaten. She could easily see that one arm had been broken, his clothing torn and covered with dirt. A knife protruded from his chest.

"Beth?" he mumbled.

"Yes, Eggerton. How can I help you? Should I remove this knife?"

"No!" he cried. "I'll bleed to death." The words were difficult to hear, his voice hoarse and slurred. "You need to find help."

She glanced around. The only person she could see was Bearstooth getting on a horse. He galloped off. "There's no one here but me." She ran her hands over his chest and midriff, feeling broken ribs. "I must get you to a doctor. Can you stand?"

"No. Leave me be. Something's broken inside me. I'm dying."

"Don't say that," she cried. Standing, she searched the landscape as far as she could see. A horse she hadn't seen before stood at the fence. "Help! Can anyone hear me? We need help!"

McCall tugged on her skirt. "Beth."

"Yes?" She crouched beside him, tore a strip from her petticoat, and tried to mop up some blood pouring out of him. The knife had cut deeply, and she feared it had struck his heart.

"I'm sorry," he said.

"Why?" she asked, though she knew.

"For trying to get you to marry…me so I could get your money. I was sneaky and underhanded. I'm ashamed. You're beautiful and kind. I tried to trick you."

"Don't worry about that now. Save your strength. You have to survive this."

"No. I deserve…what Bearstooth…gave me." The words came haltingly, his voice weak. "Sorry. So sorry. I couldn't pay Tildy. I was so…stupid."

"You made a mistake." She cleaned his face with her skirt. "Everyone does that."

"But you could have been harmed. I told… Bearstooth… couldn't give… money, that you didn't have any. I was… wrong. Forgive… me."

"Eggerton. Save your strength, please," she begged. "You can't die on me. It's my fault this happened to you."

"No. Mine." He lifted a bloody hand, trying to touch her cheek. "All mine."

Then his arm fell, and his head went slack, along with his body. His eyes stared at nothing.

Beth clapped her hands to her face, suspecting McCall had died.

With tears raining down her cheeks, Beth straightened his form and clothing so he'd look better. "I'm sorry. I'm sorry."

Then she rose and stumbled toward the gate, tripping over rocks and brush, her vision blurred by tears.

Suddenly, a man grabbed her. "Ma'am? Are you hurt? You belong at the fort?"

She blinked and tried to focus on his face. He wore a uniform. A soldier. "Lieutenant McCall." She pointed to the storeroom. "A man beat him. He's dead."

"Stay here," he said, releasing her and racing off toward the shed.

Within minutes, he returned, braced her back with his arm, and led her to the gate. "I'll get you back to the fort, ma'am. Are you married to one of the officers?"

"Colonel Webster is…my father."

"I'll get you back to him as fast as I can. Hang on and trust me." With that, he picked her up in his arms, set her in the saddle, jumped up behind, turned the horse, and headed for the fort.

Chaos broke out when they reached the row of officers' houses. People came out to see what was happening, then followed in a crowd.

Beth's father rushed out of the house, Mrs. Sparks behind him.

"What is the meaning of this, Private? What have you done to my daughter?" he demanded.

"Nothing, sir. I found her like this in the cemetery. Found Lieutenant McCall too, sir. He's dead."

In confusion, Colonel Webster stared at the young man for several seconds. Then he turned, spotted Corporal Sims, and shouted, "Get some men and go at once to the cemetery. Bring McCall back and take him to the infirmary. Agnes, get my daughter inside and clean her up. I'll speak with her later. Get my horse, Private. I'll go to the cemetery myself.

Mrs. Sparks fixed a bath for Beth, helped her undress, and climb in. "I'm sorry you had to witness that. Must have been awful."

"It was." Beth swiped at the tears running down her cheeks. "I feel so bad. It's my fault. He wanted to marry me to get my money, and I refused. If I'd given him the money he needed to pay Bearstooth, he'd be alive."

"I doubt that, Beth." For once, Mrs. Sparks' voice held kindness and understanding. "The man was a fool to gamble in the first place. He asked for what he got, harsh as that may sound."

The housekeeper washed Beth's hair, got her out of the

tub, dried off, and tucked into bed. "I'll be downstairs if you need me. Try to rest."

Beth slept through lunch. When she finally went downstairs, her father was waiting for her.

"How do you feel, Beth?" he asked.

Surprised by his concern, she said, "I'm fine, Father. Just sad about what happened to the lieutenant."

"Yes." He cleared his throat and picked up his pipe. "Well, he knew what he was getting into when he made his ill-conceived wager."

"I know." She sat in a chair across from him. "Getting the money to pay his debt was why he wanted to marry me. He knew about my inheritance."

"That was my fault. I told him. I was foolish." He lit his pipe and puffed on it a few times before speaking again. "I haven't treated you well since you arrived. I apologize for that. The truth is that having a daughter to take care of terrified me."

Beth giggled.

He harumphed. "You might find that humorous, young lady, but I don't. I was derelict in my duty to you. I shall attempt to change that."

"Thank you, Father. I have been enormously lonely here."

"Is that why you were... What were you doing in that cemetery?" He frowned.

"I had gone for a walk and saw the fence, so I investigated. Then I heard the fight and knew someone was being hurt. I had to try to help.

"That was a reckless thing to do, Beth. I applaud your concern for others, but don't do that again. You might have been harmed or killed yourself. This Bearstooth fellow appears to be a dangerous man."

"Yes. He's enormous and strong."

"Why don't you go to the commissary and look for a dress in those catalogs they have? Mrs. Sparks informed me you have few dresses, and you wore those out on your difficult trip here."

"That is true, Father. Thank you. I'll do that."

"No time like the present." He picked up a newspaper, snapped it open, and buried his nose.

Having been dismissed, Beth returned to her room, took out her stationary supplies, and wrote to Tildy, saying if she wanted to know Lieutenant McCall's fate, to write Beth. She addressed it, *care of the Woodbury Hotel, Salt Lake City, Utah Territory.*

She dawdled with her food that night at supper, her mind heavy with questions about Sparrow Hawk's continued absence, the lack of news from Francine and Tildy, and what part she might have played in Lieutenant McCall's death, as well as the fate of Annaliese and Thomas. She poked at a Brussels sprout. "Father, do you ever use Indian scouts here?"

He set down the glass of wine he'd been sipping and stared. "Heavens, no. Why would you ask such a thing?"

"Lieutenant McCall had a Snake Indian scout on our journey out here, and I just wondered if using such Indians was a common practice in the army."

Taking up his knife and fork, he cut off a bite of beef steak. "It's fairly common, but I won't have the sneaky devils here or on my patrols. Don't trust them. Can't abide them."

"I see." Despite what she'd learned of her father's attitude toward Indians from McCall, indignation filled Beth, and she had to bite her tongue not to argue.

He chewed his meat and swallowed. "I doubt you do, Elizabeth. Those damned Injuns are the vilest vermin in this country of ours. If I had my way, I'd exterminate the lot of them."

Beth swallowed hard. "But some are friendly with whites and don't cause trouble. Isn't that true?"

"Some are less trouble, but they're all scum. No mistake about it. They're relatively peaceful now, but mark my word; it won't last. Right this second—" he waved his knife at her. "—they're plotting some new evil to perpetrate on innocent people somewhere."

Spirits plummeting, Beth laid down her fork. "May I be excused, Father? I'm not hungry tonight."

"Go on." He pointed his knife toward the door. "You're excused."

She had reached the doorway before his voice stopped her. "By the way, tomorrow, there's to be a harvest ball in town. As commander of the Fifth Infantry, I have been invited. I shall be taking Mrs. Sparks as my companion, which means you'll be alone in the house. I expect you to remain indoors and admit no one. Understand?"

"Yes, Father." The news came as no surprise, but that did little to comfort Beth. She had hoped the Colonel would take her to the dance. After all, tomorrow was her birthday. She would finally be eighteen.

As she climbed the stairs to her room, Beth had to acknowledge two facts she'd long been denying—Colonel Jonathan Webster would never love her. Nor would he ever condone her marriage to an Indian, even one as fine and honorable as Sparrow Hawk.

For most of the next day, Beth moped about the house. She did go for a walk by the river and begged her father to take her to the dance. She didn't mention her birthday. It hurt too much that he didn't already know. He refused. She would go to the stables for half a penny and insist they saddle a horse for her. Then she'd do her best to ride the animal to Salt Lake City and find Tildy. From there, she would try to find Francine. Unfortunately, she had never been on a horse before, and foolish and impetuous as she might be, she wasn't fool enough to attempt such a feat alone. Perhaps she was growing up.

Somewhere downstairs, Mrs. Sparks was singing. Beth wanted to kick her.

Darkness fell. The dinner bell rang. And rang. Beth ignored it. Undressing, she crawled into bed and pulled the pillow over her head.

She tossed and turned.

Were the ladies at the dance dressed in their finest? What was the music like? Was her father a good dancer? She wondered if they'd decorated the room where the dance was to be held and how it looked. Did they have food? Frosted cakes, cookies, and punch? It could have been like a birthday party.

Mouthing a silent curse, she rose and dressed. The house was quiet. Her father and Mrs. Sparks must have left. In the kitchen, she found leftover biscuits, some cheese, and an apple. As she ate, she wandered the house, peering out the windows toward town and wondering where the dance was taking place. Halfway through her apple, she tossed it into the garbage pail, grabbed a shawl, and quit the house.

The music danced on the wind, reaching Beth before she spotted the lights from a building at the edge of town. Wagons and teams waited outside. The cheerful, rollicking music made her feet itch to move. She found a window where the curtain had not yet been drawn and peered inside. The men wore their best suits with stiff, white collars, brocade vests with watch chains, and fobs dangling. Her father, of course, wore his dress uniform. A swirl of color flashed before her as the men twirled the women past the window. Full skirts flew out, revealing glimpses of lace-edged petticoats. Feet pounded the floor.

A fiddler, an accordion player, and a pianist provided the music from a corner of the room, which had been festooned with fall branches in oranges, reds, and golds. Laughter and chatter broke through the music here and there. A familiar figure waltzed past—her father, with Adelia Sparks in his arms, wearing a lovely gold velvet gown, her hair hanging in ringlets about her face. A stab of jealousy pierced Beth. She swiftly banished it, assuring herself she did not care that her father chose to take Mrs. Sparks instead of her. What she regretted most was not being inside, dancing, and enjoying the festivities.

The musicians launched into a fresh new waltz, so lovely that Beth lifted her skirts and danced over the grass alone, humming the tune.

"Woman-Who-Dances-in-Moonlight," a familiar, gruff voice said from the shadows.

With a squeak of surprise, she spun about, froze, and stared into the darkness. Bit by bit, he emerged into the light. Leather leggings, moccasins, and a fringed leather tunic.

"Sparrow Hawk!"

"Yes, my Beth. It is me."

He laughed as she ran to him, arms outheld. Pressing her against him, he kissed her cheeks, forehead, chin, and finally, her lips. "Now, my heart is happy again."

"Mine, too. I have missed you so much."

She stepped back, her hands on her hips. "Why haven't you written? Why did you take so long to come? Is your mother all right? I worried so about her and prayed for her to recover." She paused. "You *have* come for me, haven't you?"

He studied her until she grew uncomfortable under his all too discerning gaze. "You are unhappy here." A statement rather than a question.

"I was right about my father. He does not want me. No one does. It's awful. I have heard nothing from Francine since we parted or from Tildy. Everyone deserted me."

A tender expression formed on his brown face, a half-smile curving his lips. "You sound like the child I first met in Fort Leavenworth. Yet I can see you have matured. You have become a woman."

He pulled her to him more tightly, kissing her, and she melted against him, her bones liquifying, her blood heating.

"Yes, my Beth," he whispered against her lips, "My mother has recovered, and I have come for you. I want you to be my wife, share my life, and bear my children. Is this your wish, too?"

Arms entwined around his neck, she pressed closer. "Yes. Oh, yes."

"You will go with me to my village and live with my people and me?"

"I will go wherever you want."

On a groan, he crushed her to him and kissed her hard. To Beth, their bodies seemed to meld together and become one. Synchronized heartbeats sounded in her ear. He wanted her. And, oh, sweet Heaven. She wanted him. So much.

"Then this," he whispered, "will be my birthday gift for you. We will leave this place tomorrow."

She didn't think she could hug him tighter but she did. She was so happy.

The music rose, the sound swirling around the couple kissing in the dark garden, lifting them, blessing them. Beth thought never, in all the eons that the world existed, had anyone been as happy as her at this moment. Hawk's arms around her, his lips caressing hers, his scent surrounding her, his love binding them together for all eternity. Nothing and no one could ruin this one instant in time, this glorious, perfect instant.

"Who goes there?" a man called out.

Startled, Beth stumbled back from Hawk. Her heart leaped into her throat. She felt cold suddenly. Somewhere, she had lost her shawl. But that mattered little.

The lantern's light played over her, exposing first her, then Hawk.

"Sparrow Hawk, is that you?" the intruder asked.

"*Haa'*, yes, Henry."

"Good heck, man, you eager to die?" The guard, a short, plump man, emerged into the light from the window. "What are you doing out here with her? Colonel Webster will have you whipped for this. Or shot."

"Please." Feeling as if about to jump off a cliff, Beth took a step toward Henry. "Please don't tell my father. Sparrow Hawk and I stumbled into each other in the dark. I came to watch the dancing. If my father finds out that I left the house, it will be me he has whipped."

Henry wagged his head, looking torn. "I'm sorry, miss, but... " He glanced at Hawk and leaned closer to Beth. "I saw him kissing you, and it'd be my neck getting stretched if I don't report it."

He lifted his rifle and pointed it at Hawk. "Come on, Injun. I gotta take you to the guardhouse."

"No. You can't." Beth couldn't believe what was happening. How could life be so unfair?

"Go home," Sparrow Hawk told her. "I will be all right."

The trooper poked him with his gun. With a last, lingering look at Beth, Hawk walked away, prodded by the rifle as he and the soldier disappeared into the night.

Fear pumped through Beth. Her hands shook, and hot blood coursed through her veins. How could this happen? It was so wrong. Why did the world have to be this way? Sparrow Hawk was a man like any other. They should be allowed to be together if they choose.

But no one would understand how she felt about Sparrow Hawk. Not the whites anyway, and least of all, her father. Would Hawk's people accept her?

She had to find a way to free Hawk from the stockade. They could run away, go to his village and be free. Or find Caleb and Francine and stay with them.

Please, God, help me find a way...

"Please let me in," Beth pleaded with the woman who opened the door. The music and laughter she had heard only through the window before now swirled outside and around her. "I am Colonel Webster's daughter and must speak with him."

"Wait here. I'll send him to you."

Beth bounced on her heels, too anxious and frightened to be still. Skirts in pink, yellow, blue, and red whirled inside as couples danced past the open door. The smell of lemonade and baked goods wafted on the breeze. Was she doing the right thing? She must think it through and be certain whatever she did made sense and was wise.

But, oh, she had to save Hawk.

At last, her father emerged from the crowd, scowling. "What the devil are you doing here, Beth? I ordered you to stay home."

"I'm sorry, Father, but this is important. They've arrested a friend of mine for no reason. You must intervene. Please, Father."

"What friend?" He looked incredulous, as if it were unbelievable for her to know anyone.

"His name is Sparrow Hawk. He was the scout for the Army supply train I traveled with."

The Colonel's eyes narrowed, and his mouth tightened. "You associated with an Injun on the trip here? Damn Lieutenant McCall's hide. I'd have him hanged for this if he weren't already dead."

"No. Hawk is a good man." Her heart sank, and desperation filled her. "He saved my life during a Pawnee attack."

The Colonel showed no sign of softening. "Why was he arrested?"

Heat rose to Beth's cheeks. How foolish not to have

anticipated this. She would have to lie. "I was so glad to see him, Father, because it's been so lonely here that I embraced Hawk. A guard happened by and took him to the guardhouse for touching me. It wasn't Hawk's fault. Please, have him released. He did nothing wrong."

Her father stiffened and glanced around as if afraid someone might have heard. "I will give no such order, Elizabeth. If that damned heathen touched you, he deserves to be shot."

She jerked in shock at his cruel words but couldn't give up. "Please!"

Mrs. Sparks appeared at his side. "What is the matter, Jonathan? Everyone is staring and whispering."

He turned to her. "Go back and wait for me, Adelia. I'll be there in a moment."

"But, Father," Beth pleaded. "I need your help. It's my birthday. Can't you do this one thing for me?"

His face flushed, and a tic jerked in his jaw. "Elizabeth, you will leave here this instant and go home, or I will have that filthy Injun shot now. Understand me? We will discuss your disobedience later."

In the next instant, the door slammed in her face.

Not knowing what to do, she hurried to the guardhouse, a small structure with a barred door. Skirting around it, she found a window too high in the wall to see inside. Taking hold of the bars and pulling herself up as much as possible, she called out, "Hawk? Can you hear me? Are you all right?"

"Beth, go home. You should not be here." His voice sounded hollow and small as if coming from a long distance away, though the building could not have been more than ten feet square.

"I have to be here. You're here."

"There is nothing you can do for me, Beth. Go and find Caleb. Send him here."

"Caleb? He's somewhere up north, Hawk. I don't know how to find him."

"No. He's here. He and Francine came with me to celebrate your birthday with you. They're probably waiting at your residence."

Excitement and relief filled her. "I'll go there at once." She released her hold on the bars but hesitated. "Are you sure you're not hurt?"

"Go, Beth. Send Caleb to me."

She ran home, holding her skirts out of her way, not caring if anyone saw her stockinged ankles.

In the light of a lantern, she saw Francine and Caleb rise from the porch swing as she raced toward the house.

Francine rushed down the steps.

Beth threw herself into her arms. "Francie! Oh, Francie."

Tears rained down her face as she clung tightly to her friend. "I'm so glad to see you. I thought you'd forgotten me."

"Of course, I didn't—"

Beth pulled away, seeing Caleb on the porch. "Caleb. Come. You have to help Hawk."

His smile faded, and he strode quickly down the steps. "What are you talking about? What's happened?"

"A soldier caught Hawk with me and took him to the guardhouse." Grabbing Caleb's arm, she tried to tug him toward the jail. "Come. He wants to see you."

"Oh, Beth," Francine cried.

Beth paid no attention. Her breath came in pants as her

heart ran rampant, fear and dread filling every cell of her being. She could only think of Hawk and protecting him from her father's hatred.

"I'll go." Caleb freed himself from her hold. "You stay here with Francie. You won't help matters hanging around the jail."

"But—"

"No buts, Beth. You want him cleared and released?"

"Of course. I went to Father at the dance and begged him to intervene, but he threatened to shoot Hawk."

Caleb took a handkerchief from his pocket and dabbed at the tears on Beth's face. "Don't worry. I'll find a way to get him out of this. Stay here."

Setting her aside and giving his wife a significant look, he hurried off.

Beth started to follow.

Francine grabbed her. "You heard him, Beth. Stay with me."

She knew Caleb was right, but it was so hard not to be with Hawk now he was here. "What if he can't get Hawk released?"

"Then we go to bed and try again tomorrow."

"Bed? I could never sleep while Hawk is locked up because of me."

"Whether you sleep or not, we must go to your room and wait for Caleb to return."

With one last look at Caleb's shadowy form disappearing into the distance, she allowed Francine to guide her into the house, her personal prison, where she would await word of the man she loved.

CHAPTER FIFTEEN

At breakfast, Beth pleaded with her father not to punish Hawk.

"Keep away from me, Elizabeth. I can't stand the sight of you. That my own flesh and blood should lower herself to the level of a whore and let a stinking, thieving Injun touch her sickens me to my core. Pack your bags; you will no longer live here."

"Where will I go, Father?"

"I don't know, but it won't be to some filthy Indian village. I'd rather see you dead than live with murdering heathens."

Beth's eyes still ached from sobbing through the night before. Now, the misery spread through her entire body. She tried to feel the shame her father believed she deserved to suffer, but it refused to come. Her love for Hawk was not wrong, not something to hide or apologize for. She asked what Sparrow Hawk's fate would be, terrified he would be killed, but the Colonel refused to tell her.

She learned soon enough that Hawk was to be lashed at noon, and she was ordered to watch.

Locked in Francine's tight embrace, Beth gazed at the scene in horror as each strike of the whip cut into Hawk's naked back. They had tied him to a pole with his back bared. Soldiers surrounded the scene. Beside the women, Caleb stood fiercely stiff and angry.

Hawk's body jerked with each bite of the lash, muscles quivering.

My fault. Beth's brain repeated, again and again. *My fault.* None of this would have happened had she been sensible and stayed away. Instead, she'd met with him on the journey at every chance she found. They'd hidden by lying in waist-high grass, in patches of forest, at the bottom of a gully, behind rocky outcrops, anywhere they could find, while talking of their lives, wants and needs, and fears and failures. And each time, she had fallen a little more in love with him, with his gentleness, deep respect for all living things, and affection for his family. His religious beliefs, so closely connected to nature, fascinated her. She found more sense in them than in much of what the preachers had taught back home in New York.

Now, she could no longer ignore the reality of what she'd done and caused. And Sparrow Hawk was paying the price. She closed her eyes and prayed for forgiveness, though she knew she'd never wholly exonerate herself.

His body sagged against the pole; his head lolled to one side. He barely flinched when the whip sang through the air and found its mark as if he no longer felt the pain. And through it all, he uttered not a single cry, not even a groan. But Beth did. Blood from the lip she had bitten to keep from crying out filled her mouth, its metallic flavor causing her to retch. Francine's hold on her tightened, and she murmured into Beth's ear, the words indistinguishable.

Did Hawk still live?

Her hands clenched at the thought, her fingernails digging into the flesh of her palms.

At last, it ended. Sparrow Hawk slumped to the ground

when the soldiers cut his bindings as if unconscious. She prayed he was, for then he would feel no pain.

But the fear that he was dead tore at her heart. She had to know.

"Caleb," she whispered in a shaky voice, "is he—" she could not say the words. "Is he... all right?"

"I'll find out, honey."

Two soldiers carried Hawk off on a litter. She tried to follow, but other troopers blocked her way. She could not see where they took him. The guardhouse? The infirmary? The cemetery?

Please, please, let it be the infirmary.

Caleb had trailed after the party. She had to hope he came back with good news.

Overcome by horror, regret, and fatigue, Beth allowed Francine to take her home, where they awaited word of Hawk's fate. Caleb had been invited to stay in the corporal's quarters. He visited first to tell Beth that Hawk lived, though badly hurt.

After crying her heart out, Beth fell into a nightmare-filled sleep. The moon had risen high in the sky by the time she awoke. No sound came from the house. Francine slept peacefully beside her.

Scooting off the bed, she went to the window. The only visible light outside came from the moon and stars. A tiny red-glowing arc marked the flight of a cigarette tossed away by a guard as he made his rounds. Everything else remained still and silent.

She wondered why she had ever thought her father might hold even a speck of love for her. Jonathan Webster was blind to the good in the world and too full of hate to be capable of love.

What he had done to Sparrow Hawk was unforgivable.

She looked at Francine and thanked God for her friend's presence. Never had Beth needed her more. As soon as Hawk was released, Caleb would take them all north to his home in Jackson Hole.

If they released Hawk.

Her father had threatened to have the man she loved shot at dawn.

But Beth would never again kowtow to the Colonel. She would leave Camp Floyd with a glad heart—and Sparrow Hawk.

Sitting on the bed, she mapped out a plan in her head, reminding herself that she must be sensible and clever. She could not be reckless or impulsive. Unfortunately, she had little time to put any plan into action. Francine and Tildy might tell her that she should stay out of her father's business, but in this case, she could not. She couldn't undo the harm she might have caused Hawk and the lieutenant. Annaliese Thomas appeared to have escaped, though Beth couldn't be sure. But she could help Hawk.

Not only because she loved him but because it was her fault he was in trouble, and a thorough search of her heart and conscience told her it was the right thing to do.

First, she had to get herself free. Father had locked them in. To solve that difficulty, she rose and dressed. She slid a vellum paper under the door, inserted a hat pin into the lock, and probed until the key fell out the far side. Muttering a brief prayer of thanks, she drew the vellum into her room and rejoiced at finding the key lying on the white surface.

"Beth?" Francine's sleepy voice called. "What are you doing?"

"I'm going to break Hawk free, and then we're leaving here. Will you and Caleb come with us?"

Francine slid from the bed. "Of course, we will. But, Beth, how will you do it? Your father said there would be a trial in the morning to decide if Hawk will be court-martialed or shot."

"It's a travesty." Beth handed Francine her clothing. "Hawk isn't a soldier. He volunteered to scout for the supply patrol. I'm not waiting around for Father to carry out his revenge. We're leaving tonight."

While Francine dressed, Beth packed a single valise with items she considered practical and necessary: sturdy walking shoes, her warmest wrap, sturdiest skirt, and shirtwaist. Ready, at last, the two girls crept downstairs and set their valises by the front door.

"Wait here." Beth left for her father's study. Seconds later, she returned with every penny his cash box held. She'd go to a bank and have the money returned by wire when she could. Using the rear door, they slipped from the house into the darkness, stopping first at Corporal Sims's quarters to rouse Caleb.

While they awaited Caleb in the corporal's small parlor, she took Gage aside.

"I'm sorry, Gage. I had hoped to forget what I felt for Hawk and fall in love with you, but it didn't happen. The moment I saw him again, I knew I would never love anyone but him. Will you forgive me?"

He gave her a wan smile. "Yes. I have great respect and admiration for you, Miss Webster. If Hawk is who you love, I will do what I can to help you. When I report to the Colonel this morning, I will tell him Caleb was gone when I awoke, and

I know nothing of his whereabouts or yours."

"Thank you. You are a good friend." She hugged him just as Caleb came down the stairs. They rushed out the door.

Light snow, the first of the season, peppered them as Beth, Caleb, and Francine made their way to the guardhouse. Beth called to Sparrow Hawk through the small window while Caleb went to fetch his buckboard and horses from the stable.

A rustling came from inside. "Beth?"

"Wait," she whispered back.

A whistled tune warned the night watch approached. Stowing their bags behind some barrels, Beth found the biggest rock she could fit in her hand. She and Francine formed a quick plan. Beth stepped out of the shadows as the guard came near and asked if she could see Hawk. Before he could answer, Francine crept up from behind and conked the guard on the head. He dropped like a felled tree.

"Make sure he's okay, Francie." Beth returned to the window to explain to Hawk what they were doing.

"It's too dangerous, Beth," Hawk said. "I don't want you to do it. I will survive this."

"I will not take that risk."

Francine found her and reported that the guard was unconscious but unhurt. She handed Beth the man's key ring from his belt.

"Perfect." With shaking hands, she unlocked the door and slipped inside. "Hawk?"

"Here, Beth."

She followed the sound of his voice and kneeled beside him. "How bad is your pain? Can you move?"

He replied in a guttural language.

"English," she said. "Speak English."

"You go," he mumbled. "Don't want you hurt."

Beth jerked in surprise. "No, I'm taking you out of here. Caleb and Francie are with me."

He held her away, his body trembling from the cold. He wore no shirt. "You will all be in great danger if you do this. I do not want anyone harmed because of me."

She gently wrapped a blanket around him. "If you cooperate, we won't be caught, and no one will be hurt." More determined than ever, she tried to tug him to his feet. "Come on. I'm not leaving you here."

Caleb arrived and helped get Hawk standing. Hawk groaned as they supported him while he staggered into the night. The moisture Beth felt on her arm around his waist told her he bled severely. How much blood had he already lost? A lump formed in her throat. She forced it down. Now wasn't the time for emotions and tears, only for good sense and extra precaution.

They halted at the rear of the wagon.

"We'll hide you and Hawk in the back, Beth," Caleb said. "Stow the bags around you and cover everything with a canvas tarp. I'll tell the guard at the gate that I'm taking my pregnant wife home because of the execution. We have four horses, so we can ditch the buckboard later and switch to riding to make better time."

"Pregnant?" Beth stared at Francine. She knew her friend had yearned for a baby. "Are you with child, Francie?"

"Yes, but we'll talk about that later." She squeezed Beth's hand. Getting back to business, Beth put the news from her mind and continued helping to keep Hawk upright.

A dog barking had them all whirling to see a large, mottled brown mongrel bare his teeth at them.

"Shut him up," Caleb whispered urgently.

Beth crouched in front of the mutt, ignoring the chill from the snow she kneeled in. "Hello. Nice dog." He stopped barking and stared at her while she reached into her bag, pulled out a biscuit from her father's kitchen, and held it out.

The dog sniffed, whined, and edged closer. At last, he snatched the biscuit and ran off.

"You thought of everything," Francine said.

Beth snorted. "Not really. I brought the biscuits for us."

While the women kept Hawk upright, Caleb prepared the back, spreading blankets to cushion Hawk and Beth and soft bundles for pillows. Then he helped them climb in.

"Hawk," Caleb said, "I think you should lie on your stomach to protect your wounds."

"Yes." Hawk crawled into place and lay down.

Beth took her place beside him. Caleb loaded the bags, carefully arranging them around his two passengers. He stored some lightweight items on top of them, avoiding Hawk's back, and covered them with more blankets, which Beth appreciated. The temperature had plummeted. Winter was here. Unable to see now, she listened to the snap and whoosh as Caleb unfolded and spread a canvas tarp over everything, securing it tightly to discourage anyone from looking underneath.

"With this snowfall, no one will question why we have our load covered," he said.

When all was ready, Caleb got the horses going. Francine sat beside him, bundled up against the icy temperature. They drove slowly to lessen the chance of attracting attention. Beth's lips moved in silent prayer until Caleb stopped, and she knew they'd reached the guard station at the gate.

"Good evening," Caleb greeted.

Footsteps crunched near the wagon. Beth froze and put her hand on Hawk's to remind him to stay quiet. "Where are you going this time of night, sir?" the guard asked.

"Home. I understand there's to be an execution in the morning," Caleb told him. "My wife is with child, and I won't risk her or the babe being harmed by witnessing such a horrific event."

"I'm not sure the Colonel would like this. What do you have in back?"

"My wife's trunk and other bags, including provisions for our journey. We live up north, so we have a way to go."

Beth held her breath and put a hand to her pounding heart. Silently, she prayed. Hawk squeezed her hand, and she returned the gesture to let him know she was all right, even though she wasn't. She had never been so frightened in her life.

A rifle muzzle jabbed at the bags. One poke struck Beth's leg hard, but she bit her lip and kept quiet.

At last, the footsteps receded.

"All right. Go ahead," the guard said.

Caleb spoke to the horses, and the wagon began to move. They hadn't gone more than twenty yards when a cry of alarm sounded from the area of the guardhouse halfway across the grounds. Beth's heart sank.

The warning bell on the parade ground began clanging, and the shouts of men came from all over. Doors slammed. Dogs barked.

"What the hell?" the guard muttered. "Hey, mister, hold up there."

Caleb snapped a whip over the horses' backs, and the wagon bolted forward.

Luggage and bundles bounced and slid, bumping into Sparrow Hawk and Beth. He moaned, but they held on. She shielded him as best she could from the shifting cargo.

"Stop, or I'll shoot!" the guard yelled, his voice faint with distance.

Caleb snapped the whip again.

A bullet whizzed overhead, followed by another. Beth flinched at each one, and Hawk squeezed her hand. They held tight to each other while being jounced about the wagon bed. It seemed to go on forever, and Beth knew she would bear bruises when it ended. Shot after shot exploded nearby, and she reacted the same to each. The wheels bumped over ruts in the road, causing everything to slide. She thought of the image of her mother that she had taken from her father's parlor and hoped the glass didn't break. She had wrapped it inside a dress.

At last, the firing stopped, and she knew they must be too far away to be visible from the fort. They had a good head start, but her father would send soldiers to search for them. She could only hope they could outrun the army horses.

Gradually, the night quieted, and Beth knew they had escaped the fort. They were in open country now.

What seemed like endless miles and hours later, Beth stiffened, hearing Caleb whoa the horses and wondering why. Had the soldiers caught up with them? What was Caleb doing? If only he'd speak to them through the canvas covering. Her heart raced and she desperately wanted to get out into the fresh air. The buckboard swayed as if someone had gotten down. Caleb, no doubt.

Footsteps approached the side of the wagon. Beth waited anxiously, barely breathing. Hawk heard too. She felt him tense up, and his hold on her hand tightened.

"Hawk?"

Caleb's voice. Beth let out a breath, and she and Hawk both went limp.

"Yes, Caleb?" Hawk answered. "We hear you."

"I've stopped near a farm just past the lake," Caleb said. "No one is here, or they're asleep. No lights in the windows, just horses in a field next to the road. Let's leave the wagon here and ride the horses from now on. The wagon will be too slow."

"Whatever you think best," Hawk answered.

Francine murmured something to Caleb. Soon they threw back the tarp and helped Hawk and Beth disembark. The snowfall was light here, with less on the ground. A large home loomed in the distance, too large for a single family. It must house a polygamist and his wives and children.

"We'll leave the trunk and only take what the horses can carry," Caleb directed. "Hawk, are you up to helping me find saddles in that tack shed and get them on the horses while Francine unhitches the wagon?"

"Yes." He wrapped the blanket more securely around him and followed Caleb, vanishing into stygian darkness and leaving Beth and Francine to care for the horses. Together, the women removed the harness and freed the animals. After that, they sorted through their things, choosing a few possessions and packing them and what food they had into bundles. Beth found her mother's picture, glad it was undamaged, and re-wrapped it in her dress. Caleb and Hawk returned so quietly that their arrival startled the women.

"Oh!" Francine blurted. "You scared us."

"Sorry." Caleb put down the two saddles he held and kissed her.

Beth took the one Hawk carried, frowning. It had to have pained him greatly to haul something so heavy. "You only found three?"

"I need no saddle," he answered.

"But I should ride with you," she objected. "To steady you."

"No, sweet Beth." He lay a hand gently on her cheek. "I am stronger than you think. I will be fine."

Caleb drove the buckboard beneath some trees, and the men covered it with the tarp. Their possessions were stored in saddlebags or tied in bundles to the saddles. Each of them mounted a horse. All night they rode northward, listening for sounds of pursuit and avoiding homes and people. A few dogs barked as they traveled past homes, but no one investigated. They avoided small outlying towns.

At last, they stopped by the river they'd followed to let Hawk rest, and Caleb rode back a few miles to see if the army followed. While he was gone, Beth checked Hawk's wounds to ensure they weren't bleeding badly.

"I didn't see any sign of a posse after us," he announced cheerily on his return.

They celebrated by sharing the biscuits Beth had taken from the kitchen. Then they mounted up and continued their journey.

The sky began to lighten as they passed Salt Lake City, and still, they rode on. When the reached the convergence of the Jordan River with the Great Salt Lake, they stopped to let the horses drink. Beth dismounted, lay on the river bank, ignoring the snow, and scooped water to her mouth with her hands. The others did the same.

Refreshed, Beth climbed onto a large rock to see over the bushes in the pale, pre-dawn light. "Look at that enormous lake. It appears endless."

"And salty as can be." Caleb chuckled.

"I'm glad we aren't trying to drink from it," Francine said, joining her.

Beth jumped down from the rock and grinned, turning to Hawk. "We made it. We escaped."

He did not share her smile. Somberly, he put his hands on her shoulders and gazed a long time into her eyes. "My Beth, you are certain you want this?"

She cocked her head as she stared at him. "You mean do I want you? Yes, for the rest of my life. You and the children we create are all I will ever want."

"And to live with my people? No white woman's fine clothing, no white man's food or house? It will not be easy, Beth. Your father may hunt us. People may die."

His words sobered her. "You fear for your family."

"You bet he does." Caleb spat at a sagebrush. "He's right to do so. You know my house is not easy to find, Hawk. You will be safer there than with your family. Stay with us at least until summer. I had planned to build a cabin next to ours with a dogtrot between when we got home. That way, Francine can use one for a kitchen and parlor and the other for our bedroom. In the summer, she can cook in the dogtrot, where it will be cooler. You and Beth can stay in the second room this winter.

if you decide to stay permanently, we'll build you a separate cabin."

"I'd like that." Beth gave Hawk a hopeful look.

"It would please me as well." Hawk held out a hand, and the men shook. "You are a fine friend, Caleb. Our hearts are grateful."

"Oh, I'm so excited." Francine clapped her hands together softly. "To have another woman around. It will be wonderful, especially when this one arrives." She patted her belly.

"Oh, yes, Francie." Beth grinned. "When is it due?"

"Around June, I think." Francine hugged Beth. "I'm so happy."

Caleb interrupted their small celebration. "Let's see to these wounds before we go any farther. Then we'll need to get going again." He took away the blanket Beth had wrapped around Hawk to examine the damage the whip had done. "Aw, hell. They did a right damn job. This needs cleaning and bandaging. Sit on the tailgate."

At once, Beth stepped out of her petticoat and began ripping it into strips. They bathed the wounds with water from the stream, applied some salve Caleb had, and bandaged them. Beth sensed Hawk's pain, yet he endured the torture stoically. The mass of bloody cuts and bruises sickened her, and her heart ached to think of the pain he suffered lying in that wagon, being bounced around during their flight from the fort. Yet he never complained. His courage and fortitude amazed her anew. Even riding the horse must have caused great pain.

When it was over, she drew his head down and kissed him. "I love you, Sparrow Hawk."

"As I love you, my Beth." He slid off the tailgate and drew

her into an embrace. "I have been thinking. Caleb's home is still a distance away. I would have you be my wife, even though we cannot consecrate the marriage until I heal. We can marry in the Indian way. Would that please you?"

Her heart stuttered. This was what she wanted, what she'd prayed for. Now that it had come, panic struck. Was it the right thing to do? What did marrying in the Indian way require?

No, it didn't matter. One look in Hawk's dark, expressive eyes banished the fear. "Of course. I will wed you in any manner God will accept as real."

Hawk kissed her long and hard. When it ended, he rested his forehead against hers. "Beth, my Beth. You make my heart sing with joy."

Stepping back, he took his horse's reins and held them out. "If we were in my village, I would call you from your lodge and present numerous ponies to you. Here, it will be different. If you wish to accept me as your husband in your heart, you need only take this horse to water."

"That's it?" she asked.

He nodded.

They still stood at the river's edge. She glanced at the water gurgling so close and laughed, but the sound emerged slightly edgy. This moment changed her life forever. She would never be the same woman as before. From now on, she would be married, a position that brought new responsibilities, experiences, difficulties, and bliss.

Hawk squeezed her hand as if to lend courage. What he asked seemed pointless. Yet she knew the small act meant something monumental, the equivalent of saying *I do* in a church. Her chest swelled, and tears formed in her throat. She wallowed them, took the reins, led the horse to the two feet that separated them from the stream, and then returned to him.

His smile as he accepted the reins showed Hawk's pleasure and satisfaction. "Come, Woman-Who-Dances-in-Moonlight. You belong to me now."

"And you belong to me." She kissed him. "From this day forward, nothing can tear us apart."

"And they will not. Happy belated birthday, my heart."

EPILOGUE

B eth bit into the stick in her mouth and panted, praying for the pain to end. Hawk ducked inside the tipi and smiled at her. The smile soon fled.

"My heart, you are in pain." He hurried to her, worry contorting his handsome face. "Is the baby coming? How can I help?"

The pain eased, and she relaxed on her sleeping blankets. The stick showed deep indentations from her teeth as she laid it beside her. She wished he hadn't seen her use it. Shoshone women did not show pain. At least not that Beth could see. Trying to meet their high standards challenged her, but it was worth the effort when Hawk smiled at her and spoke of his pride in having her as his wife.

They had spent the winter with Caleb and Francine, but Beth insisted Hawk needed to see his family, despite the danger that might bring. They would not stay long. Beth rejoiced at that knowledge, for she was eager to return to their Jackson Hole home. Life in a tipi offered many amenities she had not expected, but she missed Francine and worried her father might find them. He had put a price on their heads. Five hundred dollars for Beth as long as she was healthy. Five hundred dollars for Hawk, dead.

"Yes, husband. Your daughter wishes to join us today."
She stroked her enormous belly, hoping to feel the baby move
or kick. It troubled her that it had been so quiet today.

"My daughter?" Hawk grinned. "You mean my son?"

"No. I carry a girl inside me, despite your wishes." She
smiled at him. A bead of sweat rolled from her hair down the
side of her cheek.

Hawk gently removed it with his thumb. "I care not
whether it's a boy or a girl. You know that. I want only for you
both to be healthy."

"I know." She attempted to kiss his thumb before he
moved it away but failed. The attempt left her feeling silly.

One of Hawk's friends called from outside, "Come, Hawk.
We have a game to play."

"The baby is coming," he replied.

"You must leave then. Men have no part in such
happenings. Join us."

"Go, my husband," Beth told him. "I will be fine."

He frowned. His friends called again.

The men were right; Shoshone men were not allowed at
birthings. The blood could draw away his strength. Hawk
considered it nonsense, but Beth did not want to see him
criticized for not following norms.

Beth tried to give him a gentle shove, but her hand went
to her belly as a new pain began. She grabbed the stick, put it
in her mouth, and began panting like Francine had told her had
helped when her son had been born.

Beth shoved at him.

He nodded. "My mother will be eager to be here for this
event. I will fetch her."

The pain attempted to sever Beth's body in half. She bit harder on the stick. She did not want Hawk to see her like this.

He jerked his chin, which was his way when agreeing, and left.

Finally, the agony eased, and she relaxed. She already loved this child more than she had imagined possible and had not even laid eyes on her yet.

Yes, it would be a girl. She felt sure of that, and it pleased her. She did not believe Hawk's claim not to care about the sex of the child. All men hoped for boys, and she'd heard his friends tease him about whether he was man enough to produce a boy or only a girl. Hawk assured her they meant nothing by it, and he didn't take it seriously. It annoyed Beth.

A scratching came at the large hide that operated as a door flap. Tipis had no wooden doors. Or windows. Beth missed having windows.

"Come," she called, hoping the visitor would be her mother-in-law.

"My son sent me to check on you, daughter. How are you doing?" Little Beaver looked happy today. Perhaps she was eager to become a grandmother.

Beth caressed her belly with both hands. "The baby wants out, I think."

"This is good to hear," Little Beaver said. "Lay back, and let me check to see how close you are to giving birth. I must know when to call our medicine woman."

Beth did as asked. She knew Many Tongues, the woman Little Beaver spoke about, was not a real medicine woman, but she came very close. She knew herbs and potions better than any man, could heal most ailments, and had a part in delivering early all the babies born to the tribe.

Little Beaver lifted Beth's skirt and cried out, "*Aiieee.* I can see the head. Your daughter will be here soon. I must tell Many Tongues. I hope she won't mind coming. She has a special visitor today, a famous *Newe, Shoshone* woman. I will be back soon."

She ducked through the door and vanished.

Beth would rather have only Little Beaver present. Her mother-in-law would be less critical should Beth lose control and cry out in pain. Despite sending Hawk off with his friends, she wished he was here. To her mind, he should be. After all, he put this baby inside her. Should he not have some part in seeing it born?

She thought of Francine in Jackson Hole. Beth had been with her when Francine's son came into the world. They would not see each other again until the moon when the leaves left the trees, two moons away. The men had completed the dogtrot and second cabin, where she and Hawk lived. Thoughts of Francine brought other memories.

So much had happened since the night she and Francine had caused the fire in their school dormitory, and Beth learned of her mother's death. Her father had sent Lieutenant McCall to fetch her to Utah Territory to live with him, and during the long journey, she had fallen in love with their kind and gentle scout, Hawk. It struck her as odd to think of who she had been then, so innocent and naïve compared to now. She had lived a great deal in the moons since she, Francine, and Caleb rescued Hawk from the Camp Floyd guardhouse.

They had almost died that night. The soldiers had done their best to shoot them as they hurried away in Caleb's buckboard, with Hawk and Beth hiding in the back.

She had heard rumors that her father hunted for her still and viciously ravaged Indian villages in his determination to punish her and Hawk. It terrified her and filled her with guilt and sorrow for the people her father hurt, and out of fear, not all Sosone villages would welcome her or Hawk. Soon after they had moved into their Jackson Hole home, a hunting party came to warn them that her father and his army were nearby and heading their way. It was early winter, the month she still thought of as October, almost a year from when Lieutenant McCall had delivered her to her father. Hawk took her up the mountain to hide. She had been so scared and cold that Hawk had held her, whispering reassurances into her hair. Beth believed that time away had seen the conception of the child about to enter the world today.

A new contraction stole her attention. She didn't hear the scratching on her door. Three visitors let themselves inside and came to her bed, Little Beaver, Many Tongues, and a shriveled but regal older woman.

"Dances in Moonlight, you know Many Tongues." Little Beaver gestured to the medicine woman.

"Of course I do. We met at Fort Laramie."

Many Tongues nodded, reached inside her neckline, and pulled out a red ribbon holding a beaded medallion. Her grin displayed missing teeth but lots of humor. "You remember I say you be important to our people someday."

Beth smiled back, remembering how she'd given the ribbon to her at Fort Laramie. She hadn't recognized Many Tongues at first.

Little Beaver gestured to the third woman then. "This is

Walks Far. She is famous for guiding the men called Lewis and Clark to the great water. We are honored to have her here."

Beth's pain eased, and she struggled to sit up to show deference to the proud woman. Little Beaver slipped an arm around Beth's back to help.

Walks Far raised a hand to halt them. "Let her rest, but get her into the proper birthing position."

They helped her to kneel over a hide. A knotted rope hung from the lodgepoles overhead. Beth had heard that Indian women kneeled while giving birth but hadn't truly believed it. The knotted rope was for her to clutch during the birth

A new contraction struck. She thrust the stick between her teeth and began to pant.

"Push, Dances in Moonlight," Many Tongues said. "Push. The child is almost out."

Beth thought she might die; it hurt so badly. Three pains later, Little Beaver cried out in triumph, "It is here. You have a daughter, Dances in Moonlight, as you said you would."

At that moment, a lark sang somewhere outside. It sounded beautiful and significant to Beth. Exhausted, she tried to lie down and reach for her baby.

"Stay as you are," Many Tongues told her and cut the cord. She cleaned the baby, wrapped her in a cloth, and handed her to Walks Far.

Beth wanted to complain and demand they give the baby to her. An unexpected pain stopped her. A rush of liquids emptied from her womb. Many Tongues carefully picked up the hide beneath Beth, which now held the afterbirth, and carried it outside for Hawk to bury.

Little Beaver handed a piece of the cord to Walks Far.

Beth frowned, confused. Why would a stranger want her baby's cord? The question fled her mind as Little Beaver placed the tiny fussing baby in her arms. After that, the other women and everything around her faded while Beth studied her incredible child. She kissed each pea-sized toe, touched a diminutive hand that clasped onto her finger with surprising strength, and peered deep into dark eyes, seeking some resemblance to Hawk or herself. "I had thought to name her Rosebud. Now, I want to call her Lark, after the one that sang as she was born."

Beth saw her husband most in her baby's eyes. She noted the absence of a birthmark with gratitude until she saw the back of Lark's neck, and there it was, a mark almost exactly like Beth's. At least it would be out of sight once the hair grew longer. No one would notice it.

Warmth filled Beth, along with love more profound than she could have imagined feeling for anyone. She hadn't believed she could love a person more than she did Hawk. Now, she felt doubt. This small creature in her arms was a part of her, created by the love she and Hawk shared, and would always need her mother in a way no one else would.

Beth would protect her child with her life. She would never send her off to some cold, unfeeling school or ignore her. She would beg Hawk to take them back to Jackson Hole, where they would be safer, and she could be with Francine. The summer had fled, and it would soon be time for them to go back anyway for the winter.

A voice in her head said she was selfish, that she and Hawk should go somewhere and live alone so her father's continued search for her would not endanger anyone else.

There were moments when she asked herself if she should return to Camp Floyd to stop her father from killing more *Sosone*. Those moments filled her with terror, which banished all notions of going to her father. She worried about Hawk's safety most. Her father wouldn't harm a baby. She doubted her ability to go on living without Hawk. Now, she had a new reason to stay, never to leave him.

Little Beaver placed a hand on her shoulder and gestured to Walks Far. Beth glanced up and saw that the old woman was offering her something. Taking it, Beth realized it was a beautifully beaded necklace made of leather. "This is lovely. Thank you so much. I will wear it always."

"It is not for you," Walks Far said. "Hang it from your baby's cradleboard. It will protect her."

"Oh," Beth said. "Thank you. My heart is happy to accept this token from you."

"You are important to the Newe, Granddaughter. No other white woman has chosen to take a Newe man as her husband. You are a sign of better times to come for our people. This is why I came to this village, to see you and give you this symbol of her importance to us all. Raise Lark with pride."

"I will, Grandmother." Beth wanted to hug the woman but couldn't move yet, not with her baby nuzzling her breast, seeking nourishment. She opened the blanket wrapped around her and let her daughter nurse. A fresh wave of love washed over her as Lark's little mouth clamped onto her nipple. "I am grateful to you for visiting me and giving us your blessing. It means much to all of us."

Walks Far jerked her chin in acknowledgment, rose, and left, followed by Little Beaver and Many Tongues.

A new visitor took her place.

"Hawk," Beth cried. "Come see your daughter. Is she not beautiful?"

"Yes, my heart. She looks like you."

Beth laughed. "You are silly or crazy; I'm not sure which."

"Perhaps both," he said as he snuggled next to her and the baby.

"I am so happy," Beth said.

"Both our hearts celebrate this new life we have made." He kissed her and then the babe. "Nothing will ruin this joy we feel. We will raise her and watch her grow until the day she leaves our lodge for that of her husband."

"That will be a long way off," Beth said. "But it will happen someday."

"We have a lifetime of somedays ahead of us, my heart."

AUTHOR'S NOTE

Although *Dances in Moonlight* is a more recent book, it is a sort of prequel to a contemporary romantic suspense novel titled *The Girl in the Mirror*. In this later book, the heroine is an artist, Carissa, who has reoccurring dreams about a girl named Elizabeth who travels across the U.S. in an army ambulance to live with her father in 1859 and falls in love with a Native American scout. The story relates Carissa's efforts to find out who Elizabeth was and what happened to her. It parallels *Dances in Moonlight* in certain ways and answers questions about Beth's later life. I hope to have *The Girl in the Mirror* published soon.

ABOUT THE AUTHOR

Charlene Raddon fell in love with the wild west as a child, listening to western music with her dad and sitting in his lap while he read Zane Gray's books. She never intended to become a writer. Charlene was an artist. She majored in fine art in college.

In 1971, she moved to Utah, excited for the opportunity to paint landscapes. Then her sister introduced her to romance novels. She never picked up a paintbrush again. One morning she awoke to a vivid dream she knew must go into a book, so she took out a typewriter and began writing. She's been writing ever since.

Instead of painting pictures with a brush, Charlene uses words.

Visit Charlene on Social Media

Website charleneraddon.com

Sign up for Charlene's newsletter

Book Cover Site silversagebookcovers.com

Facebook www.facebook.com/charleneb.b.raddon

Amazon www.amazon.com/Charlene-Raddon

Goodreads www.goodreads.com/author/Charlene_Raddon

Twitter twitter.com/craddon

Bookbub: www.bookbub.com/charlene-raddon

OTHER BOOKS BY CHARLENE RADDON

Printed in Great Britain
by Amazon